Dane Thorburn

and

NATURE'S REVENGE

By Matt Galanos

A catalogue record for this book is available from the National Library of Australia

Publisher:
ASPG (Australian Self Publishing Group)
P.O. Box 159, Calwell, ACT Australia 2905
Email: publishaspg@gmail.com
http://www.inspiringpublishers.com

National Library of Australia Cataloguing-in-Publication entry

Author: Galanos, Matt

Title: **Dane Thorburn and Nature's Revenge/**_Matt Galanos_

ISBN: 978-1-922792-09-9 (Print)

ISBN: 978-1-922792-10-5 (eBook)

ISBN: 978-1-922792-11-2 (Hardcover)

*For Caroline,
Melissa and Michael*

VALENTALAND

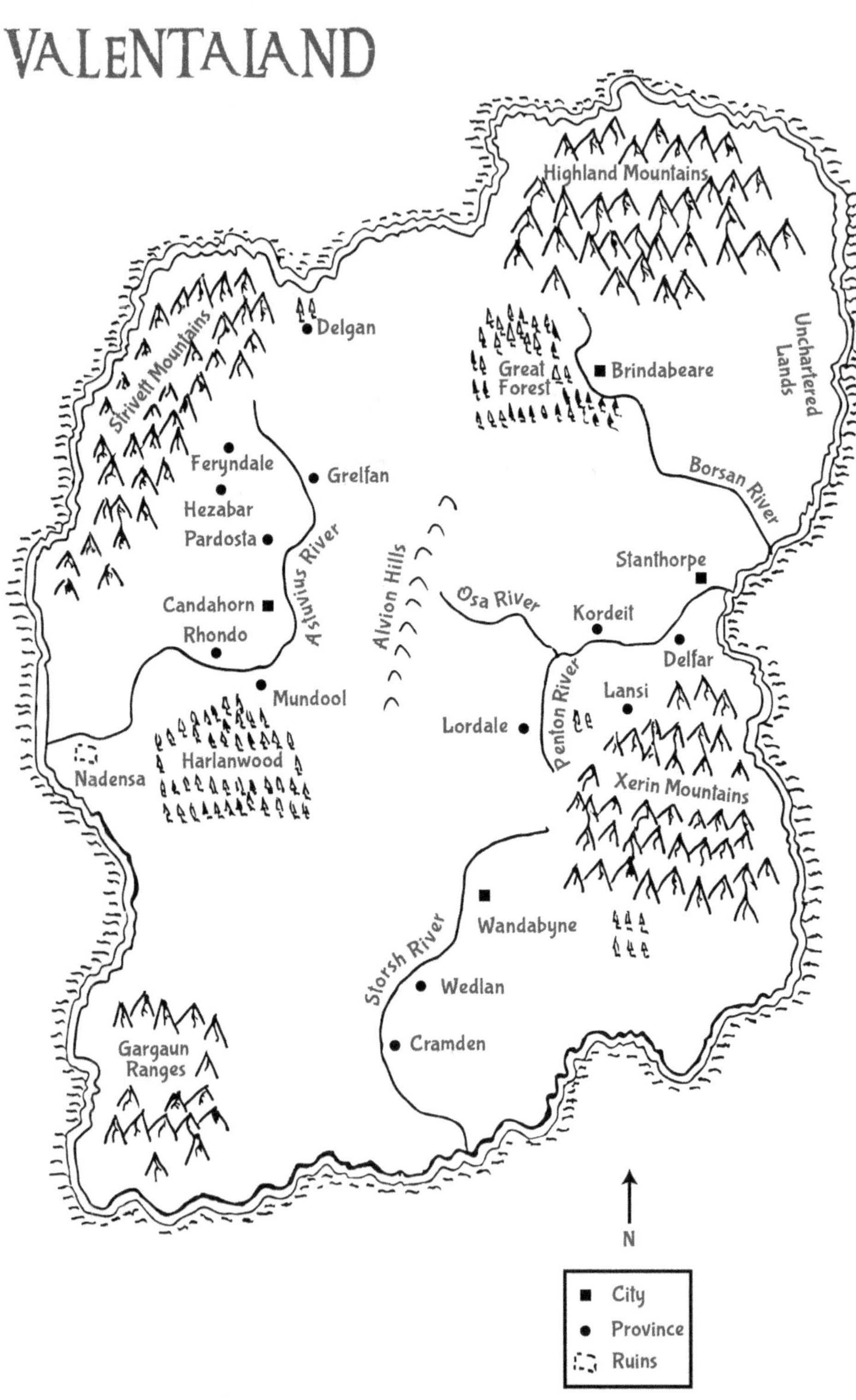

Chapter 1

A NEW KNIGHT

Darkness swallowed the land. People slept in the warmth of their beds. Horses were tethered, the stables silent. A gentle breeze wandered the streets, passing with nothing but the faintest whisper. Perimeter guards manned their posts, staring into the silence around them. Forests and rivers were still, the sounds of night buried in the dark. Wherever you looked, it appeared as though nature itself was asleep, resting from the rigors of another day ...

A crack appeared in the mountainside, breaking through a thin layer of ice. Pushing itself outward, the crack turned into a small hole. A flame appeared in the opening, melting the ice.

With a burst of energy, the surface around the flame broke away, shooting into the sky. Covered in a clear, oozing slime, a small creature emerged, shivering for a few moments as its body adjusted to the late-night air.

Hidden from prying eyes on a westward ledge, the afternoon sun kept the area fertile and soft. Tucked in a nook in one of the trees, buried under twigs and foliage, the egg was invisible to all.

No one saw it rock gently in the night, with more and more force, before falling to the ground, cushioned in the soft grass. Its purpose served, the outer shell dissolved, releasing its tiny occupant; wet, featherless and blind.

From within the forest floor, a patch of ground about an inch around caved in. Hidden within, under the cover of night, it emerged after a moment's hesitation. To the naked eye, it appeared as though the ground itself was moving.

Sliding on its belly until it was out of the hole, it stood on its hind legs, sniffing the air uncertainly.

Several feet below the surface of the Astuvius Falls, near the ruins of the wizarding city of Nadensa, the threshold of a small cave had lain undisturbed for its entire existence. Being so close to the falls, nothing ventured close enough to know it was there.

On this night, when something ancient and reptilian emerged from within, it encountered no resistance as it swam frantically towards the surface, seeking its first breath.

From the base of the ranges, it walked on wobbly legs, struggling to put one foot in front of the other. Its vision shifted in and out of focus, trying to adjust to the darkness. Despite its thick coat, it felt the cold of the night air as it wandered on, unsure if its next step would be its last ...

Despite the early hour, Dane Thorburn was wide awake, fully dressed, and ready for whatever the day had in store. Splashing some water on his face, he left his quarters, heading towards the castle proper.

Moving through the hallways, past the sound of pots and pans in the main kitchen, he saw attendants extinguishing wall torches and others pottering around as the castle woke from its evening slumber.

Nodding to the Royal Knights on duty as he made his way to the first floor, he arrived at his destination and waited.

It had been six months since his return from rescuing Princess Vanessa from the ancient wizard prison known as the City of Lost Souls. Hidden in the Gargaun Ranges, according to legend no one had escaped in the entire history of the land. Kidnapped by exiled Firelord wizard Raegan's Black Knights, Vanessa had been left in the city to die.

Dane and his friend and fellow knight, Will Hevenshire, had been in the party sent to find her; and with the help of Blaze, his messenger and hunting eagle, Dane had found her and brought her home.

As a reward for their efforts, Dane and Will were now in the senior ranks of the Royal Knights.

A maid emerged from Vanessa's quarters, a bundle of laundry in her arms.

'Good morning, Genevieve,' said Dane.

'Good morning, Dane,' the maid replied with a smile as she approached him.

'We were well behaved last night,' said Dane. When Genevieve gave no response, he added, 'Will and I. We were only at the Staghorn Inn for a short time.'

Genevieve nodded.

'I know. He came to see me after you came back.'

Dane's eyes widened in surprise.

They're getting serious!

'She will be with you in a moment,' Genevieve added as she walked past him.

Admiring her as she walked down the hallway, he didn't see the others until he heard a familiar voice behind him.

'She's taken.'

Smiling, he turned and saw Vanessa, accompanied by her Mistress – his mother, Marilena Thorburn, standing in front of him.

Vanessa looked radiant; a few inches shorter than Dane and slightly taller than her Mistress, her azure-blue eyes sparkled in the pre-dawn light, the warmth in her face and smile seeming to spread to every aspect of her demeanour – emitting an energy, a sense of presence, lighting not only herself, but those around her.

Marilena had been through a difficult and trying ordeal herself – consumed with worry from the time of the kidnapping, she had come close to a complete breakdown until Vanessa returned. Like Dane, she had also had to cope with the scandalous reality of Dane being falsely accused of aiding the kidnapping, until Masterlord wizard and Brindabeare's High Governor, Lord Frederick, had seen through Raegan's plot and proved Dane innocent.

Today, despite her relative calm, she had a scowl on her face; the mood in her eyes as dark as the grey dress she wore.

Dane smiled.

'Mother,' he said, knowing the source of her discontent, 'it's appropriate for Vanessa to dress like this.'

Marilena's scowl deepened.

'She is the future Queen of Valentaland,' she said. 'Not some common knight.'

Vanessa put a hand on Marilena's arm.

'We've talked about this,' she said. 'I need to be able to lead my army in battle, and I can't do that in a dress.'

Marilena let out an exasperated sigh, eyeballing Vanessa's uniform, complete with chest armour, gauntlets and leggings, and her long, dark hair, drawn into a braided ponytail – looking very unlike a Princess.

'I know,' she said. 'But I don't think I'll ever get used to it.'

'She's in good hands,' said Dane. 'I promise to bring her back safe and sound, and you can spend the whole morning and afternoon pampering and playing dress-ups.'

Marilena scowled again.

Vanessa slapped Dane's arm.

'That's out of order,' she said with a smile. 'Another remark like that, and you may find yourself on stable duty, where you can share those comments with the horses and hounds.'

Dane laughed.

'My apologies, your Princess-ness,' he said, bowing. 'Please, forgive me.'

'Let's go,' said Vanessa with another slap.

They left Marilena behind, heading towards a courtyard near the Royal Knight quarters. They'd first sparred together in secret, in the time before Dane became a knight, and after her ordeal in the City of Lost Souls, the King and Lord Frederick had allowed Dane to train her privately.

They had been fitting her training in during the hour before dawn, trying to cover as much as they could in that short time each day. Competent with a sword and an accomplished rider, in recent days they had moved to mounted sword fighting.

Arriving at one of many stables clustered on this side of the castle, making their way down the aisle separating the stalls on each side, nodding to the stablehands as they passed, they saw their horses were saddled and ready for them.

As always, Dane had Thunder, a tall, black, knight-bred stallion who'd been with him from the time Thunder was a weanling. Now fully-grown and battle-hardened, Thunder was the perfect complement to his rider, who stood just over six-feet tall; his short hair and eyes a dark brown, and who, despite his relative youth, bore the strong, fit build of a seasoned knight.

Vanessa had also been given a knight-bred horse; one she had chosen specifically for its colour – a silver she named Razor.

'I want to be seen in battle, where my army knows exactly where I am,' she'd said over the protests of others – Dane, Marilena (who'd gone a whiter shade of pale on hearing it), Lord Frederick and the King among them – who'd argued that being so conspicuous would make her a target.

'I'm not concerned about that,' she'd replied. 'My army will want to know if I'm there, fighting with them, and that's more important. If everyone knows I'm on the battlefield and they can see me, they'll be in a better position to protect me. And if I'm trained properly, none of it will matter.'

Unable to find fault with her line of thought, the debate had ended, and in the time since, she and Razor had bonded.

Walking towards their mock battleground, they heard horses behind them.

Turning, they saw two knights in full armour – Will and Aidan Hindmarsh, Commander of the Royal Knights, approaching.

'Good morning,' said Dane as they drew level.

'Good morning,' they replied.

Slightly shorter and thinner than Dane, with black, wavy hair, Will had been Dane's close friend since their cadet days; his laid-back, almost care-free nature betraying a fearlessness and strength Dane had seen in the many battles they'd survived together.

Hindmarsh was the stockiest and most experienced of the three, his sharp eyes peering out from the thin layer of stubble on his face.

'What are you doing here?' asked Vanessa.

'We want you to get used to fighting in cramped spaces,' said Dane. 'Fighting on horseback is not as simple as a one-on-one battle. You can be bumped and buffeted by others around you. You need to be able to cope with that and beat your opponent.

'It's also something Razor has to deal with. Although he's knight-bred, he needs to get used to moving in a tight space and helping to keep you balanced.'

Vanessa nodded.

'Very well,' she said. 'What are we going to do?'

'We will fight as we have the last few days,' said Dane. 'And while we're doing that, Will and Commander Hindmarsh will move in and out, bumping and trying to knock you off balance. Once you get used to it, they'll start fighting as well, so you learn to keep your focus with other swords moving around you.'

Moving into the field, a fifty-yard square ringed by a wooden fence, Dane and Vanessa were handed their swords. Apart from being blunt, they were the same light-weight swords made by Will's father and used by the entire army.

Will and Hindmarsh waited as Dane and Vanessa moved to the middle of the field.

'Ready?' said Dane, raising his sword.

Vanessa raised her sword in response.

In the next moment, Dane swung hard across Vanessa's body from right to left, pushing Thunder forward in the same motion. Vanessa leaned back, bringing her sword up just in time.

Dane swung in the opposite direction, using his momentum to keep her off balance. Raising her sword again, she blocked the blow, allowing Razor to step back and sideways at the same time, negating some of Dane's advantage.

Dane grinned.

'Well done,' he said.

In the next instant, he had Thunder mirror Razor's movement, and he was on the attack again. He used the same moves as before – swinging from right to left, then left to right.

Vanessa blocked the blows once more.

'Well done, again,' said Dane.

Another turn, and Dane used the same strategy.

This time, when he swung from left to right, Vanessa raised her sword as she had before; only she felt a bump from the side and was thrown completely off balance. Not only did Razor swing away, she fell forward in the saddle, nearly dropping her sword in the process.

With a yell, Dane swung his sword and whacked it against her exposed chest.

Stunned for a moment, Vanessa gathered herself and looked at Dane.

'I don't understand,' she said. 'All of a sudden, everything went wrong.'

Dane smiled.

'Exactly. That can happen on horseback. You have to be able to react and stay in control. Let me show you.'

Dane nodded to Will and Hindmarsh.

Hindmarsh stepped forward and Vanessa moved away from the line of battle.

Raising their swords, Dane and Hindmarsh engaged.

Giving no quarter, both rained blows at each other, horses snorting as they twisted and turned. One would be on the attack, then the other. After several exchanges, Dane appeared to have Hindmarsh in a defensive position, when he felt a bump from Will to his left.

Without hesitating, he turned Thunder in the same instant, maintaining his attacking position and forcing Hindmarsh back. There was a bump to his other side as Will moved in again. Dane reacted, and Vanessa could see that although he was in a defensive position, it didn't distract or deter him.

In a couple of moments, he had the advantage again.

Will moved again – only this time, not only did he bump into Dane, he'd drawn his sword.

It was two on one.

Vanessa watched on.

He's done for. He can't possibly beat two of them ...

His mind and body as one with his blade, Dane heard no sound as he responded to the moves of his attackers, the flashes of steel swirling around him in slow motion as he parried the blows; one smooth, fluid fighting force.

The battle continued, and Vanessa saw Dane backing away as Will and Hindmarsh came at him. With two swords coming at him, he had to swing with short, sharp defensive thrusts to keep them at bay – and he could only do that for so long.

In the next moment, to her surprise, Dane smacked Hindmarsh hard in the chest; and after a few more blows, he'd beaten Will as well.

Mouth open, she made her way over.

'How –'

'It's about balance,' said Dane. 'Reacting in time with what's going on around you. There were a lot of times I was off-balance, where there didn't appear to be a way out, but I kept working with what I saw; reacting as things changed, until a chance presented itself and I could fight my way back.'

Vanessa nodded.

'There was a moment when the Commander had his side exposed,' said Dane, 'and I took advantage of it. That changed the fate of the whole battle. But if I hadn't been able to keep my balance, it would never have happened.'

'And he has some kind of magical power when he fights on horseback,' said Will. 'If I didn't know better, I'd say he was accessing the Fire Element and sourcing the same increase in strength as the Black Knights.'

Everyone smiled.

It was well-known throughout the land that Raegan gave his Black Knights an increase in strength by accessing dark elements within his dominant Fire Element, making them harder to defeat in battle.

'It's difficult, but not impossible to win in a situation like that,' said Hindmarsh.

Vanessa looked at Dane, who said nothing.

Will nodded his agreement.

'Some, like Thorburn,' said Hindmarsh, 'have an almost unnatural ability, which is why he is best suited to train you.'

'Are you ready to try again?' said Dane.

'Yes,' Vanessa replied.

Hindmarsh and Will moved away.

Dane and Vanessa engaged.

Dane swung from his right to left, then left to right.

Vanessa nervously blocked each blow, waiting for the bump.

'Don't think – just react,' said Dane.

Coming at her again, he changed his strategy, forcing her to concentrate on his sword.

'Remember, it's a two-way fight,' said Dane. 'If you see an opening – take it.'

Right to left, right to left, high to low, left to right; Dane kept coming.

She found her rhythm, blocking each blow, until she felt the bump.

She didn't fall forward as badly as the first time, but it was still enough for Dane to slap her on the chest.

'Better,' said Dane.

Vanessa grunted in frustration.

'You'll get used to it,' said Dane. 'With time, you'll be able to adjust and keep fighting.'

After a few more exchanges, the sun had crept over the horizon.

'That will do for this session,' said Dane.

Dripping with sweat, Vanessa nodded.

'Thank you, Will. Thank you, Commander.'

'Thank you, Princess,' Will and Hindmarsh replied together.

Walking the horses back to the stables, Vanessa wondered how she could possibly become as good in the saddle as Dane.

Wiping her face with her arm, she said, 'you're brilliant. You must know that.'

Dane said nothing.

'I'm serious,' she added. 'Everyone says so. Father, Lord Frederick, General Silvers. Even Commander Hindmarsh, just now.'

'I think they're exaggerating,' said Dane. 'You can be as good as anyone.'

'Not likely,' said Vanessa.

'Yes, you can,' said Dane. 'We'll keep practising. And once you get used to it, we'll change the routine. We'll find other times, other circumstances for you to spar. So you can fight in any conditions.'

Vanessa sighed.

She couldn't remember when she'd felt so tired.

Reaching the stables, Dane handed his reins to a stablehand, dismounted, and started untying his saddle.

Next to him, he heard a thud, and saw Vanessa leaning awkwardly against Razor's stall.

Rushing to her side, he took Razor's reins, passing them to a stablehand.

'Vanessa?' he said nervously. 'What's wrong?'

'I don't know,' she said, standing. 'I feel ... a bit ... dizzy.'

Dane held her arms to help her support herself.

'Did we do too much?' he said, looking her up and down. 'Maybe we rushed this?'

'I don't think so ... It's strange ... I haven't noticed it until now.'

'You sound like you're out of breath,' said Dane, scanning her again.

Nodding to the stablehands, they continued unsaddling and tending the horses.

'Let's wait for a moment. Relax, take some deep breaths. We don't have to rush.'

'No,' said Vanessa. 'I'm fine. I was just a little dizzy at the end. Really, I'll get used to it ... I'm ... fine.'

'Let's see how you are during the day,' said Dane.

'No. I'm fine ... I feel better. I don't know what all the fuss is about.'

She pulled out of his grip, starting towards the castle.

Dane watched as she took a few steps.

Following, he had almost caught up when he saw her stagger for a moment, before collapsing to the ground.

Chapter 2
MUSINGS AND BRIEFINGS

Plentiful portions of food and wine lined the table, but none had been touched. Neither the host nor the gathered guests were in the mood for dining. The evening light mirrored the dark mood in the room. The guests sat nervously, eying each other in turn, waiting for someone to break the brooding silence.

Governor Mortensen, leader of Candahorn, looked around the room.

'Gentlemen,' he said. 'Now we are all here, I suggest you raise whatever it is you deem so important to discuss.'

The others averted their eyes, wanting someone else to be the first to speak.

Mortensen waited.

'Hazelwood,' he said, locking his eyes on the Governor of Hezabar. 'You are never one to hesitate when you have something to say.'

The man two seats to his left hesitated, stroking his bearded chin and trying to look away.

'Maynard? Farrington? Norton?' said Mortensen, looking to the Governors of Pardosta, Rhondo and Mundool in turn.

'It's ... delicate,' said Norton, the weakest and most insecure among them.

'Delicate?' said Mortensen.

'We ... don't want to question why ... but we wish to know.'

'Know what?' said Mortensen, his eyes focused with an intensity that had Norton shifting in his seat.

No one answered.

'Know what?' Mortensen said again, knowing exactly what Norton wanted to ask, addressing him so directly to see how he would respond, and whether any of the others would support him.

'Well ...' said Norton, doing his best not to squint through the sweat dripping down his forehead.

'Lord Raegan,' said Hazelwood suddenly. 'It has been over six months ... and there has been no sign of him.'

Norton sighed with relief.

The others relaxed.

The question had finally been asked.

Mortensen looked at the governors in turn.

'Where is Lord Raegan?' he said. 'That's why we're here?'

The others stared at their hands.

'It's ... unusual,' said Farrington, the nerves he felt hidden behind his full-length beard as he spoke up. 'Since we declared our allegiance, it's unusual for so much time to have passed without any ... contact ... any ... communication from him.'

The others nodded.

'I see,' said Mortensen. 'Our Lord, our Supreme Ruler, has not been in contact – *communication* – with you, and you deem that so unusual, so important, that you request a meeting?'

The others shrunk into their chairs, averting their eyes.

'And what is it you want from me?' asked Mortensen. 'Do you wish me to inform you how many times I have seen Lord Raegan in the last six months? Or would you care for a daily account of his activities?'

Maynard, Farrington and Norton lowered their heads, staring intently at the table.

Hazelwood frowned, his face twitching, trying to maintain his self-control.

'What do you wish to say, Hazelwood?' said Mortensen, seeing his obvious discomfort. 'Are you questioning Lord Raegan's actions? His motives? His objectives? Are you questioning your *loyalty* to Lord Raegan?'

The room lay deathly still.

Hazelwood raised his gaze.

Staring defiantly at Mortensen, he said, 'my loyalty to Lord Raegan is beyond question. If you, or *any* in this room, question my loyalty again, I will kill you where you stand.'

Rising from his seat, standing to his full, towering height, fist clenched, he continued.

'When Lord Raegan requested a force to draw the Advance Regiment into the open while he attacked the castle, it was *I* who volunteered. When he wanted a force sent to the Gargaun Ranges to ambush the party searching for the girl, it was *I* who responded.

'It was *I* who suffered those losses. It was *I* who was abandoned and left with no support.'

His voice rising, he went on.

'When my forces fought a Brindabeare army of over one hundred, I did not have the benefit of a Candahorn Regiment and a horde of Black Knights at my back to fend off a party of *twenty*, who arrived at my front gate to conduct nothing more than an *inspection!*'

Slamming his fist on the table, he glared at the man opposite, who had had both those forces with him when a Brindabeare party, including Dane, arrived at Mundool, searching for Vanessa.

'They were our orders!' said Norton, the strength of his voice hiding the fear he felt as he rose from his seat, shaking a little as he stared up at his taller and more imposing counterpart.

'Enough!' said Mortensen.

Norton let out a relieved sigh, wiping his brow as he sat down.

Hazelwood glared from Norton to Mortensen, before turning away and slumping into his seat with a defiant thud.

'We are aware of the sacrifices you made,' Mortensen said to Hazelwood. 'It is all part of Lord Raegan's plan, and we follow his orders without question.'

'With all due respect,' said Hazelwood, 'we would like to hear those words from Lord Raegan.'

'As you can see, Lord Raegan is not present,' said Mortensen. 'Are you questioning my authority on such matters?'

'I am not,' said Hazelwood. 'But it has been more than six months since any of us have seen him. I am sure it was not his intention for the girl to be rescued. He told us escape was impossible - that she would die in the city.'

The others nodded, glancing at Mortensen for a moment, before turning away.

'He said he would support my forces in the ambush of the Brindabeare Army,' said Hazelwood. 'Yet he abandoned us. And, even more concerning - none of our men with the power can transform.'

The others nodded.

Along with the increase in strength Raegan's Black Knights received from the Fire Element, their entire appearance changed whenever they were in that state, transforming from ordinary knights to men who wore black from head to foot, with their faces masked by black warpaint.

'I am aware of that,' said Mortensen. 'And in response, it is clear Lord Raegan has found it suitable to direct his energies elsewhere.'

'But, why?' said Hazelwood. 'That –'

'I have told you before,' said Mortensen. 'It is not your place to ask questions. *Any of us.* We obey Lord Raegan's orders, no matter what they are, no matter what time or in what circumstance we receive them – no matter the perceived cost. *Is that clear?*'

Looking at each in turn, all, including Hazelwood, nodded their acceptance.

'Maynard?' said Mortensen, eyeing the Governor of Pardosta, the youngest and most inexperienced among them. 'Have you come all this way to say nothing?'

'Everything I was going to raise has been said by others,' said Maynard.

'Very well,' said Mortensen, in a much lighter voice, the discussion over. 'Now, please, eat.'

Hands reached nervously for the food and wine in front of them.

Mortensen let out a slow, deep breath.

Thank the Gods, he said to himself, glancing around the room. Reaching for the pulse within, he swore to himself as he noted it had never felt so faint.

My Lord – where are you?

'She just collapsed,' said Dane.

Crowding around Vanessa as she slept, all eyes in the room were looking at him.

'She didn't say she was unwell?' asked King Winston Meriwether, pacing the room.

Dane met the King's gaze; his eyes a sharp, azure blue, exactly like those of his daughter, emitting a welcoming and commanding look at the same time. Although not as intimidating as others from a physical point of view, he stood at the same height as Dane; his demeanour and presence removing all doubt as to who ruled the land.

'No, Sire,' said Dane. 'And I didn't notice anything until we were at the stables. She said she was dizzy; we were walking towards the castle, and she passed out.'

Masterlord wizard and Brindabeare's High Governor, Lord Frederick stepped forward, as always, dressed in grey and wearing his multi-coloured Masterlord cape; with Scarafuse, his powerful, magical sword at his side.

'There appears to be no fever,' he said after placing his hand on Vanessa's forehead. 'From what I can see and feel, there appear to be no weaknesses or ailments that give cause for concern. She may have simply over-exerted herself.'

'I told you!' Marilena said to Dane. 'You worked her too hard! She is not as strong and fit as you!'

Dane thought for a moment.

'It was no different than the last few days,' he said. 'The basics of mounted sword fighting.'

Marilena and the Queen cringed at the words, no doubt horrified at the images they were conjuring of Vanessa fighting on horseback. Like her daughter in every way, except for her auburn hair and grey-green eyes, the Queen had been stoically accepting of Vanessa's training, but now, Dane saw deep concern on her face, no doubt thinking through the wisdom of it.

'She can't be expected to have your strength and energy!' Marilena protested.

'You are not at fault,' said the King, coming to Dane's aid. 'At some point training takes its toll. It happens to all of us.'

'But she's a lady!' said the Queen.

'I am well aware of that,' said the King, taking her hand gently and leading her away. 'I suggest we let her rest and see how she is when she wakes.'

Along with their aides, Harold Salsbury and Patrice Whiltshire, the King and Queen left the chamber; the King chuckling to himself as Marilena's tirade faded into the background.

'– and don't think because the King let you off the hook that I'm going to be so easy!'

'While there have been no disturbances of late, we must remain vigilant,' said General Laramer Silvers, Commander-in-Chief of the Brindabeare Army.

Standing to his full height of well over six feet tall, leaning forward and seemingly staring through his dark eyes into the very soul of every knight in the room, Dane felt a slight shiver pass through him as the General said, 'although the last sighting of Black Knights was upon the Princess's return from the City of Lost Souls and our informants report no activity to cause concern, we must remain on guard.'

Exchanging a look, Dane and Will nodded, well aware that they, Vanessa, Lord Frederick, and the King knew something about Raegan's possible whereabouts that had not been shared with anyone else.

Over a quiet meal that evening, careful to avoid the ears of others, they talked about it between them.

'It's strange, isn't it?' asked Will. 'Nothing from the rebel forces, the Black Knights, or,' he said, lowering his voice, 'Raegan.'

Dane raised his eyebrows knowingly.

'Yes,' he replied. 'The more time that passes, the more I ask myself – did I kill him? Did he die during that disturbance? Did he escape? Was he even there at all?'

'Until something happens, I don't think we'll know,' said Will.

'I know,' said Dane. 'But, until "what" happens exactly? He shows himself? There's another attack? Or we grow old and grey, having never heard from him again?'

Will shrugged.

'I can't stop thinking about it,' said Dane. 'One moment I'm sure he's dead, and in the next, I just don't know. I should have killed that wolf.'

'Remember what Lord Frederick said about Black Knights and their link to Raegan?' said Will, doing his best to calm his friend. 'Given there have been no sightings since we killed the last four, it's possible the link has been broken; so you may have killed him.'

Dane shook his head slowly, picking at his food, considering it all, until others joined them, effectively ending the conversation.

Royal Knights Harvey Rosenthal and Richard Lovell, both a couple of years older than Dane; Harvey slightly taller and his hair a darker brown than his colleague, along with Advance Regiment

Officers, (formerly, fellow cadets), Donovan Braidwood and Albert Webster had healthy servings in hand as they sat down.

'What did you think of the briefing?' asked Donovan, his long hair, large frame and equally large hands giving the look of a wild beast as he bit into a piece of meat and tore it off the bone he was holding.

'We were just talking about it,' said Dane. 'It's the right thing to do – it's better to be cautious and safe, than ignorant and dead.'

'I agree,' said Albert, the only one with light hair and a stubbled face among them. 'We can't trust them. Who knows what they'll do next?'

'They could attack us, or one of the provinces,' said Donovan. 'Somewhere like Feryndale or Grelfan.'

'They won't attack us,' said Harvey. 'They've tried several ways to do that already. They even had one of us on trial.'

Will, Donovan and Albert glanced at Harvey in surprise as Dane and Lovell exchanged a look; Lovell diverted his gaze as Dane fumed at him, daring him to say what Dane knew he was feeling.

He still *thinks I'm guilty ... after all this time.*

'It still bothers me,' said Harvey, ignoring what was going on around him. 'I could have sworn, and still do – the image looked *exactly* like you. I can't believe I wanted you to hang.'

Will, Donovan and Albert gaped at Harvey.

Continuing to stare at Lovell, Dane felt his anger rising.

'Image or no image,' said Albert, trying to defuse the situation, 'everyone should have known better. He's been friends with the Princess his whole life. There shouldn't have been the slightest doubt.'

Harvey nodded slowly, as though he was still trying to sort it out in his mind.

Lovell said nothing, seemingly frozen to the spot.

'Some will never change their minds,' said Dane, leaning forward and slamming his fist on the table.

Will, Donovan and Albert exchanged a nervous look as Dane and Lovell stood, glaring across the table at each other, breathing heavily, a mixture of anger, resentment and hate on their faces.

Without a word, Lovell grabbed his food and walked away.

'Keep walking,' Dane hissed at Lovell's back.

'Relax,' said Will, grabbing Dane by the arm and easing him down to his seat.

'He's never going to forgive me,' said Dane, shaking his head. 'You'd think he was the only one who's lost a friend in all this.'

'Don't let it bother you,' said Donovan.

'He's not the only one who feels that way,' said Dane, glancing around the room.

'It's as I said,' said Albert. 'You're innocent, and you saved the Princess. That should be enough.'

'But it's not,' said Dane. 'Not for Lovell, or Southwell, or –'

'If they have an issue with you, it's their problem, not yours,' said Will.

With a deep sigh, Dane nodded, stabbing at his food and lapsing into a brooding silence.

Ladies Madeline and Genevieve approached the group.

'The Princess wishes to see you,' Lady Madeline said to Dane.

Pushing his plate aside, Dane stood.

'You too,' she said to Will.

With a quick farewell, the four departed.

Making their way along the torchlit corridors, nodding to the guards posted along the way, no one said a word until they turned towards Vanessa's chambers, and Dane saw Genevieve take Will's hand and head in another direction.

'Very clever,' he said, as Will and Genevieve slunk away.

'If it were anyone else, I would simply refuse,' said Lady Madeline. 'But Genevieve is the best maid I have, and she deserves an occasional ... indulgence.'

'So does Will,' said Dane.

'I remember when I was that age ... Brandon and I ...'

'*Lady Madeline!*' said Dane with feigned shock in his voice, recalling the crush he'd had on her as a young boy, 'you're breaking my heart!'

'Just you mind yourself,' said Lady Madeline with a mischievous smile, wiping her hands on her dark blue tunic, no doubt remembering some of the many times she'd been the victim of Dane and Vanessa's pranks and games over the years.

Nodding to Marilena as they approached, Lady Madeline took her leave.

'She's waiting for you,' said Marilena.

'Thank you,' said Dane, nodding past the guard at the door.

Entering the chamber-proper, he found Vanessa, dressed in an evening gown, reading under a wall-torch and candle at a small table near the bed.

Seeing him enter, she lowered the parchment and smiled.

'How are you feeling?' asked Dane.

'Better,' Vanessa replied.

Dane wasn't convinced. She looked well enough, but something wasn't quite right; some of her usual radiance and glow was missing.

'I'm fine,' she said, seeing the suspicious look on his face. 'Really. Lord Frederick has examined me a couple of times now, and he says there's nothing I should be worried about. He thinks it may be over-work and a little fatigue.'

'He said that before. When we first brought you here. How long were you asleep?'

'I'm not sure. Marilena said it was several hours.'

'And you feel better than before? When you were in the stables?'

'I don't really remember it,' said Vanessa. 'I didn't feel anything while we were sparring. I remember entering the stables, but nothing after that.'

'Well, I guess it puts a hold on training for a time.'

'No,' said Vanessa. 'We're going to keep going.'

'Are you sure?' said Dane. 'What did Lord Frederick say? The King? I don't want to get you into any trouble. I don't want to get *me* in trouble if Mother finds out you're training when you're not supposed to.'

'We can always –'

'No,' said Dane, raising his hands. 'I'm not sneaking you out. It's not like using the secret room.'

'But –'

'No,' Dane said again. 'I'm sorry. Believe me, I am. I enjoy our sparring time. But your health is more important. We're not young rascals anymore. I can't do it. Not unless Lord Frederick grants permission.'

Vanessa scowled.

'You sound like your mother.'

Dane laughed, relaxing a little.

'That's a bit severe,' he said.

Vanessa smiled mischievously.

'Well, it's –'

She stopped mid-sentence, her mouth slightly open, a strange look on her face.

'What?' said Dane.

She continued to stare blankly past him, looking beyond the window on the far side of the room.

'I've never –'

She stood, as though in a trance, her body following her eyes as they drew her across the room.

'What?' said Dane. 'What's the matter?'

'I think I saw something,' said Vanessa, walking across the room.

Falling in step with her, they walked to the window, gazing into the distance.

It was dark outside; the last slivers of sunlight blinking out on the horizon.

The window faced north, towards the Highland Mountains. Some of the peaks were just visible in the distance, the ice-caps a dull grey against the sky.

'There's nothing out there,' said Dane. 'Nothing for miles.'

'I thought it was, something like, like a –'

'*Flame!*' they said to each other at the same time, their eyes wide with shock.

Chapter 3
HIGHLAND RUMBLINGS

Fuelled by the fire within – from very core from which it came, it had already grown to half of what would be its full size – twenty feet in length and nearly seven feet tall, its wingspan close to fifty feet from tip to tip. Snorting through its large nostrils, it turned its head, looking for more food, its large, dark eyes having no trouble seeing into the night.

The remains of what it hunted the last few days lay scattered around; a collection of bones and rotting carcasses. Although it had eaten its fill of those, no creature was courageous enough to approach for the remains.

The ice caked around the peaks where it nested was no more, melted into the water that lay pooled in the surrounding outcrops. For as long as it needed, there would be plenty of water here, and more in the streams winding their way through the valleys below.

Turning to the south with a swish of its tail, its hind legs stamping into the ground, a cloud of dust rose in its wake, the bones of the carcasses scattering like leaves in the wind.

At the same time, something roused deep from within; and, as though suddenly awakened, it raised its head, staring intently into the distance. Sniffing the air, it picked up the scent for the first time.

With a thundering roar, it let loose a ball of flame.

'You're sure?' asked Lord Frederick, glancing out the window.

'Yes,' they replied.

Lord Frederick and the King looked doubtful, seeing nothing but a peaceful night outside.

Along with Salsbury, they were the only people in the room; the King telling Marilena to wait outside the chamber.

'And you haven't seen it since?'

'No,' said Vanessa.

Dane shook his head.

'It was only there for a moment. There's no way to know exactly what it was.'

Pacing the room, head bowed, his mind locked in thought, Lord Frederick considered what he'd heard.

'There are several possibilities,' he said. 'At the time of the Great War, there were stories of scattered settlements. No one from Nadensa, or Brindabeare for that matter, ever had reason to venture further than the base of the mountains. The area beyond our northern walls is barren and empty, and with the Unchartered Lands to the east, there has never been a reported sighting or disturbance from anything in or around the Highland Mountains - certainly no flame that could be seen from so far away.'

'Except when Vrenin did his damage during the Great War,' said Dane.

'Even then,' said Lord Frederick. 'The extent of what Vrenin was said to have done remains unconfirmed.'

'He flies on the Highland Dragon,' said Dane. 'It's one of the first stories we're told from the time we're old enough to know. Vrenin on a dragon, Arclos on a giant kestrel, Emilene on –'

Vanessa looked at Lord Frederick.

'You don't think it could be?' she asked.

'Without more information, we have nothing to act on,' said Lord Frederick. 'It could have been anything. A spark from a rock-fall, for example.'

Dane and Vanessa looked at each other.

'I don't discount what you saw,' said Lord Frederick, 'but there's nothing more we can do at the moment.'

'What about Raegan?' asked Vanessa.

Dane felt his blood run cold.

Raegan!

'We don't want to let our imaginations run wild,' said Lord Frederick.

'We tell no one of this,' said the King, stroking his chin as he paced towards them.

Dane and Vanessa nodded.

'And I mean *no one*. Mistress Marilena, the maids – *no one*.'

'Yes, Father,' said Vanessa.

'Forgive me for asking,' said Dane. 'Hasn't meeting like this already made people suspicious?'

'We can create a cover for it if the need arises,' said Lord Frederick.

As if on cue, swaying for a moment, Vanessa's eyes rolled back and she fainted, crumpling in a heap on the floor.

'What aren't you telling me?' Marilena demanded.

'Nothing,' said Dane.

'I don't believe you,' said Marilena. 'And let me remind, you, I am her Mistress; I am to be informed of anything and everything concerning her well-being.'

Dane maintained his neutral expression.

'I'll ask again,' said Marilena sternly, her hands firmly on her hips. 'What aren't you telling me?'

'Mother,' said Dane with a sigh, 'I told you. We were talking, she looked out the window, and when she turned away, she fainted.'

'You are my *son*, Dane Thorburn!' she spat, straightening and stamping her foot. 'And you take me for a fool! I can see through you like a tawdry silk cloth!'

Dane remained still, his face a mask.

'I have nothing more to say,' he said.

Marilena glared at him, her face red with rage.

'I'll come and see her in the morning,' Dane said quietly.

Marilena continued to stew before him.

'Goodnight, Mother,' Dane said with a gentle nod, before turning away.

'Dane –'

'Goodnight,' he said, without looking back.

Leaving Vanessa's chambers, he found Lady Madeline hurrying past him.

'Is everything all right?' she said, grabbing him by the arm.

'Vanessa fainted again,' said Dane. 'And Mother's being, well ... Mother.'

✧ ✧ ✧

'She collapsed again?' Will asked at the morning meal.

'*Shh!*' said Dane nodding. 'It's being kept quiet.'

Will nodded.

'The healers and Lord Frederick don't know why. It's a mystery. When I saw her last night, she still didn't seem herself. She looked well enough, but something about her didn't seem right. I can't really say what it was, but she was … different.'

'Are you patrolling today?' asked Will.

'Yes,' said Dane. 'Out past the northern wall.'

'The northern wall?' asked Will. 'There's nothing there.'

'Orders from General Silvers,' said Dane with a shrug. 'Remember the briefing? Better to be cautious and safe.'

'I'll see you later then,' said Will.

Parting ways at the end of the main hall, Dane headed to the stables, had Thunder saddled, and met his patrol at the rendezvous point at the north-west gate. There were seven others, Harvey among them.

'We have our orders from General Silvers,' said Dane. 'I can tell by the looks on your faces that you're less than impressed and wondering why we're here.'

A couple nodded.

'I know there's not a lot to see,' he said, looking across the open land towards the Highland Mountains in the distance. 'And while the Great Forest and other areas have more appeal, it's prudent we patrol this area as well. You never know, Vrenin and the Highland Dragon may swoop down from the Highland Mountains.'

The other knights laughed.

Dane smiled inwardly.

Let's hope I'm not pre-empting anything.

Guiding Thunder forward, the group fell in behind him.

They were following a sandy-dirt trail, leading a few miles towards the mountains, with little more than an occasional shrub, and perhaps the odd sand-runner, a beetle-like creature that ran on its hind legs, to distract them. Despite the cloud cover overhead, the air was warm and dry, enough to make the ride sweaty and unpleasant.

Boredom set in within the hour, and with the exception of its leader, the group appeared to have lost interest in their work.

In usual circumstances, Dane would have been harder on them, speaking at regular intervals, reminding them why they were here, keeping them motivated and interested. Today, though, he was content to appear as flat as they were, keeping his real intentions to himself.

Whenever he thought he could do it without drawing attention, he looked skyward, towards the Highland Mountains, searching for anything resembling what he and Vanessa had seen the night before. Lord Frederick had seen to it that a patrol, led by Dane, would be sent to this area.

Dane hoped his earlier levity about Vrenin and the Highland Dragon had been enough to convince them that, however unlikely, it was at least plausible for them to be here. But even with his higher sense of purpose, he found himself struggling to stay motivated.

Stopping for their morning break, the group dismounted, keeping their horses reined in while they walked around. Dane moved Thunder away from the others, looking directly into the mountains as the clouds darkened overhead.

In a matter of moments, the sky went from grey to black, and in the next instant they found themselves being pelted with rain. With a collective groan, they looked at Dane, who nodded for them to re-mount and start back towards the castle.

Turning Thunder around, he placed one foot in the stirrup, and as he hoisted himself up, he saw it.

Stunned, he stood there, half-in, half-out of his saddle, his eyes transfixed by what he'd seen. Looking again, it was gone. Hit by a sudden increase in the intensity of the rain, he gathered himself, and along with the others, made his way back towards the castle.

'With due respect to the General, that was a waste of time,' said Harvey as Dane rode level with him.

'Orders are orders,' Dane replied, hearing, but not really listening.

'I thought you had more influence than this,' said Harvey. 'That you would be able to get us out of these tasks.'

Dane wasn't paying enough attention to know whether Harvey was being serious.

'We all have our share of unpleasant tasks,' he said, giving Thunder a short kick to the ribs. 'And I don't have any more influence than anyone else.'

Dane found who he was searching for in one of the small meeting rooms adjacent to the council chambers, a pile of papers scattered around him.

'I need to see Lord Frederick,' he said to Laidlaw, Brindabeare's Clerk of Court.

A man of middle years, with a balding scalp and a portly face, Laidlaw gave Dane the slightest of glances before returning to his papers.

'Lord Frederick is at Council,' he said.

'Do you know how long he will be?' asked Dane, shivering before him, droplets of water pooling on the floor.

'They're scheduled to finish before sunset,' said Laidlaw, 'but they could finish any time – earlier or later.'

Dane grunted in frustration.

'Surely they don't have that much to talk about?' he asked.

Looking up from his papers, Laidlaw said nothing for a moment, before raising a knowing eyebrow; something Dane knew would be followed by a response designed to make him realise it was a foolish question.

'The Leader's Convention will be held in a short while,' said Laidlaw. 'That alone will keep them occupied for a time.'

Dane cringed.

Held every year, the Leader's Convention was an event where all governors across the land travelled to Brindabeare for a series of meetings and social events, held over a period of two weeks.

Dane wondered for a moment how much time they would spend talking about Vanessa's rescue from the City of Lost Souls during this year's convention.

Grunting again, he realised the council meeting may, indeed, take a while.

'Is there any way Lord Frederick can be disturbed?' Dane asked hopefully. 'For a few moments? He's expecting me. He asked me to report once I came back from my patrol.'

'May I ask what is so important to warrant an interruption?'

'Not really,' said Dane. 'Just tell him it's important.'

Laidlaw shook his head.

'I can't do that,' he said.

Dane muttered to himself.

'I beg your pardon?' asked Laidlaw.

'Nothing,' said Dane. 'I guess it will have to wait. Can you ask if he will see me after the meeting?'

'That I can do,' said Laidlaw. 'But I can't promise anything.'

'Just pass on the message,' said Dane.

Laidlaw leaned back in his chair, glaring at Dane.

'Please,' Dane added quickly.

'I will see what I can do,' said Laidlaw, looking at his pile of papers once more.

'Thank you,' said Dane, doing his best not to let his frustration get the better of him.

Laidlaw nodded.

'You look like a drowned rat,' he said.

'Nice seeing you, too,' said Dane, turning and leaving the room.

Making his way towards barracks, a knight stepped in front of him, and he found himself confronted by his old foe, Martin Fenwick; as always, in the company of his two thuggish companions, Vincent Winslow and Austin Harrop.

'Look who it is,' Fenwick sneered.

'I have nothing to say to you,' said Dane.

'But I have something to say to you,' Fenwick replied, blocking Dane's path; his cohorts fanning out behind him.

Dane looked into the skinny, weasel-like face in front of him.

'It seems your plot didn't work,' said Fenwick.

'What?'

'Not only is he wet, he's also deaf,' said Fenwick.

Winslow and Harrop laughed.

'I said your plot didn't work.'

'I have no idea what you're talking about,' said Dane.

'Not only is he wet and deaf, he's also a liar,' said Fenwick.

'What *are* you talking about?' asked Dane.

'You tried to get me thrown out of the Advance Regiment,' said Fenwick.

'What?' said Dane.

'You tried to get me thrown out of the Advance Regiment. When you were leaving to search for the Princess. You had me thrown out of the regiment. We were all there, and we all saw it.'

Winslow and Harrop grunted their agreement.

'I did no such thing,' said Dane. 'It was your own fault.'

'It was a ruse,' said Fenwick. 'You and Hevenshire provoked me, and you did it so Commander Hawthorne would expel me from the regiment.'

Shaking his head in disbelief, Dane saw Fenwick blink sharply as a couple of drops of water splashed into his eyes.

'You had yourself expelled,' said Dane, leaning towards Fenwick. 'And Commander Hawthorne expelled you, not me.'

'Well, Commander Hawthorne is *dead!*' said Fenwick with a smile and great delight in his voice.

'I was there,' said Dane, anger starting to rise within him. 'I know that.'

Hawthorne had been killed during the ensuing quake-like disturbance that had occurred shortly after Vanessa's rescue. To see Fenwick revelling in his death was sickening.

Dane placed a hand on his sword.

'You wouldn't,' said Fenwick, taking a step back.

'You dare to gloat about the death of a Brindabeare Knight?' Dane growled. 'The Commander of the Advance Regiment, no less?'

He took a menacing step towards Fenwick, his hand tightening around his sword.

'If you do that again,' he said, taking another step forward, 'no matter where we are,' he said, taking another step, 'I will cut out your tongue, and feed it to the dogs.'

With a final step, Dane had Fenwick pinned against a wall; Winslow and Harrop splayed out beside him.

Brushing past them, he stalked away.

'Well ... I'm back in the Advance Regiment,' Fenwick said in the distance.

'How do you feel?' Dane asked gently.

'Well enough,' Vanessa replied, sitting forward and pouring herself some water.

'What did Lord Frederick say?'

'The same as before. He can't find anything wrong with me.'

Seeing the uncertainty in her face, Dane asked gently, 'how do you *really* feel? No heroics: no trying to talk your way into training. Just you and me.'

Kneeling before her, he took her hands in his.

'Vanessa,' he said, his voice barely more than a whisper. 'Talk to me.'

With a quivering voice, she said, 'I don't know. I can't say how I feel – but it's ... strange. I don't feel like myself. I know how that must sound, but it's true.'

Dane nodded.

'I know,' he said.

Vanessa's eyes widened.

'What do you mean?' she asked.

'I saw it yesterday, and I see it today. I can't say what it is either; but you don't *look* like yourself. Not in a bad way, but it's as though something's not quite right.'

Vanessa sat back, looking at herself.

'No,' said Dane, seeing her reaction. 'That's not what I meant. Something *about you*, about *who you are*, is missing. Not in a bad way, and I can't describe it exactly; but you seem to be ... different – not your full self – in some way or another.'

Vanessa relaxed, considering what Dane was saying.

'That's about as well as I can explain it,' she said, fear and uncertainty in her eyes.

Dane rubbed her hands gently.

'I'm sure it will pass,' he said.

Vanessa smiled weakly.

Changing the subject, she asked, 'did you see anything today?'

'Yes,' said Dane. 'I was just telling Lord Frederick about it.'

Vanessa's eyes widened.

'At the time it started to rain. I'm sure I saw it. Something lifted into the sky, very briefly, and there was a puff of smoke.'

'What was it?' said Vanessa.

'I really don't know,' said Dane. 'It was only for a moment. Part of me wonders if I saw anything at all. It could have been a cloud. But the more I think about it, the more I'm sure of it.'

'A dragon?' asked Vanessa.

'I only saw it for a moment,' said Dane. 'But, if we wanted to put the pieces together, and use our imagination, then, we could say it was a dragon.'

'The Highland Dragon?'

'Who's to know?' said Dane. 'It's all myth and legend. It would be strange to suddenly appear like this.'

Standing, unsteady for a moment, but righting herself, Vanessa took a step towards the window.

'What?' said Dane, stepping in front of her. 'What are you doing?'

'I want to look out the window,' Vanessa replied.

'But, should you? Are you well enough to walk? Why not just stay here?'

'I'm all right,' said Vanessa. 'I just want to look.'

Dane saw the same wistful, almost trance-like look come over her he'd seen the night before.

'Vanessa,' he said taking her arm, 'I don't think this is a good idea.'

'Of course, it is,' she replied, leading them across the room.

Reluctantly, Dane walked with her to the window.

Looking towards the Highland Mountains again, they searched the night sky.

It was a little colder tonight; the cloud cover making it harder to see into the distance.

'I can't see anything,' said Vanessa, after a time.

'No,' said Dane, standing behind her. 'Neither can I. It's too dark.'

'Are you all right?' he asked.

Vanessa nodded mechanically, as though she hadn't really heard him.

Looking towards the mountains again, Dane couldn't understand why, but something seemed to be different.

It was as black as night, but there was something, something eerie about it.

It felt very quiet; too quiet; as though everything had stopped, when, in the next instant there was a blur as the darkness suddenly charged towards him, followed by a tremendous roar and a thundering *CRASH!* that sent everything spiralling out of control.

Chapter 4
DRAGON

The whole of the north tower shuddered.

The sheer force of the collision threw Dane and Vanessa back into the chamber.

Glass from the window shattered, raining down on them. At the same time, chunks of stone around the window crumbled, falling away; some into the chamber, others to the ground outside.

The mouth of a large beast burst into the gap; trying to force itself into the chamber.

Dane looked up.

The jaws of the beast opened, sending a chill down his spine as it roared again, louder and more fearsome than anything he'd heard in his life. The size of its mouth, the razor-sharp teeth glistening in the light above him, highlighted by a pair of large fangs on its lower jaw, looked large enough to swallow him with a single bite.

Pieces of stone and mortar continued to crumble as it continued to push forward, trying to force its way inside.

Unable to do so, it started growling again.

Guessing what would come next, he grabbed Vanessa, lying in front of him, and rolled away from the window.

With another roar, a ball of flame burst from the creature's mouth, filling most of the chamber, setting the furniture on fire.

Huddling in a corner, Dane took stock of what was happening.

All their hunches, their wild thoughts, no matter how fanciful, were true.

A dragon!

The Highland Dragon!

It wasn't the night rushing at him in those last moments – it was the dragon; its sheer size filling his entire line of sight as it flew into the tower.

Stunned from the force of the impact for a moment, as he brushed glass and stone fragments from his hair and arms, apart from a few scratches, he saw he was unscathed.

Vanessa groaned next to him.

Moving her into a sitting position, he looked at her closely.

Having taken more of the blunt force, she had an open cut on her forehead dripping down her face and onto her clothes. A smaller cut on her cheek bled freely. Glass fragments were embedded in her hair, and her hands and arms were bleeding.

'Wh-what –'

'The Highland Dragon!' said Dane. '*The Highland Dragon!*'

It roared again, another scorching flame filling the chamber.

Vanessa screamed, rolling into a ball, hugging herself to Dane's chest.

'*It's trying to get in!*' Dane yelled.

Squeezing herself smaller, Vanessa held on to Dane for all she was worth.

Dane heard more stones falling away as the dragon sought to remove its head from the window. For a brief moment the space was empty, and he felt the full night air gusting into the open room, before, with another shuddering *CRASH!* the head slammed into the opening again.

Dane looked around.

Everything was on fire, and he could feel its heat and the stench of the smoke starting to choke the air around him.

The Royal Knight assigned to the chamber came charging in, sword drawn, running straight at the dragon.

'NO!' Dane yelled a moment too late.

Another roar, followed by a fireball filled the chamber.

The guard fell where he stood.

Vanessa screamed.

Trying to understand what was happening, Dane's mind raced.

It's trying to get into the chamber!

The dragon growled again.

More debris fell into and away from the chamber.

It can't turn its head …

From his crouched position, he could see the dragon had only been able to fit its jaws into the chamber. He couldn't see its eyes, or its neck, which meant there was nothing vulnerable he could strike at.

He and Vanessa were stranded – anyone entering would suffer the same fate as the guard, and at the moment they would be foolish to move from where they were.

'Princess! *Princess!*' voices screamed from the entrance of the chamber.

The dragon backed its mouth from the chamber again.

The smoke and flames were quickly destroying everything.

With another CRASH! Dane felt the tower shudder again as the dragon's head tried to force itself through the gap once more.

Outraged at its lack of success, another roar and fireball erupted, the heat and noise more intense than before.

Vanessa balled herself tighter against Dane, coughing against the smoke and sobbing uncontrollably.

Dane scanned the chamber, his eyes watering from the heat and smoke, becoming more and more desperate to find an escape.

While they were relatively 'safe' from the dragon at the moment, he and Vanessa had to get out before the smoke and flames took them.

The latest fireball ceased, and with a flash of light and a *BANG!* Lord Frederick appeared. Seeing Dane and Vanessa huddled in the corner, he raised his hand.

'Stay where you are!'

Dane nodded.

Lord Frederick stepped forward. With a flick of his wrist, a thin argent light shot from his fingers, creating a swirling wind that extinguished the flames and sucked the smoke from the chamber.

While this was happening, the dragon withdrew its jaws once more.

Lord Frederick raised his hand again.

The room pulsed, an invisible force pushing towards the window.

'Behind me!' he said.

Dane rose to his feet, picking Vanessa up in his arms.

Wrapping her arms around his neck, Vanessa buried her face in his chest.

With his back to the window, they made their way behind Lord Frederick.

In the next moment, there was another shuddering *THUMP!* and Dane stumbled for a moment as the dragon slammed its jaws through the gap again.

With another roar, it let loose another ball of fire.

This time, it travelled no further than a foot, blocked by the barrier Lord Frederick had created.

'Get her out of here!' he said.

Hurrying away, Dane made it halfway to the entrance, when a group of Royal Knights and others appeared, rushing into the chamber.

Seeing a couple of healers with them, he tried handing Vanessa to them.

'No!' she screamed, turning away.

'You have to go with them!' said Dane, letting her down gently and taking her hands from around his neck. 'They'll take care of you.'

Reluctantly, she let go, before staggering into their arms.

Dane saw her continuing to bleed from the wounds on her face, cheek, and hands.

'You'll be all right!' he said, as the healers led her away.

Another grabbed his hand.

It was covered in blood, as were his clothes. How much of it was his, and how much Vanessa had smeared on him, he had no clue.

'I'm fine!' he said, tearing himself away and drawing his sword.

He ran to Lord Frederick and the others – Will, Hindmarsh, Harvey and Lovell among them. Swords drawn, they looked with horror and disbelief at the massive mouth in front of them.

'What in the name of the Gods are we dealing with?' Will whispered.

'Vrenin's dragon!' said Dane. '*Vrenin's Dragon!*'

'What –'

Will's voice was smothered as the dragon roared and let out another burst of flame.

Behind Lord Frederick's barrier, they were in no immediate danger.

Lord Frederick flicked his fingers, and a rope-meshed net the size of his hand shot forward, increasing in size as it sailed through the air. By the time it reached its target, it had become large enough to wrap itself around the dragon's jaws, turning to steel and clamping tight.

With nothing more than the slightest twitch of its mouth, the net snapped to pieces, falling harmlessly to the floor.

The dragon roared its outrage, and as it opened its mouth, Lord Frederick released a bolt of azure, straight into its throat, the flash of light blinding the whole chamber for an instant when it struck.

There was no reaction from the dragon indicating it had had the slightest effect, and in the next moment another stream of fire spewed from its mouth.

For a moment no one moved, and then, with a giant sniff, the dragon withdrew its head once more. This time, it didn't reappear.

With a roar at the night, it tilted its head, sniffing the air around it.

Those in the chamber heard the smashing and felt the shaking around the tower where new sections of the wall were breaking.

'It's moving!' said Hindmarsh. 'To the roof!'

'Go!' said Lord Frederick. Grabbing Dane and Harvey as they turned, he said, 'you two, with me!'

The others raced from the chamber.

'Let's see what it's doing,' said Lord Frederick, stepping onto the ledge that was now the remains of the window.

Dane and Harvey followed.

The damage created by the dragon had left a hole several times larger than when it had been a window. Large chunks of stone had been torn away, most of it reduced to rubble on the ground below.

Looking from the massive hole, taking in the enormity of the beast attacking them, Dane's eyes widened in sheer terror, his breath catching in his throat.

A dark vert-green, with tinges of brown and grey, perhaps thirty feet from head to tail, it stood about nine feet tall. Its legs were the size of small trees, each with five huge claws that were tearing more and more chunks from the tower as it moved around, scrabbling its way along the wall.

Large spikes along its spine stuck out through its thick, scaly skin, from the top of its neck to an arrowhead tail, which was ripping chunks from the wall as it swished and slapped against it. Finally, he noticed the wings; thick, yet partly transparent, stretching over seventy feet from tip to tip, with a single claw about two-thirds along the top.

Dane watched as it continued sniffing the night air, turning its head in swift, jerky movements.

'It's as though it's looking for something,' he said.

Lord Frederick pointed his hands at the dragon.

Twin shots of azure again shot out; this time mixed with a tinge of gold.

Hitting the dragon in the neck and side, the points of impact drew small wisps of smoke. The dragon immediately twisted its head towards them, turning its body in one swift motion. There were several loud *BANGS!* as its claws sank into new pieces of the wall, showering debris onto the ground below.

With a roar of defiance, a huge fireball leapt towards the ledge where Dane, Lord Frederick and Harvey were standing.

Leaning into the chamber, it passed them without incident.

'How are we going to defeat that thing?' asked Harvey.

In the next moment, there was a grinding noise from above, and a huge boulder landed on the dragon, hitting it squarely between its eyes with a loud *SMACK!* before falling away. From the way it reacted, it appeared to Dane as though it had the impact of a pebble.

Next, the contents from a huge cauldron of liquid fire spewed over the roof.

Instead of burning into the skin, Dane heard little more than a sizzle, like a freshly cut sword being placed in water, before the fiery liquid simply disappeared.

'It did nothing!' he yelled in disbelief. 'None of it!'

Although it appeared to be unscathed, the attack angered the dragon. In one swift movement it leaped away from the wall, more rock and mortar trailing in its wake. With a single flap of its wings, it swept itself around to face the tower again, its tail swishing around like a huge whip. It kept a position about a foot from the wall of the castle, tilting its head upward.

A moment later, raising itself slightly, tilting its head further, a huge flame roared skyward. Longer than any it had loosed so far, Dane heard anguished screams above him as it found its target.

Lord Frederick unsheathed Scarafuse.

With a wave of his hand, his mighty sword glowed a pure gold, lighting the night sky around him. With a smooth throwing motion, Scarafuse went sailing through the air, the light spinning as it turned over and over, before bouncing harmlessly off the dragon's thick hide, and falling towards the ground.

With a flick of his wrist, the sword shot back to its owner, returning to Lord Frederick's hand.

'*How are we going to defeat that thing?*' Harvey screamed.

Lord Frederick turned away from the ledge.

'Outside,' he said. 'Gather as many as you can find.'

Harvey raced away.

'With me,' Lord Frederick said to Dane.

Running towards the north entrance, they passed people yelling and screaming in the hallways.

'*Where is Will?*' Dane heard Genevieve cry out as he and Lord Frederick ran by.

With a moment's memory of what had happened on the roof, he could only hope Will had survived.

'*A dragon!!!*' he heard someone yell. '*We're being attacked by a dragon!*'

Dane felt his sword, sweaty and loose in his hand, and saw blood running down the hilt and blade.

With no time to do anything about it, he, Lord Frederick and several others ran into the north courtyard.

By now, there were perhaps fifty defenders at varying points. Some were on the ramparts, others were on the ground, spread from one end of the courtyard to the other.

Stepping around the remains of what had been torn from the wall, Dane and Lord Frederick looked up and saw the dragon hovering near the open ledge of Vanessa's chamber.

From here, Dane could see the full extent of its destruction.

In addition to Vanessa's chamber, huge holes had been dug out of the wall, some the size of the boulder that had been dropped on the dragon. Given the dragon's size, the area of damage spread over large expanses of the wall. Pieces were also missing from the ramparts surrounding the north tower, torn away by falling debris.

Dane drew another sharp breath as he understood the destruction the dragon had wrought on the strongest and most fortified area of the entire castle. It had been built from the strongest stone, to provide maximum protection for the Royal Family, and the dragon had torn into it as though it were nothing more than a pile of sticks.

'Lord Frederick, what are your instructions?' asked a Royal Knight.

'We need to get it down here, to the ground,' he said.

'How do we do that?'

'Let's try there,' he said, pointing to the ramparts.

In the next instant a volley of arrows shot through the air. They found their mark but did nothing, bouncing away like twigs.

Another stream of arrows had the same result.

'They're worthless,' said Dane.

Lord Frederick nodded.

'Come with me,' he said to Dane.

Racing to the base of a rampart, Dane followed Lord Frederick up the steps.

A couple of Royal Knights came to meet them.

'It's no use,' said one to Lord Frederick. 'I've seen everything from the moment it struck the tower. Nothing we've tried has had any effect.'

'We're not beaten yet,' said Lord Frederick. 'Get me some arrows, a bow and some rope.'

The Royal Knight ran to his companions.

'What are you going to do?' asked Dane.

'One arrow may not have the desired effect, but this just might.'

The Royal Knight returned, handing over a few arrows, and a short coil of rope.

'Your sword,' said Lord Frederick, holding out his hand.

While Lord Frederick worked, the dragon roared again.

Dane looked up and saw it sniffing and looking around as it had before.

What is it looking for?

Another ball of flame struck the tower.

If we don't do something soon, it's going to kill us all!

'There,' said Lord Frederick.

The tips of the arrows had been broken away, moulded into one larger, stronger arrowhead. Next, all the shafts were joined together, creating a single, longer length of arrow.

Fixing the arrowhead to the shaft, Lord Frederick ran his hand from the arrowhead to the end, which he'd tied to the rope. With another touch of his finger, the shaft became a thickened steel from end to end.

Dane noticed hints of azure; the same as the bolt Lord Frederick had shot into the dragon's mouth. Looking again, he also saw faint traces of vert mixed in.

Rubbing the rope with his thumb and finger, Lord Frederick had increased its length, which lay coiled at his feet. It was long enough to travel the length of the courtyard.

Finally, the bow had been changed. It had increased to several times its size, but rather than the usual archer's bow, Lord Frederick had turned it sideways, creating a large crossbow, and moulded the steel from the Royal Knight's sword to create a powerful firing mechanism, with small stands on each end.

Looking across the courtyard, Dane noticed people spilling out of the castle; either curious, or eager for a look at the dragon.

The dragon turned its head, roaring and releasing another burst of flame.

'Let's give this a try,' said Lord Frederick, 'and hope it fires truly.'

He and Dane raised the weapon onto the rampart.

Looking at the dragon, Dane saw it continuing to hover in the same position, ignoring everyone and everything around it, as if it were waiting for something.

The Gods help us, let this work.

Lord Frederick moved the bow, lining up his target.

With a snap, the weapon fired.

Streaking through the air in an arc across the courtyard, it struck the dragon in its belly, just behind its right foreleg.

The dragon seemed to freeze in the air.

Elated for a moment, Dane watched, horrified, as he saw the arrow bounce off the dragon's hide, dropping harmlessly to the ground. From what he could see, it didn't leave so much as a puncture wound.

'I've never,' said Lord Frederick.

A deafening roar burst from the dragon, followed by a fireball so bright and intense it appeared to singe the walls a shade of black.

Tossing and turning its head, it roared again.

Turning towards Dane and Lord Frederick, it appeared to raise itself up, almost vertical, lauding itself over everyone, its powerful wings and tail maintaining its position, while it sniffed the air.

With a sense of dread and horrifying certainty, Dane saw the dragon look directly at him.

With another roar, it leaned forward and shot through the air, straight towards him.

Royal Knights screamed, running and ducking for cover.

Dane dropped behind the rampart.

Lord Frederick crouched beside him.

'Our only hope is if I can strike truly with Scarafuse when it attacks,' he said.

A blur of thoughts buzzed through Dane's mind.

Raegan wins after all …

I didn't kill him …

He's released the Highland Dragon on us …

It's all my fault!!!

The rampart above him broke apart as the dragon landed several feet away.

In the next instant, Lord Frederick was gone.

It's all my fault!

I did this!

Everyone is going to die because of me!!!

The dragon lowered its head, sniffing the air.

From where he was, Dane could smell its hot, dry breath.

Any moment now, it would unleash a ball of fire, toasting him and everyone around him. It would force its way into to the castle, whatever it took, until it found what it was looking for, until …

The dragon growled, lowering its head towards him …

There was a flash of light behind its head …

Lord Frederick.

Lord Frederick … I have to help Lord Frederick!

With a yell he sprang to his feet, his sword pulled back.

The dragon lowered its head …

Lord Frederick dropped from the sky above him, slamming Scarafuse into the dragon's eye …

Dane swung his sword upward as hard as he could …

With no more than a gentle scrape, Lord Frederick and Scarafuse glanced harmlessly against the dragon's face …

Dane's sword sunk into the dragon's throat, embedding itself to the hilt …

Lord Frederick dropped to the ground …

Dane pulled his sword out.

The dragon let out a blood-curdling scream and rocked back, its neck wobbling as blood poured from its wound, before toppling backwards from the rampart and crashing into the courtyard, where it burst into flames.

Chapter 5
BLOOD RELATION

With the warmth of spring spreading across the land, people in the province of Lansi spent most days outdoors. Located towards the northern end of the Xerin Mountains, the closest settlements were either side of the Penton River, at Delfar and Kordeit, at least a day's ride away.

The city of Stanthorpe was another four days to north, with Brindabeare the better part of two weeks away.

Charles Wardsworth had his hands full, re-shoeing his horses while tending his two children: six-year-old Warren, and Charlotte, four, who were running rings around him, chasing hens across the yard.

'Be careful!' he scolded as Charlotte tore past him.

Charlotte giggled, running mindlessly, eyes only for the hen, her fair hair flailing from side to side.

He smiled. Even at this age, she reminded him of her mother, who he spotted walking towards him from the corner of his eye, the sun shining on her as she clutched a basket to her side.

Stepping away from the horse and standing to his full height to greet her, shielding his eyes from the sun; at first, he didn't realise what was happening.

The sky darkened, blotting out the sun as his wife walked towards him.

In the next moment it was visible again, the light bursting onto the ground in front of her.

A penetrating screech pierced the sky, and the creature soared in from behind her.

Others stopped what they were doing, looking in the direction of the strange noise.

Larger than any bird he'd ever seen, at first Charles thought he was dreaming as it flashed into view.

Blinking again, his mind cleared.

'Serena!' he screamed.

Swooping in above her, the giant creature shot past like an arrow.

Snapping his head around, he followed its path as it ...

'No!'

Without breaking speed, with a jolt that knocked the breath out of her, the giant bird snatched Charlotte off the ground.

No one watching could tell the difference between the screech of the predator and the terrified scream of the little girl in its talons.

Soaring into the air, in a wide arc, the giant bird headed back from where it came, blotting out the sun once more.

Norton had his suspicions.

Someone had been stealing from the flocks, and it was only a matter of time before they were caught.

Farrington has always been envious of us.

Whenever he has trouble with his own, he always comes begging to us – and now he's stealing them.

Arrogant, pompous old fool – always so smug and proper, acting as though he's so superior to everyone else.

I won't stand for it!

I'll wipe that look off his face once and for all ...

A man knocked urgently.

'Yes?'

'Governor, you must come quickly!'

'What is it, Brendley?' said Norton, annoyed at the interruption.

'The flock!' said Brendley. 'We've found what's attacking the flocks!'

'Don't you mean, who?'

'No!' said Brendley. 'Quickly! You must come!'

'What do you mean –'

'Quickly!' said Brendley. 'There's no time!'

Hustling from the room, the two ran to the courtyard, where a couple of horses were waiting.

'Quickly!' said Brendley, spurring his mount towards the river.

Bewildered, Norton scrambled into his saddle and followed.

A short time later, they approached the flock, wandering in the fields outside the boundary fence.

Spotting a large herd of sheep, at first, Norton saw nothing unusual.

'Why have you –'

His words caught in his throat.

Was the ground moving?

His face aghast, as he looked again, the creature crawled into his vision.

Its head raised off the ground, its round, scaly body slithering behind, blending with the colour of the ground.

As he watched, spellbound, it stood. If not for the fact it was standing, he would have called it a serpent. In its next movement, the creature's head shot forward, its neck extending, mouth opening wide, before latching onto one of the hapless herd.

Bleating helplessly in the clutches of its captor, Norton could only stare in dumb wonder as the lamb was hauled back towards the body of the serpent-creature, like a fish on a line. As it reeled in its catch, the creature retreated, lowering itself onto its belly and slithering towards the shelter of the woods from where it came.

The smell of meat drew it ashore, wafting to the river on the evening breeze.

Taking its first steps on land, its legs pivoting in their sockets, in a couple of strides it felt as natural on land as it had in water. It had no trouble seeing either, its eyes tilting forward and sliding towards the front of its face.

Rushing towards its prey, it crashed into a stone wall, something it had never felt before. Stunned for a moment, it struck again, the wall bending, but remaining in place. The smell was so strong, so close, yet it couldn't quite break through.

It moved to its right, following the wall until it came to a small opening.

Rushing in, the guards at the gatehouse thought it to be nothing more than a large dog.

At a full sprint, it raced towards the smell.

It could hear them grunting and squealing ahead and saw movement behind another structure.

Desperate for its meal, it charged, hurling itself at the barrier in front of it.

With a crash, the wood-fence crumbled, and it found itself surrounded by a litter of piglets.

With utter relish, it looked around, enraptured by what looked like an endless supply of meat. Snapping its jaws around the middle of the nearest piglet, it broke it cleanly in half. Leaving one piece behind, it turned away, running towards the opening from where it came.

Arriving at the gate once more, the guards watched on as the dog ran past the flickering torches with its meal.

Plants and herbs bubbled in a small pot, hanging from a stick over a small fire.

Despite the night's cold, the space was warm enough that it had stopped shivering, an evening comfort it had not had in months. Lying on its side by the fire, it stared dully at the wall, panting.

The old lady pottered about, muttering to herself. She hadn't had company in a long time, much less something as magnificent as this.

'Such a fine creature,' she said. 'A fine one indeed. And where did it come from? Wandering around on its own like that. It's wounded. Yes. It's wounded.'

Shuffling to the fire, she clutched a small cloth in her withered hand.

Bending down, wiping bits of her long, dusty hair out of her eyes, she studied its neck.

Despite the dried blood on its coat, the wound was still festering, a mixture of blood and gooey pus.

'That doesn't look good at all,' the old lady said soothingly.

She placed the cloth in the pot, letting it drop to the bottom and soak, before retrieving it and wringing it out over the fire, wiping her hands on her old, brown, dirt-ridden raggedy dress.

Easing herself beside the wolf, she lowered the cloth towards the wound.

The wolf was growling, alerted by the sizzling sound it had heard moments before. It tried to raise itself.

'There, there,' said the old lady, placing her other hand on the wolf's head, applying a gentle pressure to push it down.

The growl grew louder.

'It won't hurt,' she said.

A drop of water leaked into the wound, spreading its way rapidly through veins and arteries, all the way to the heart.

With an anguished yelp, the wolf sprang up, mouth open, biting down hard on the old lady's arm.

'How is she?' asked Dane.

'She says she's feeling better than she's felt for the last few days,' said Marilena.

'What?' said Dane. 'She's been attacked by a dragon! How can she be better?'

Entering the chamber, he found Vanessa sitting up in bed, pillows puffed around her, rays of morning sunshine streaming into the room. The wounds on her forehead and cheek had been treated; they were now little more than surface cuts, well on their way to healing. She looked tired, yet calm, as though a burden had been lifted.

Lord Frederick and the King were seated around her.

Vanessa looked up as Dane approached.

'You look well,' she said with a glowing smile.

'I was just about to say the same of you,' said Dane, watching her closely. 'How are your wounds?'

'Almost healed,' she said with an appreciative glance at Lord Frederick. 'And you?'

'A couple of scratches,' said Dane.

'Is it true?' she asked with a hint of wonder.

'What?' said Dane.

'What they're saying,' said Vanessa, her voice full of admiration. 'That you killed the dragon.'

Dane nodded.

Vanessa beamed, her face full of wonder and awe.

'But ... how?'

'Mistress,' interrupted the King, 'forgive us, but there are some matters we need to discuss privately.'

Marilena frowned.

'Sire,' she pleaded, 'after the events of the last days, she *needs* me here.'

'I'm afraid not,' said King, after a moment's pause. 'We must talk with the Princess alone.'

Marilena looked desperately to Lord Frederick, who offered his sympathies with the smallest nod.

With a final look at the King and a despairing glance at Dane, with a restrained, *'very well,'* she departed, closing the door a little too loudly on her way out.

With the north tower substantially damaged from the dragon's attack, the Royal Quarters had been relocated to the east side of the castle.

'Princess,' said Lord Frederick, 'there are some matters we need to discuss. And in the same vein as our conversation two evenings ago, they are to remain in strict confidence.'

Vanessa nodded.

'We're trying to understand everything about the dragon,' said the King.

'What do you mean?' Vanessa replied.

'There are several things we don't quite understand,' said Lord Frederick. 'While you were resting, we held a debrief with Council, but there are some unresolved matters we need to discuss.'

'Very well,' said Vanessa.

'The behaviour of this dragon was most unusual,' said Lord Frederick. 'While there are many myths and legends of dragons, there has rarely, if ever, been a sighting in the history of the land. Nevertheless, there are sufficient recordings in the *Annals of Creation*, and other information that has been passed through the course of time, as to how dragons behave.'

With a knowing glance at Dane, she nodded. They had both laboured under Councillor Lindstrom's tutoring on the subject.

'What was so unusual about it?' she asked.

Lord Frederick nodded to Dane.

'Well, from the way it acted, we think it was looking for something,' said Dane.

Vanessa's eyes narrowed.

'Looking for something?' she replied. 'How can you be sure?'

'The way it attacked,' said Dane. 'It flew straight into the tower – to your window.'

'I remember,' said Vanessa. 'It struck right where we were standing. Are you saying it meant to do that?'

Dane nodded.

'It didn't just strike once. Do you remember it hitting the tower several times?'

Vanessa frowned, trying to remember.

'Not, really. I think I remember something, like, an aftershock.'

'That was it,' said Dane. 'It was trying to get *into* the chamber. When it didn't succeed the first time, it tried again.'

'What?' said Vanessa. 'How?'

'It kept butting the tower,' said Dane. 'When it couldn't get in, it pulled itself out and butted the tower again and again, several times, trying to force its way in. They were the shocks you felt.'

'It was trying to get into the chamber?' said Vanessa, dumbfounded. '*My* chamber?'

'It would appear so,' said Lord Frederick. 'Dragons aren't usually so determined, so persistent in their hunting. Although their size usually means they can crash through trees and other foliage to catch their prey, when their prey proves elusive, they move on. They wouldn't try to force their way into a cave or under a ledge to find an elk that managed to hide there – they would simply turn to the next one.'

'And once the healers took you away,' said Dane, 'it stopped trying to force its way in.'

'Why?' said Vanessa, as she started putting it together. 'Because ... because ... I wasn't ... are you saying, it was trying ... to, to find ... *me?*'

Dane hesitated.

'Well –'

Slapping her hands to her mouth, she was aghast.

'That's not ...' she said, horrified at the thought. 'How can that possibly be true?'

'On its own, it would be hard to say,' said Lord Frederick. 'But when we follow everything to the end, it makes more sense.'

'Once you left the chamber,' said Dane. 'It gave up trying to get in, and moved around the tower, sniffing around, as though it was trying to find something. It seemed as though it was trying to find your scent again.'

'They took me to the hospital wing,' said Vanessa.

Lord Frederick nodded.

'And it was probably well that they did.'

Located on a lower floor in a corner on the opposite side of the castle, it was as far from the north tower as anywhere in the entire castle.

'It kept moving and hovering around,' said Dane. 'As though it was trying to get its bearings; as though it was looking for something.'

'It's very strange behaviour for a dragon,' said Lord Frederick. 'And there are a couple of other factors we have to consider.'

'Such as?' said Vanessa, her eyes wide.

'Well,' said the King. 'You. How you have been feeling these last few days. Your fainting spells.'

'How can that have *anything* to do with this?' said Vanessa, thinking they'd lost their minds.

'It's not just the fainting episodes,' said Lord Frederick.

'What?' said Vanessa, taken aback.

'Two nights ago,' said Dane quietly. 'When we first saw the flame. Do you remember?'

Vanessa nodded.

'And last night?' said Dane.

'Of course.'

'What do you remember?'

'We saw the flame,' said Vanessa. 'The first night. From the window.'

'Do you remember anything else?'

Vanessa thought for a moment.

'No,' she said. 'What else is there? We were looking out the window, and we saw the flame in the distance.'

'And last night?'

'We were standing at the window, and the dragon attacked.'

'You don't remember anything else?' said Dane.

'No,' said Vanessa, her eyes narrowing in suspicion. 'What are you trying to say?'

'Well,' said Dane, 'both times; last night and the night before; you didn't walk to the window in a way that was, what I would say … normal.'

'Wh-what?'

Vanessa's face contorted in shock; her eyes widening, her cheeks flushed and her skin clammy.

'It was as though you were in some sort of *trance*,' said Dane gently. 'I don't know how else to explain it.'

Leaning back, Vanessa couldn't believe what she was hearing.

'You seemed to be drawn to the window,' said Dane. 'You didn't seem to be yourself. It was only for a moment or two. But you weren't yourself.'

'I don't understand!' she said desperately.

Dane lowered his head, struggling to keep his composure. With the King and Lord Frederick here, he couldn't offer her any comfort.

Lord Frederick touched her arm gently.

'We don't mean to upset you,' he said. 'But once we get through it, I think we'll all understand.'

'Vanessa,' said the King. 'Earlier, before Royal – before Dane arrived, you mentioned you felt better than you had for the last few days.'

Vanessa nodded.

'Well,' said the King, 'from what we've pieced together, you started to feel better about the same time the dragon was killed.'

Vanessa gasped.

'What?' she stammered. 'But ... how? How can they possibly be related?'

'At the moment, we can't say we're sure about any of this,' said Lord Frederick. 'The last thing we believe connects you to the dragon, is the way it was killed.'

Looking at Dane, she said, 'he killed it. What's so unusual about that?'

'What you don't know,' said Lord Frederick, 'is that I tried and failed to kill it several times.'

Vanessa sat speechless, her mouth open in shock.

'I tried several spells,' said Lord Frederick. 'As a Fire-sourced creature, we know the strongest counter-measures are Water-based. I struck the dragon with several of these – spells to paralyse, cripple and kill it. I also used blunt force: a large arrow, and Scarafuse.'

Shaking his head slowly, Lord Frederick seemed in his own state of disbelief.

'Every measure failed,' he said. 'They had no effect on the dragon at all. They were strong, powerful spells, and Scarafuse is wizard-forged, with a power and capability no other sword possesses.'

'So, then, how –' said Vanessa.

'And yet, despite those failings,' said Lord Frederick, 'Dane killed it with a single stroke, which, although a great feat on his part, simply does not make sense.'

Vanessa looked at Dane, confused.

'We think it was because I was with you,' said Dane. 'When it attacked.'

'What –'

'I had blood all over me. *Your blood.*'

'What?' said Vanessa, bewildered. 'My blood killed the dragon?'

Dane, Lord Frederick and the King nodded gently.

'When you put it together, you can see it makes sense,' said Lord Frederick. 'When this dragon was created, it had one purpose – to find you. In the time before it found you, while it was growing, it was drawing power – essence, from you. This explains your fainting spells, and why we were not able to find anything wrong with you.'

'I've only been ill the last few days,' said Vanessa. 'Are you saying it was only alive for four days?'

'We don't know how long it was alive before it attacked,' said Lord Frederick.

'I've been told it was over thirty feet long!' said Vanessa. 'Surely it can't grow to that size in three or four days?'

'We will never know,' said Lord Frederick. 'But I'm led to believe, given everything we know, that this dragon lived a short life, and grew to size rapidly.'

'It's not Vrenin's Dragon – the Highland Dragon?'

'We don't believe so,' said Lord Frederick.

Vanessa didn't know whether to be relieved or frightened.

'So, it grew in three or four – a short space of time. And then?'

'It found its way to you,' said Lord Frederick. 'Drawing on your essence, it became more attuned, more sensitive to it. And then, two nights ago, you were drawn to the window, and it picked up your scent – connected to it directly.

'Last evening, it drew you to the window again, knowing exactly where you would be, and tried to force itself into the chamber. Once you left, it kept searching for you, until it found your scent on Dane.'

'It thought Dane was me?'

'Possibly.'

'But ... how did he kill it?' said Vanessa.

'There were traces of your blood all over me, and on my sword,' said Dane.

'I'm still confused,' said Vanessa. 'Because Dane's sword had my blood on it, he could kill it?'

'Yes,' said Lord Frederick. 'Given the other efforts to kill the dragon failed so dramatically, I believe this dragon was created from the very core of the Fire Element itself, with a specific purpose – to kill you.'

Vanessa rocked back, gasping in shock.

'And I believe, when this is the case,' said Lord Frederick, 'the essence within the object it is has been created to kill – in this case, your blood – is also the means – perhaps the only means, by which it can itself be killed.

'Traces of your blood fused with Dane's sword, enabling it to penetrate the dragon's skin, and he was able to kill it.'

Vanessa nodded, somehow making sense of it in all the madness she'd heard.

'I don't know whether to laugh or cry,' she said.

'You are well, and the dragon is no more,' said Lord Frederick with a wry smile. 'I would lean towards the former.'

Dane gave her an encouraging nod and a smile.

'It's over,' he said.

Vanessa nodded slowly, not convinced.

'What do we do now?' asked Vanessa.

'Among other things, we work out where this dragon came from,' said Lord Frederick.

'Where do we start?' said Dane.

'I need you to show me exactly where you saw it,' said Lord Frederick, beckoning Dane from the room.

'I'll come with you,' said Vanessa.

Lord Frederick looked at the King.

'I'm coming with you,' she said, climbing out of her bed and disappearing into the dressing room.

Knowing better than to argue, Dane, Lord Frederick and the King waited while she dressed.

Making their way to Vanessa's chambers, with an insistent Marilena joining them, both Dane and Vanessa shook their heads in disbelief at what remained. Although the furniture had been removed, the walls still bore the scars left by the flames that had torched the room.

Walking to the large hole that had been the window, they looked briefly at the damage they could see outside.

The stones that had fallen from the castle and walls were gone, some of the holes already filled in. Repairs had commenced on the outer wall, and they could see the masons preparing to replace the damaged sections around the window.

Directing their gaze to the mountains, with a flick of his wrist, Lord Frederick sent a light into the air.

'Tell me when the light lands where you saw the dragon.'

'A little to the left,' said Dane.

'A bit more,' said Vanessa, following the path of the light.

'There!' said Dane. 'That's where I remember first seeing it.'

'I think so, too,' said Vanessa.

Lord Frederick lowered his hand.

The light remained where it was.

'Very well,' he said.

'What are you going to do now?' asked Dane.

'Take a short journey to the Highland Mountains,' Lord Frederick replied.

With a final nod, he dematerialised in a flash of white light and a *BANG!*

Watching the mountains, Dane and Vanessa saw the light hover in the air for a few moments before it disappeared.

Walking from the room, Vanessa took Dane by the hand.

'Thank you,' she said. 'For protecting me.'

Dane nodded.

'All part of a knight's duty,' he said.

Chapter 6
CORE CONNECTION

In a far corner of the castle, a thin stream of light filtering through a solitary window, they waited.

Mortensen read the note a second time.

Dismissing the messenger with a wave of his hand, he smiled. Anxious looks filled the chamber.

'A dragon has attacked Brindabeare,' he said.

A collective gasp filled the room. Mouths fell open; eyes were wide-eyed in shock. No one spoke for a moment.

Ainsley Thurman, Mortensen's Senior Councillor, a stout middle-aged man with a greying beard, broke the silence.

'When?' he said quietly, coming to grips with the enormity of Mortensen's words.

'Two nights ago,' replied Mortensen.

'A dragon?' said Thurman, his eyes wide with wonder.

'What happened?' asked Hinchcliffe, a younger version of his counterpart, his eyes full of hope. 'Casualties? Damage?'

'We don't have all the details at this time,' said Mortensen. 'It attacked the castle – specifically the girl's quarters, causing considerable damage. Several died trying to kill it.'

All eyes were glued to the Governor, ears hanging on every word.

'The dragon was killed?' asked Hinchcliffe.

'Yes,' said Mortensen.

'By Lord Frederick?' asked Thurman.

Mortensen shook his head, a mixture of amusement and wonder on his face.

'No. By all accounts, it wasn't Lord Frederick.'

Everyone in the chamber looked at Mortensen, stunned.

'Then who?' asked one.

'Dane Thorburn,' said Mortensen.

All looked at each other, disbelief on their faces.

'How is that possible?' asked Thurman. 'He's a common knight. How could he kill a dragon if Lord Frederick could not?'

'I know as much as you,' said Mortensen. 'Lord Raegan has wanted Thorburn killed for some time. Clearly, he is more than he appears.'

'What action are they taking?'

'There are no reports on that,' said Mortensen. 'But I suggest they will be quite preoccupied trying to unravel exactly why they were attacked by a dragon from the Highland Mountains.'

The room gasped again.

'The Highland Mountains?' said Thurman. '*Vrenin's* dragon?'

'At the moment we don't know,' said Mortensen. 'Although, given there have been no reported sightings of the God of Fire, I doubt it was his dragon, or something he had a part in.'

'But it's possible?' asked Hinchcliffe.

'Perhaps our Lord has chosen to reveal himself at last,' said Mortensen.

'What do you mean?'

'He hasn't been sighted since the girl was rescued from the City of Lost Souls,' said Mortensen. 'And he made no effort to attack when they brought her back. I have always believed he had a reason for this; that he had moved on to a larger purpose. What larger purpose could there be, than to unleash a dragon capable of destroying the entire city?'

'You think Lord Raegan controlled the dragon?'

'I have no doubt,' said Mortensen. 'It explains everything.'

'Be that as it may,' said Thurman, 'they killed it.'

'You disappoint me,' said Mortensen. 'Do you think he's going to stop with one? If he can do it once, we can be sure there will be more; perhaps many. Imagine – an attack on Brindabeare by a horde of dragons. They wouldn't stand a chance.'

Mortensen saw looks of hope and wonder on the faces of those around him. Smiling to himself despite no change in the pulse within, he could only hope his instincts were correct.

Word spread through the city like wildfire.

'Vrenin's unleashed his dragon! We're doomed!'

'The castle is damaged! The whole north wing has to be torn down! If the castle isn't safe, what hope is there for any of us?'

'But it's dead. We killed it. We're safe now.'

'How do you know there won't be more!?'

'What will Vrenin do, knowing we killed his dragon!?'

'I heard the Highland Mountains were alight with fire. That means there's more of them.'

'They think Raegan has convinced Vrenin to get his dragons to attack us. We're all going to die!'

'As long as we have Lord Frederick, we're safe. He killed the dragon.'

'No! They say he couldn't kill it!'

'Then, who did?'

'Everyone's saying it was Dane Thorburn!'

Dane felt the eyes of everyone following him in wonder and awe wherever he went. Doing his best to ignore it, the whispers were also following him.

'*Dragonslayer,*' they were calling him.

Bound to silence by the King and Lord Frederick, his telling of what happened disappointed the masses wanting to hear a first-hand account from the one who killed a dragon by his own hand.

'There's not much more to say,' he said, doing his best to stay calm in the face of the latest barrage of questions from his group of knights as they tended their horses at the end of the morning patrol. 'It flew to where Lord Frederick and I were standing on the rampart, and we killed it.'

'Not *we,*' said Harvey. 'You're too modest. It was you.'

Dane shrugged, hanging his gear and giving Thunder a final pat before heading towards the dining hall.

Harvey and the others looked on as he walked away, stable-hands bowing reverently as he passed.

'Probably the most significant event in the history of the land,' Harvey muttered. 'As if rescuing the Princess from the City of Lost Souls wasn't enough. And he acts as though it's no more important than tending his horse.'

'He simply gives no time to consider such things,' said Bernard Devine, an older and wizened member of the patrol who stood a few inches shorter than Harvey. 'In that and many other things, he carries himself the same way his father did.'

'That may be,' said Harvey. 'But his father never killed a dragon.'

All in the dining hall watched as Dane took his meal.

Gripping his plate a little tighter, he did his best to ignore it, relieved when he spotted Will at a far table.

'I don't know if I can deal with this,' said Dane as he sat down.

'What?' said Will.

'This!' said Dane, gesturing to everyone in the dining hall. 'Everyone looking at me like I'm some kind of mystical being.'

'Well, you did kill a dragon.'

'Don't you start! These are the same people, the very same people who were convinced I was guilty of treason. The same people who wanted to see me hang.'

'People can be fickle,' said Will with a shrug. 'Don't let it bother you.'

'Easy to say – hard to do,' said Dane. 'Lord Frederick told me not to worry about it too. But when everyone's looking at me like this, it's hard to ignore.'

'Did you hear about Lovell?' asked Will as Dane bit into his bread.

'What about him?' said Dane, his temper on alert.

'He's dead,' said Will. 'The dragon. When we went to the roof. Southwell, too.'

Dane found himself breathing a sigh of relief.

At least I won't have to worry about them looking at me like I'm guilty ...

'That's ... a shame,' he managed to say.

'I know you never liked them,' said Will.

'It's not that I didn't like them,' said Dane. 'They never believed I was innocent. How can I be friendly towards people like that?

Especially Lovell. He still thinks I killed Oppen, and you saw how he acted the other evening.'

Will nodded.

'Still, that doesn't mean I'm pleased they're dead,' said Dane, as much to convince himself as anyone else.

Neither said anything for a few moments.

Glancing around the room once more, Dane saw Lord Frederick approaching them.

'I don't mean to intrude,' said Lord Frederick, 'but I have a matter I need to discuss with you.'

'Of course,' said Dane, standing to leave.

'I'll see you later,' said Will.

Dane nodded as he and Lord Frederick departed.

Making their way towards the Royal Chambers, Lord Frederick turned down a familiar hallway.

'Are we going where I think we're going?' asked Dane.

'Indeed,' said Lord Frederick.

Moments later, they stood at the entrance to a secret room very few knew about, and once the hallway was clear, Lord Frederick reached up and pulled on the torch on the wall above them.

The entrance to the room slid open, closing and blending back into the wall once they entered the passageway.

After a short walk, they entered the chamber, finding Vanessa waiting for them, partly hidden in the darkness of the room.

With a flick of his hand, Lord Frederick had the wall torches alight.

'I didn't expect to find you here,' he said to Vanessa.

'I will not be treated like a child,' she said. 'If father is not able to accompany you, that duty falls on me.'

Lord Frederick nodded.

'It's only that you're –'

'I'm fine!' said Vanessa. 'I won't be coddled like an old maid.'

Lord Frederick raised a hand.

'Very well,' he said. 'We are not here to argue. Let's direct our attention to the matter at hand.'

Vanessa nodded, the anger draining from her face.

She glanced at Dane.

'I'm fine,' she replied, reading the look on his face.

Dane couldn't see her clearly in the light of the chamber, but something about the way she looked and spoke gave him pause to wonder if she was telling the truth.

Lord Frederick beckoned Vanessa to a spot to the right of a ledge protruding from one of the walls. Standing on the other side, he touched the wall in a spot about six feet off the ground, and with a low hum, the ledge started moving out from the wall. Tracing its path to the centre of the room, it lowered to the floor, a hole opening as it did so.

Another minute passed while the ancient, leather-bound *Annals of Creation* emerged on a dais from beneath the floor.

Lord Frederick opened the great tome and started flicking through the pages.

'What are you looking for?' asked Vanessa.

'Something about the Elements of Nature. More specifically, anything that may give a clue as to how they may be moulded or shaped to form shapes or living things.'

'Like a dragon?' said Dane.

'Exactly,' said Lord Frederick.

'Who do you think created it?' asked Dane.

'At the moment I don't know who or how it was created,' said Lord Frederick. 'My time in the Highland Mountains didn't show me anything to indicate whether anyone had any involvement in the creation of the dragon.'

Directing their gaze to one of the walls, he waved his hand.

A bright light appeared, with an image filling the space a moment later.

'Once I arrived in the mountains, it took a short while, but from the directions you gave me, this is what I found.'

They saw the remains of what appeared to be the dragon's nest. Rotting carcasses and bones littered the area. Parts of the ground in and around the surrounding area had the same scorch marks as the walls in Vanessa's chamber.

'Look carefully here,' said Lord Frederick, enlarging an area of the image.

'What are we looking at?' said Vanessa.

With a flick of his wrist, a white circle appeared on the image, around what appeared to be an opening in the earth.

'What is it?' said Dane.

'Look closely,' said Lord Frederick.

Staring intently, Dane couldn't make out anything conspicuous.

'It looks like a hole,' he said.

'That's exactly what it is,' said Lord Frederick.

'What about it?' said Dane.

'Look at this image,' said Lord Frederick.

With a flick of his hand, another image appeared on the wall.

Taken from above the hole, it had been lit to enable them to see inside, although from what they could see, it revealed nothing other than an empty space.

'There's nothing there,' said Vanessa.

'Yes,' said Lord Frederick. 'But that's what's relevant. It goes into the depths of the mountain, to the very core.'

'I still don't know what that means,' said Dane.

'I believe it's where the dragon first appeared,' said Lord Frederick. 'Where it hatched.'

'So ... it came from within the earth?' said Dane.

'Yes,' said Lord Frederick.

'How can that happen?' asked Dane.

'In the same way all living things are created,' said Lord Frederick. 'From the interactions of the Elements of Nature.'

'But what would lead them to create a dragon?' asked Vanessa. 'Here? Now? Unless something, or some*one* helped. Someone like Raegan.'

'Could Raegan create a dragon?' asked Dane.

'At this stage anything is possible,' said Lord Frederick.

'*A dragon!*' said Dane. 'We're not talking flame or fire; we're talking about a forty-foot living, breathing, *dragon* that he somehow created to search for Vanessa? Not even Edan did that.'

'Edan created the Fire-Walkers,' said Vanessa.

Dane stopped cold; his mouth open, frozen in mid-thought.

'Gods,' he breathed. 'It *is* possible.'

Dane and Vanessa looked at each other, stunned.

Dane's mind raced.

Could it be?

Could Raegan have penetrated to the very core of the Fire Element, the same way Edan had done?

Are we on the verge of a repeat of the Great War?

All because ...

'*No!*' he yelled.

Vanessa and Lord Frederick turned to look at him.

'It can't be,' he said. 'If Raegan has penetrated to the core of the Fire Element and created a dragon ... all because I didn't kill him in the City of Lost Souls ... it's all my fault.'

Rocking back, he staggered into a wall, barely able to stand.

Vanessa rushed over.

'No!' she said. 'We've been through this before. Don't do it to yourself.'

Dane continued staring ahead, the enormity of his guilt bearing down on him.

'I can't believe I had the chance to kill him,' said Dane, his voice little more than a whisper. 'I had the chance to kill him, to end all this, and I didn't do it.'

'Dane,' said Lord Frederick gently, resting a hand on his arm. 'The Princess is right. There is no way to know if you confronted Raegan in the City of Lost Souls. You gain nothing by allowing yourself to worry over something that may not be true. As we stand here, nothing has been proven, and you won't do yourself or anyone else any good by worrying about it.'

Dane took a couple of steadying breaths, glancing at each of them in turn.

Nodding slowly, he gathered himself, moving away from the wall.

Lord Frederick returned to the *Annals of Creation*.

Vanessa smiled reassuringly.

'If it wasn't Raegan,' Dane said slowly. 'What else can it be?'

'All we know at the moment is it formed within the earth,' said Lord Frederick. 'From the very core of the earth.'

'How could something from the core of the earth create a dragon you believe was sent to attack me?' asked Vanessa.

'That's why it has to be Raegan,' said Dane quietly, his guilt rumbling to the surface of his thoughts again.

'Let's not rush to conclusions,' said Lord Frederick, locking his eyes in a penetrating stare as he looked at Dane.

Dane nodded, breathing deeply again.

Vanessa took his hand in hers, looking at him with a gentle smile.

'Remember,' she said, 'you saved me. Twice. I wouldn't be standing here if not for you.'

Dane smiled ruefully, letting the soft glow in her eyes, the warmth of her smile and the touch of her hand relax his mind. He still thought she didn't look her usual self, but she calmed him nonetheless.

No one spoke for several minutes as Lord Frederick continued working his way through the *Annals of Creation*.

Reaching the end, he turned the back cover over, before flicking his wrist and flipping the book right-side up once more.

'Well?' asked Vanessa, stepping back to her place next to the wall so Lord Frederick could send the *Annals* back to its resting place.

'There is a lot of information about the need for Nature to keep itself in balance,' said Lord Frederick. 'The need for Nature to always be in harmony with itself. As we saw in the Gargaun Ranges, there are times when Nature responds to a disruption in the balance of the Ruling Elements.'

Dane and Vanessa nodded, remembering the massive disruption and destruction they survived shortly after returning from the City of Lost Souls.

'How does that relate to the dragon?' asked Dane.

'Dragons are Fire creatures,' said Lord Frederick. 'There may have been a disturbance that has upset the balance of the elements, specifically the Fire Element, that may have led to the creation of the dragon.'

'But why would it be sent to kill me?' asked Vanessa.

'That I don't know,' said Lord Frederick.

'A disturbance in the Fire Element,' said Vanessa. 'Brought about by the actions of a Firelord wizard?'

'Or his death?' said Dane, looking at Lord Frederick, daring to hope.

'Anything is possible,' said Lord Frederick. 'What I've found here hasn't really given us any new information. There's more we need to understand before we get to the bottom of this. The patrol sent to the Highland Mountains may find something useful, and I myself will be returning at dawn.'

With the ledge resuming its resting place once more, the three of them headed for the entrance, Lord Frederick extinguishing the torches as they left.

None of them spoke as they made their way along the passageway.

Dane stopped for a moment, allowing Lord Frederick to move past to check the hallway was clear.

Stopping at the entrance, Lord Frederick hesitated.

'What's wrong?' asked Vanessa.

'Someone is coming,' said Lord Frederick.

Placing his hand on the wall, the faintest vert light spread from his fingers, working its way through the stone.

A moment later, he pulled down on the torch above his head.

Stepping into the main hallway, Dane saw Marilena and the King walking towards them.

'Sire?' said Lord Frederick.

With no guards in the hallway who could overhear him, the King didn't hesitate.

'There's been another attack.'

Chapter 7
ANOTHER THREAT?

With the Brindabeare coat of arms looming over them on the far wall, Dane, Vanessa, the King and Marilena joined the rest of the Brindabeare Council in the smaller chamber. In addition to Salsbury, Councillors Maurice Fairbrother, Patrick Medhurst and Reginald Lindstrom were present, as were Silvers and Hindmarsh; with Carruthers, Head of the Royal Guard, stationed at the entrance.

Taking his place at the centre of the table, flanked by Vanessa and Lord Frederick's empty chair, with the councillors in the other seats on that side of the room, the King motioned Dane to a chair opposite, next to Hindmarsh. Marilena and Salsbury stood to the right of Vanessa and the King.

'The message states a large kestrel seized a child from the streets of Lansi,' said the King, placing the note on the table in front of him.

Nervous looks spread across the chamber.

'That's impossible,' breathed Medhurst, trying to sit taller, glancing at all except the King in turn, looking for others to agree with him and trying to work out if one of them had made up what they'd just heard at the same time.

Dane felt their eyes meet, the hostility Medhurst held towards him visible for the briefest moment, before he spoke again.

'A child?' said Medhurst. 'No kestrel is large enough to be able to do such a thing.'

'The message has been verified by our Falconer and Clerk of Court,' said Fairbrother, his warm, friendly face and taller frame a direct contrast to his counterpart.

'And Lansi has never wavered in its loyalty,' said Vanessa.

'You don't think it could be a –'

Before Medhurst could finish, Lord Frederick materialised behind the King with a flash of white and a *BANG!*

'I have spoken to many in Lansi,' he said, taking his seat, 'including the father and mother of the kidnapped child. All spoke of a large kestrel, the size of which they have never seen before. They say its size blotted out the sun when it flew away.'

'Where did it come from?' asked Lindstrom, a furrowed brow crossing his age-worn, wizened face.

'It appears to have emerged from somewhere in the Xerin Mountains, and once it seized the child, it flew back from where it came, and has not been seen or heard since.'

'When did it happen?' asked the King.

'In the middle of yesterday,' said Lord Frederick.

'They're sure it wasn't a dragon?' asked the King.

'They are,' said Lord Frederick. 'As large as it was, they say it's a kestrel.'

The King shook his head nervously.

'First a dragon, and now a kestrel,' he said. 'There has to be some reason for it.'

'Vrenin?' said Fairbrother. 'Raegan?'

Dane shuddered.

Raegan?

A giant kestrel?

'Forgive me,' he said without thinking, 'but it can't be Raegan.'

Heads turned towards him; Silvers bristled at his audacity to interrupt.

'Why do you say that?' asked the King.

'Kestrels are Air creatures,' said Dane.

Looking at Lord Frederick, he asked, 'Firelords can't create Air creatures. Can they?'

Lord Frederick answered with an approving nod.

'It's very difficult for a wizard to create any creature,' he said, raising a hand as he saw Medhurst moving to interject. 'And before you tell me about Edan and the Fire-Walkers, I am not saying it's impossible; just extremely unlikely. And as Royal Knight Thorburn has stated, even more unlikely a Firelord wizard would be able to create an Air-sourced creature.'

'But if Raegan created the dragon, perhaps he's worked out how to create other creatures?' said Medhurst.

'I think you're giving him too much credit,' said Lord Frederick. 'We have no proof Raegan created the dragon. The complexity involved to create any creature is beyond the capability of the most intelligent wizarding minds – except, as legend says, for Edan, and despite all the tales, there is no evidence he did what the stories say.

'Raegan and I saw nothing to prove it one way or the other. The Fire-Walkers certainly wreaked havoc on Nadensa, destroying everything in their path. Nonetheless, neither of us can say without a trace of doubt that they were created by Edan.'

'But we know Raegan can transform into a wolf,' said Lindstrom. 'If he can transform into an animal, doesn't that mean he can create one?'

'The two are not related,' said Lord Frederick. 'Being able to transform oneself involves reorganising one's physical being, which is quite different to creating a new creature from nothing.'

'Arclos?' said Medhurst.

'The God of Air sent his kestrel to kidnap a helpless child?' asked Fairbrother.

'Well,' said Medhurst uncertainly, 'Arclos is said to ride a kestrel. We have to consider it.'

'That's like saying a swordsmith kills every man who dies at the hand of his weapons, no matter who wields it,' said Fairbrother.

'Why would the Gods unleash their own creatures on us?' said Lindstrom.

'Enough!' said the King. 'We need to focus our thoughts on what to do if this kestrel attacks again.'

'A patrol, Sire?' said Silvers. 'We could send a patrol to Lansi. Perhaps a regiment we could deploy through the Stanthorpe region. We would include some accomplished archers among them, and we could send another group into the Xerin mountains.'

'A regiment might induce panic,' said Medhurst.

'If the kestrel attacks again, there will be plenty of panic,' said Lindstrom.

'Stanthorpe has responsibility to defend the region,' said Medhurst. 'It has a sizeable army it could deploy to help the others.'

'If we're seen to have done nothing, we will appear to be weak,' said Vanessa. 'We are the ruling city of the land. We have to take control and show we're capable of solving it.'

Looking on, Dane saw Vanessa speaking very much like her father – as a ruler. He saw the King and Lord Frederick offer approving nods in her direction.

'It's a sound plan,' said the King. 'They are to depart as soon as they can be ready.'

All in the chamber nodded in approval.

'We need to be careful how we deal with this,' said the King. 'Rumour and gossip have their own way of causing fear and unrest. We need to find out what we're dealing with and resolve it as soon as possible.'

Leaning towards Salsbury, he said, 'Send word to the Stanthorpe region.'

With a bow, Salsbury left the chamber.

'I will visit the Xerin Mountains as well, Sire,' said Lord Frederick.

'Very well,' said the King. 'We're done here. Dismissed.'

'Princess,' said Lord Frederick as the chamber emptied. 'A word please. Royal Knight Thorburn? You as well. Carruthers, please ask Royal Knight Hevenshire to join us.'

Dane and Vanessa waited, wondering what Lord Frederick wanted to talk about.

Carruthers followed the others out of the chamber.

'I need to discuss something among the four of us,' said Lord Frederick.

'Four?' asked Vanessa.

'Once Will joins us,' said Lord Frederick.

Looking closely at Vanessa, Dane asked, 'Are you sure you're well? You look a –'

'I'm fine,' said Vanessa, glaring at him.

'But –'

'I'm *fine*,' she said again.

Deciding not to push it further, Dane changed the subject.

'A dragon and a kestrel,' he said. 'It's as though nature has lost its mind.'

'What do you mean?' asked Vanessa.

'The disruption in the Gargaun Mountains; a dragon; and now a kestrel. Nothing like this has ever happened before, and suddenly it all happens in a very short time. And who knows what else may be out there?'

The chamber doors opened, stopping Dane mid-sentence.

Turning towards the sound, he saw Will walking towards them.

'You sent for me?' he asked Lord Frederick.

'I did,' Lord Frederick replied. 'A regiment is being readied to travel to the Xerin Mountains and the Stanthorpe region. I want you and Dane to be part of it.'

Glancing at each other, Dane and Will turned to Lord Frederick with surprised looks on their faces. Royal Knights were not part of regimental patrols unless they were accompanying Vanessa or the King.

'Why?' asked Dane.

'Let me share our recent conversation with Will about why we believe you were able to kill the dragon,' said Lord Frederick.

Dane and Vanessa waited in silence while Lord Frederick spoke again.

Looking at Dane once Lord Frederick finished, Will saw him nod in agreement with what Lord Frederick had told him.

'I see,' said Will.

'You are two of our most accomplished archers,' said Lord Frederick. 'I want you to be there and to take something with you. Something that will only be in your possession.'

Looking at Lord Frederick in confusion, they had no time to react before, with a dull thud, Vanessa collapsed in a heap to the floor.

'Vanessa!' said Dane, rushing to her side.

Leaning next to him, Lord Frederick took Vanessa's limp hand in his, before looking to Dane and Will.

'I will take her to her chamber,' he said.

'I knew she didn't look well,' said Dane, as he and Will helped Lord Frederick lift Vanessa off the floor. 'But she's too stubborn to admit it to anyone.'

Lord Frederick nodded.

'Please make sure you see me before you depart,' he said. 'Allow me some time to inform the General you will be part of the regiment.'

With a flash of light and a *BANG!* Lord Frederick and Vanessa disappeared.

'We'd better get to barracks,' said Dane.

'Do you think Lord Frederick's right?' said Will as they left the chamber. 'About the dragon?'

'I don't know what to think,' said Dane. 'But there's no other reason that makes sense.'

'A kestrel?' asked Mortensen. 'You're sure?'

'I've seen the message,' said Thurman. 'It's reliable.'

'What are they doing about it?' said Mortensen.

'They're sending a regiment to the Stanthorpe region.'

'Interesting. I wonder if they're related?'

'Governor?'

'The dragon and the kestrel,' said Mortensen. 'It's too unusual to be a coincidence.'

'A giant kestrel is going to attack us!'

'We're doomed!'

'Raegan's unleashing all these creatures and Lord Frederick can't stop them!'

'There's no hope, we're all going to die!'

'We stopped the dragon, and the kestrel is in the Xerin Mountains. It's nowhere near us.'

'The dragon was in the Highland Mountains, and it still attacked!'

'And we killed it.'

'It took a child! The Gods are angry! They're angry with us, and we're all going to die!'

'How is she?' asked Dane, as he and Will met Marilena in Vanessa's antechamber.

'She's awake,' Marilena replied. 'It's the same as before. Lord Frederick and the healers have examined her and haven't found anything to explain it. As far as they can tell, there should be nothing wrong with her.'

Seeing the concern on her face and the anxiety in her voice, Dane gently placed a hand on Marilena's arm.

'They'll solve it,' he said. 'Lord Frederick told us to meet him here.'

'Yes,' said Marilena in an unhappy tone. 'And he told me to leave. I want to know what's going on. Why can't I be part of what he has to tell you?'

Dane shrugged, looking at Will, who wore a similarly puzzled expression on his face.

'We don't know,' said Dane. 'He was about to tell us when Vanessa collapsed.'

'Well, you excluded me the last time, so I know you know some-thing,' said Marilena.

'Mother, please,' said Dane.

With a final exasperated look, Marilena left the room, closing the door with a slam.

Will raised an eyebrow, a knowing smile on his face as he and Dane entered the chamber, where they found Vanessa propped up in bed, surrounded by pillows, a goblet in her hand.

Lord Frederick sat in a chair next to her.

Smiling weakly when she saw them, she put the goblet down.

'How are you feeling?' asked Dane.

'It's like the last time,' Vanessa said weakly. 'No one can find anything wrong with me. And yet, here I am.'

Do I tell her I thought she was unwell?

'I'm sure you will be well after you rest some more,' said Dane.

'You're a terrible liar,' said Vanessa.

Dane smiled sheepishly.

Will stared at the floor.

'What do you need to see us about?' Dane asked Lord Frederick, changing the subject. 'What is it about this expedi-tion to the Stanthorpe region you want us to be part of that's so secretive?'

'I want you to take these,' said Lord Frederick, picking up two of four vials from Vanessa's bedside table. 'Once I fill them.'

Dane and Will looked at each other.

'Fill them with what?' asked Dane, noticing the other two con-tained what looked like a grey liquid.

'You know my thoughts as to why you were able to kill the dragon,' said Lord Frederick, nodding to Vanessa.

'Yes,' said Dane and Will together.

'Well, perhaps this kestrel has been created in a similar manner.'

'From the core of the earth?' said Dane.

Lord Frederick nodded, glancing to the wall on his right, and with a flick of his hand, an image appeared.

'I found this is the Xerin Mountains.'

Dane saw a tree with what looked like a hole in a nook of its trunk.

'Are you saying it came from there?' he asked. 'Like the dragon came out of the earth in the Highland Mountains?'

'I'm not sure,' said Lord Frederick. 'But it's possible.'

'But kestrels are Air-creatures,' said Will, 'wouldn't it have been created from air?'

'Indeed,' said Lord Frederick.

'Then it can't come from within the earth,' said Dane, following Will's lead.

'No?' said Lord Frederick.

Glancing at each other, Dane and Will wondered how they could possibly be wrong.

'Wait,' said Vanessa in a quiet voice.

All eyes turned towards her.

'Air is everywhere,' she said. 'Not just in the sky above, not just in the air we breathe. Air gives space to everything. It can be below the earth – it can be anywhere. Otherwise, there would be no place or space for anything to be created, for anything to be able to move.'

'There's your answer,' said Lord Frederick.

Thinking it through, Dane repeated Vanessa's words in his mind.

'I see,' he said.

Looking at Will, he saw he'd also understood.

'So, what do you want us to do?' asked Dane.

'I will fill these with the Princess's blood,' said Lord Frederick, holding the vials up to them once more.

'Why?' asked Will.

'If the kestrel attacks, you may find your weapons have no effect; sword, arrow, or knife; no matter how true your aim.'

'But if they have Vanessa's blood on them, you think we will be able to kill the kestrel, the same way I killed the dragon,' said Dane.

'Exactly,' said Lord Frederick.

'What about the other two?' said Dane, pointing to the table.

'They contain a fusing element,' said Lord Frederick. 'Spread them on your weapons first, then add the blood. A little of each at a time. They will dissolve into the steel.'

'Can we do it for the whole regiment?' said Will.

'At the moment, it's only a theory,' said Lord Frederick. 'We don't know if the dragon and kestrel are related. The kestrel has not approached the castle; so, at least for the moment it hasn't picked up any sense of the Princess and tried to find her. And we want to contain our knowledge of what we may know, until we're sure.'

Dane and Will nodded.

'Are you sure it's a wise thing to do?' asked Dane, glancing at Vanessa. 'In her current condition?'

'With the amount of blood we need, I don't think it will cause any harm,' said Lord Frederick.

'Very well,' said Dane. 'What if the kestrel attacks a province and we're not there?'

'Again,' said Lord Frederick, 'it's only a theory.'

Turning to Vanessa, he placed a hand on her arm for a few moments, before drawing it away. Taking one of the vials, he held his hand above it, and as everyone watched, a small sliver of blood leaked from his middle finger, dripping into the vial.

Once full, Lord Frederick stoppered it, before handing it to Will.

Repeating the process to fill the second vial, Lord Frederick handed it to Dane.

'You leave at first light?' Vanessa asked.

Dane nodded, taking a vial with the fusing element from Lord Frederick.

'We'll do this before we leave,' he said, gripping the vials tightly.

Standing, Lord Frederick put a gentle, reassuring hand on Vanessa's shoulder.

'You need to rest,' he said, before heading towards the chamber door. 'I will come and see you again in the morning.'

Dane and Will turned to follow.

'Dane,' said Vanessa. 'A moment. Please.'

Beckoning him towards the bed, Dane sat on the chair next to her.

Once Will and Lord Frederick left, Vanessa looked at Dane, her mouth quivering.

'I don't know what's wrong with me,' she said. 'I've never felt so helpless, so scared.'

Reaching over, brushing her hair out of her face with his hand, Dane let her lean her head to his chest, hugging her to him.

'I'm sure it's nothing,' he said quietly. 'Lord Frederick and the healers will work it out.'

'Please don't lie to me,' said Vanessa, turning to look him in the eye. 'I want an honest conversation, not another telling me what they think I want to hear.'

Looking past the anxiety and fear on her face, Dane saw she meant it.

'Very well,' he said quietly. 'When we were looking at the *Annals*, and in the chamber. You didn't look well.'

'I wasn't,' said Vanessa. 'I didn't feel faint, but I didn't feel … normal.'

'Like the last time?' said Dane.

Vanessa nodded.

'I don't know what's wrong with me,' she said. 'And it's not something Lord Frederick and the healers can fix. That's why I'm worried.'

'You weren't well before I killed the dragon, but you felt better once I killed it?'

'Yes,' said Vanessa with a gentle nod.

'And in the last day, you started to feel unwell again?'

Another nod.

'Is there anything you can think of; something you did; something you ate – anything unusual in that time that may have made you feel unwell?'

'You sound just like the others.'

'I'm trying to help,' said Dane. 'You said you felt unwell in the secret room. Can you think of anything before you went there that may have made you unwell?'

'No,' said Vanessa. 'If anything, I've been more careful.'

'You have to trust Lord Frederick and the healers,' said Dane.

'I –'

'I mean it,' he said, looking her squarely in the eye. 'Lord Frederick has been to the Xerin Mountains, but he isn't going to the Stanthorpe region with us. For the moment, he's not leaving the castle, and you can be sure he won't rest as long as you're unwell.'

He waited a moment, letting his words sink in before continuing.

'They will solve it,' he said. 'But you have to do something to help them.'

'What?'

'No more lies,' said Dane. 'If you're not well, you have to tell them. You have to stop letting your pride get in the way of them looking after you.'

Vanessa drew away, looking at Dane as though he'd slapped her.

'You asked for honesty,' said Dane, seeing the look on her face.

Relaxing a little, a thin smile crossed Vanessa's face.

'I didn't expect you to be so blunt,' she said. 'But you're right.'

Chapter 8
THE KESTREL'S TRAIL

With dawn's light creeping over the horizon, preparations for departure to the Stanthorpe region were well advanced.

Taking his morning meal with Will, Genevieve and a group of gawking maids, Dane noticed Genevieve looking at Will and fidgeting uneasily.

'Is something wrong?' he asked.

Genevieve looked nervously at her plate.

Reaching over, Will took both her hands in his.

With a deep breath, Genevieve looked at Dane.

'We're to be married,' she said.

'What?' said Dane, stunned for a moment, looking at them both in turn.

Will nodded with a grin.

Dane slammed his goblet on the table, his face breaking into a smile.

'That's wonderful!' he said, jumping up.

They were all on their feet, others looking on, not sure what was happening.

Springing to the other side of the table, Dane gave Genevieve a warm hug.

'That's wonderful!' he said again.

Back to Will, he shook his friend's hand, wrapping him in a bear-hug.

'Congratulations to you both!' he said.

'I want you to be my guardsman,' said Will when they sat down.

Dane grinned as they bound the arrangement with a charging of goblets.

'I promise to do my best to ensure he stays in one piece,' he said to Genevieve.

Genevieve nodded with a smile.

They chatted for a few minutes, Will talking proudly about receiving consent from Genevieve's father for their upcoming nuptials, and how he'd told his mother and father the night before.

The other maids left the table, their eyes lingering on Dane as they huddled away.

'I have to get Blaze,' said Dane, gathering his empty plate and goblet. 'Congratulations again.'

Will nodded and Genevieve smiled as Dane walked away.

Heading towards the cages, lost in thought; a jolt from some-one bumping him brought Dane's mind back to the present.

'Don't think for a moment you're as special as you think you are, Thorburn,' Fenwick spat, as Dane gathered himself. 'You were lucky with the dragon; and while you have everyone else fooled, you haven't fooled me.'

'I'm busy at the moment,' said Dane, trying to bump his way past.

'Wait,' said Fenwick, forcing himself in front of Dane. 'You need to get me in the regiment going to the Stanthorpe region.'

'Not that I can, but why would I want to do that?' said Dane.

'I'm one of the best in the entire army,' said Fenwick. 'I have to be there.'

'Fenwick, this regiment needs archers,' said Dane, thinking back to their time as cadets for a moment, 'and from what I remember, my mother can shoot a straighter arrow than you.'

'That's not –'

'I don't have time for this,' said Dane, grabbing Fenwick by the shoulder and pushing past. 'I suggest you take it up with the General.'

'I will,' said Fenwick. 'And you'd best pray you never need me to save you.'

Stopping in his tracks, Dane stood for a moment, before turning and grabbing hold of Fenwick.

Leaning in close, eyes hot with rage, Dane stared directly at him.

'First, you make light of the death of a knight,' he said, gripping Fenwick tighter, 'and now you threaten to abandon another. I ought to have you tried for treason.'

Grabbing him tighter still, Dane leaned right in, his face glancing off Fenwick for a moment, before, with a violent thrust, he threw Fenwick to the ground.

Tumbling in a heap, Fenwick could do nothing as Dane stalked away.

Taking a couple of soothing breaths, Dane smiled as he approached the cages holding Brindabeare's hunting and messenger birds.

'Hello, Angus.'

'Master Dane!' said Angus Flitson, Brindabeare's Falconer, rushing to shake hands, his plump face, as always, looking as though he were in a constant state of wonder and surprise, and his clothes full of clawed holes and tears.

'She's ready?' said Dane.

'Yes, yes, yes!' said Angus, disappearing inside.

Looking at the cages lining the enclosure from floor to roof, Dane noticed fewer occupants than usual.

'You have a lot of ravens out,' said Dane.

'Yes, Master Dane,' said Angus, walking towards him. 'With all the talk about the dragon and the kestrel, there are a lot of messages across the Stanthorpe region and the rest of the land at the moment.'

Turning towards the familiar squawk of the bird being walked towards him, Dane beheld the sight of the eagle on Angus's wrist.

Charcoal-black and now fully-grown, Blaze had been assigned to Dane and Vanessa when he'd first been promoted to the Royal Knights. She had been instrumental in freeing Vanessa from the City of Lost Souls – penetrating the invisible barrier into the city, then leading Dane to her and helping them escape.

'Here she is, Master Dane,' said Angus, handing her over.

Allowing Blaze to perch on his wrist, Dane raised her to eye level.

Squawking gently in recognition, Blaze stood proudly for a moment, before walking up Dane's arm and settling on his shoulder.

'The Stanthorpe region know we're coming?' asked Dane.

'Yes, they do,' said Angus. 'Ravens were sent last evening.'

'Tell me, Angus, do you know anything of giant kestrels?'

'They would be like any other bird of prey, Master Dane. And due to their size, more dangerous.'

'Have you ever heard of one attacking a child?'

'No, Master Dane. Unless they're desperate for food, hunting birds will only attack prey they know they can kill, and they have to be able to carry it away.'

'The messages say it blocked the sun,' said Dane. 'Have you heard of anything growing to such a size, apart from the tales of Arclos?'

'Anything is possible,' said Angus. 'If it's true, it would be larger than any I have ever seen.'

'So, if it is as large as they say, it could attack a child?'

'Yes, indeed,' said Angus. 'A child, or a scuttler.'

'A scuttler?' said Dane.

'Yes, Master Dane,' said Angus, nodding. 'Just this morning, a message came in from a settlement near Lansi. They say a man and child were at the edge of the woods, when the kestrel attacked them. A scuttler tried to help them, and the kestrel took the scuttler instead.'

'Is it the same one?' said Dane.

'We think so,' said Angus.

'How do we kill it?' asked Dane, considering what he'd heard.

'You want to kill it?' asked Angus, shocked.

'If it's attacking children and scuttlers, there's no other alternative,' said Dane.

Nodding slowly, muttering to himself, Angus paced nervously.

'To kill a bird,' said Angus, 'even a kestrel –'

'We're not doing it by choice,' said Dane, 'but we can't have something like this roaming the land. Like the dragon – we had to kill it, too.'

'Very bad, that dragon,' said Angus. 'Very bad.'

'So is this kestrel,' said Dane.

Nodding again, Angus looked at Dane, despair etched on his face.

'We have to stop it,' said Dane.

'Yes,' said Angus.

'So, how do we kill it?' asked Dane.

'It's no different to killing any other bird,' said Angus quietly.

'You're sure?' said Dane.

Nodding again, Angus looked at Dane forlornly.

'Might you consider trapping it?' he said. 'And bring it here? I could train it.'

'Angus,' said Dane, 'I don't think we'd be able to –'

Dane stopped, seeing Angus's eyes welling with tears.

'Well,' said Dane, 'if we can, we'll try and trap it.'

'Thank you, Master Dane,' said Angus.

'I can't promise anything,' said Dane.

A sound to Dane's right distracted him. Glancing in that direction, he saw Will walking towards him.

'I have to leave,' said Dane.

'Very well,' said Angus. 'Keep her safe, won't you?'

'I will,' said Dane.

Raising his arm, Blaze walked down to his wrist, and with upward thrust of his hand, took to the sky.

'We have to go,' said Will.

Heading towards the stables, Dane and Will watched Blaze rise higher and higher in the sky.

'I wouldn't have believed it, had I not seen it with my own eyes,' said Norton. 'It looks like a serpent; only, it has legs, so it doesn't always slither along the ground. It can stand and raise itself, and when it attacks, its neck shoots forward, like an arrow.'

Looking at his colleagues, Mortensen said nothing.

'Go on,' said Thurman.

'If that wasn't enough, the last time it attacked, it breathed fire and killed one of my men.'

'Anything else?' asked Thurman.

'As I said when I arrived,' said Norton, 'my entire flock is in danger.'

Waiting until he was certain Norton had finished, Mortensen said nothing for a few moments, looking at his colleagues in turn, rubbing his chin as he considered what he'd heard.

'Well?' said Norton, exasperated at Mortensen's lack of urgency. 'Are you going to help me?'

'What is it you wish me to do?' said Mortensen.

'My entire flock is in danger!' said Norton again, waving his arms, spittle spraying from his mouth. 'You have to help me!'

Raising an eyebrow, Mortensen remained unmoved.

'I do?' he said. 'And what is it you need?'

'I need you to send knights to find this creature and kill it before I lose my entire flock!' said Norton, in a tone that suggested anyone in the land knew the answer.

'You have knights of your own, do you not?' said Mortensen.

'Well, yes,' said Norton, 'but –'

'And they are not capable of finding this beast?'

'But,' stammered Norton, 'you're the ruling city – in a situation like this, you have to help me!'

'That is quite presumptuous of you,' said Mortensen. 'I'm well aware of my responsibilities, and I'm afraid I have more important matters to deal with than your sheep. If your own knights are incapable of defending your flock from such a threat, I wonder what use you are to me at all.'

'But surely when such a threat emerges, you have an obligation to assist – as Candahorn has done throughout the history of the land.'

'Spare me the oratory,' said Mortensen. 'When there is a real threat to our survival, I will offer whatever aid is required. This meeting is at an end.'

'But –'

'This meeting is at an end,' said Mortensen again, nodding at Thurman, who rose to escort Norton from the chamber. 'If you are not satisfied, you can always take your grievance to Brindabeare.'

Knowing his last comment had struck a nerve, Mortensen smiled at the scathing look on Norton's face.

'It's a shame that dragon didn't wipe them out,' said Norton, his anger at Mortensen dissolving in thoughts of the greater hatred they both shared.

'There may yet be more awaiting them with regard to that,' said Mortensen, smiling again.

'Are you sure Lord Raegan is behind it?' asked Norton. 'Those of my knights with the pulse still say they still feel nothing.'

'We do not question our Lord,' said Mortensen. 'I am sure time will prove me right.'

Arriving at Stanthorpe, the nearest city east of Brindabeare, the regiment followed their escort towards the castle. On a large, flat expanse of land about a quarter of the size of Brindabeare, with a strong stone outer wall, they saw the castle in a far corner of the city, protected by its own walls and other defences.

Making their way through the gatehouse and along a short pathway, they emerged into the castle proper. Dane, Will and Ernald Norwood, the tall, ginger-haired Commander of the regiment dismounted, following their escorts towards a chamber to the left of the main courtyard.

Inside, they were greeted by the governors of the Stanthorpe Region, who, clearly anxious for them to arrive, wasted no time filling them in on all that had happened.

The three exchanged nervous glances as the tale unfolded.

'The entire province is anxious, not knowing how to defeat it,' said Governor Beasley of Lansi, a tall, thin man and the most youthful of the governors. 'Since the poor girl was taken, we've had the streets patrolled, and people have been scared to leave their homes. We have knights in the streets and fields, but they can do nothing until it attacks again. If the threat is not removed soon, our entire crop is at risk.'

'We've seen it too,' said Governor Moore of Delfar, stroking his beard as he spoke. 'At dusk about two days ago. It had an elk in its clutches.'

'A couple of settlers saw us several days ago,' said Beasley. 'Before we started our journey here. They said their children were attacked near the woods, and a scuttler tried to help them. The children escaped and the scuttler was taken.'

'Your knights have not been able to kill it?' asked Dane.

'It hasn't come close enough,' said Beasley.

Moore nodded his agreement.

'Well, in addition to your knights, we will deploy our regiment among you,' said Norwood. 'We have also sent a patrol to the Xerin Mountains.'

The Governors nodded their thanks.

'We will leave ten here,' said Norwood, 'and ten in each of the provinces.'

'How do you plan to kill it?' asked Beasley.

'It will have to be from close range,' said Dane. 'We'll have to lure it to us.'

The Governors drew a collective gasp.

'Surely not?' said Governor Cooper of Kordeit, a portly, middle-aged man with a wide-eyed look on his face.

Dane watched him shifting uncomfortably in his seat, shuffling and shifting as though he'd never worn armour before.

'If it's as large as it's said to be,' said Dane, 'our arrows won't be able to knock it out of the sky from long range, as we could with others, such as my eagle.'

Dane saw the Governors nodding as they considered what he'd told them.

'So, we need to draw it out. We'll set some bait, something to entice it towards the ground.'

'You don't mean –' said Cooper with a gasp.

'We will kill some prey, and leave it in the open, where it will be easily spotted,' said Dane.

Relaxing in his chair, Cooper let out a sigh of relief.

'You will have to kill some of your flock,' said Will, breathing a sigh of relief when Norwood offered an approving nod.

'I'll gladly give a couple of lambs, if it guarantees the safety of my province,' said Moore.

'It will need to be somewhere open enough to pose no threat, and at the same time, allow us to kill it without being seen,' said Dane.

'Outside the walls?' suggested Beasley.

'Maybe,' said Norwood. 'While it would be away from the rest of your flocks, we need somewhere to hide. I don't think it would be the right thing to leave the bait outside your gate on open ground.'

'Does it matter if we're not hidden?'

'We don't want it mistaking our knights for prey,' said Dane.

'You think it could attack a man?' said Beasley.

'It may see anything on the ground as a meal,' said Will. 'It's better we don't give it any option but to attack the bait we set for it.'

'Very well,' said Norwood. 'Are there any other questions?'

'Where is Lord Frederick?' said Governor Preston Kavendish of Stanthorpe, speaking for the first time. 'Why isn't he here?'

Dane, Will and Norwood looked at each other.

Dane couldn't help but notice Kavendish's considerable girth, visible despite the loose garb that he wore; the only unarmoured man in the chamber. Together with his long, unkempt hair, the bulging eyes and the wide smile on his face, Dane found himself comparing the Governor to an overgrown toad.

When none of them offered a response, Kavendish stood, glaring at them over the table.

'We are under attack by a giant kestrel, and Brindabeare's Masterlord Wizard is too preoccupied to help us?'

'He's detained at the castle,' said Dane.

'We believe with our combined forces, we will be able to kill it,' said Norwood.

'That's all very well,' said Kavendish with a simpering smile. 'But Lord Frederick is bound by oath to serve the entire land.'

'I'm sure Lord Frederick gave the matter great consideration,' said Dane carefully. 'As did the King and the Brindabeare Council.'

'If Lord Frederick were here, he could sniff out the kestrel in a matter of moments and be done with it,' said Kavendish.

'I don't think it's that simple,' said Dane.

'He took care of the dragon well enough.'

'No,' said Cooper, pointing at Dane. 'It was him.'

'A likely story,' said Kavendish, 'trumped up by Brindabeare to keep their wizard for themselves.'

'Governor, please,' said Dane, trying to keep his voice calm. 'Princess Vanessa is unwell. Lord Frederick and the healers are tending to her.'

The chamber fell silent.

Beasley spoke first.

'Unwell?' he said.

Dane nodded.

'She's been unwell lately. Lord Frederick and the healers are looking after her.'

'It must be serious indeed, if it is stopping him from coming here,' said Beasley.

Glancing at Will and Norwood, Dane found himself struggling for words. The last thing he wanted was a long conversation about Vanessa.

'Very well,' said Kavendish. 'If the Princess is unwell, I understand their decision. It hasn't been all that long since she returned from her ordeal in the Gargaun Ranges.'

Dane and Will looked at each other uneasily.

'And sending Royal Knights, including the dragonslayer himself, shows they have given due cause to our situation. All in all, I'm confident we will be able to deal with the kestrel.'

Crossing the Penton River on their way to Delfar, Dane glanced towards the Xerin Mountains in the distance.

Rounding a bend, they saw a group of three small thatched wooden huts in a dirt-crusted clearing ahead.

At the sound of their approach, a couple of men emerged, running towards them.

'Stop!' they yelled. 'Stop!'

Waving their hands madly, rushing alongside the regiment, they yelled again.

Reigning their horses to a stop, Dane, Will, Norwood and several others dismounted: the rest remaining in their saddles.

'The kestrel!' one said, pointing madly. 'It comes! It comes!'

'What?' said Dane. 'Where?'

Looking skyward, everyone searched for it.

'It comes!' said the man again. 'My boy! Please! My boy!'

Beckoning them towards the first hut, Dane, Will and Norwood followed.

Once inside, their attention drawn towards someone crying, they saw a woman sitting on the ground in a corner, a small child cradled in her arms.

Crouching, Dane reached to the woman, trying to see the child she was holding.

'No!' she screamed. 'No!'

Thrashing her body from side to side, the woman refused to let Dane touch her or the child.

Standing after a couple of moments, Dane saw all he needed to see. The child had been badly injured, its raggedy clothing torn by a scratch stretching from the top of its neck and diagonally to the waist, a couple of large puncture wounds continuing to bleed.

'When did this happen?' he asked one of the men.

'Not more than half an hour ago,' he said quietly, struggling to be heard over the woman's sobs. 'Not far from here. Tending to our plants. Kestrel attack. Try to take my son. I beat it off.'

Looking at the man more closely, Dane could see he had a gash of his own on one of his arms, and blood smeared down his shirt.

'Where did it go?' he asked.

Beckoning Dane outside, with Will and Norwood following, the man led them about fifty yards from the edge of the huts.

Pointing, he said, 'Attacked here.'

Dane, Will and Norwood could see signs of some kind of struggle; the ground trampled, plants uprooted, a couple of feathers and a piece of the boy's clothing on the ground.

'Then there,' the man said, pointing towards the Xerin Mountains.

'What did it look like?' asked Will.

'Big as the sun,' said the man.

The three from Brindabeare looked knowingly at each other.

'Well,' said Norwood. 'If it didn't get its meal from here, it will try somewhere else.'

Walking back to the rest of the regiment, Norwood found Governor Moore among them.

'Are there any other settlements between here and Delfar?' he asked.

'Yes,' said Moore. 'Two. Just like this one. The first is about an hour's ride from here.'

'Then we haven't a moment to lose,' he said.

Separating from the rest of the regiment, Dane, Will and several others raced ahead. Spurring Thunder again once they saw the settlement, Dane arrived moments before the others.

Dismounting, to his dismay, there was no one there to greet them.

Running inside the first hut, he found it empty. Searching the others, he found them deserted.

'Where are they?' he asked Will, his eyes searching desperately.

'Over here!' they heard one of the group yelling in the distance behind one of the huts.

Making their way over, they saw the rest of the group standing still, backs towards them, blocking the view ahead.

As they approached, the group stepped aside.

Dane's breath caught in his throat.

Glancing at Will, he saw the same shock on his face.

A man and a woman lay on the ground in front of them.

Her body twisted at an awkward angle; the woman had a deep gash in the back of her neck. Looking closer, Dane saw what looked to be a burn mark on her skin and on part of her dress. The man had a large cut on his face and a deep wound at the point where his neck met his collarbone.

Glancing from one to the other, and to the knights gathered around him, it took Dane a couple of moments to gather his thoughts.

'The woman,' he said. 'Bury her.'

A couple of knights bent down to the woman's body.

Looking at the rest of the group, he said, 'Don't let anyone, especially the Governors, come around here.'

Dane approached the man, crouching beside him.

The man's breathing was short, sharp and strained, each breath a struggle.

With the state of the man's wounds, Dane could see it would only be a matter of moments.

'It ... took ... my ... son ...' the man whispered.

With a vain, hopeless look towards the Xerin Mountains, Dane and Will saw nothing.

Looking around them, they could see the same signs of struggle as the other settlement.

'It ... took ... my ... son ...' the man whispered again. 'Gabriella ... Gabriella ... we ... tried ...'

With a final sigh, the man slumped to the ground.

Bowing their heads, Dane and Will were silent for a few moments before standing.

'Bury them together,' said Dane.

As the others continued their work, Dane and Will stood to one side.

'Where have they gone?' said Dane, looking at the deserted settlement.

'They probably fled when it attacked,' said Will.

'Now we've seen what this thing can do,' said Dane. 'A man and a woman, and it wasn't enough to stop it, even if they had no weapons.'

'Killing it won't be easy,' said Will.

'It looks to be incredibly powerful,' said Dane. 'It didn't just fend them off, it nearly tore them to shreds. I've never seen marks like that. And the boy at the other settlement.'

'It's beak and its claws must be enormous,' said Will.

'Did you see the burn marks on her neck?' asked Dane.

'Yes,' said Will. 'There were scorch marks on the ground at the other settlement. I didn't think anything of it, until I saw what we found here.'

'You don't think it can breathe fire?' asked Dane, considering the possibility for the first time.

Will shrugged.

'Let's hope not.'

'Kestrels don't breathe fire,' said Dane, lost in thought.

'Kestrel or not, it's certainly leaving a trail of destruction,' said Will.

'Whatever it is,' said Dane, 'we have to find it and kill it as quickly as we can.'

Chapter 9
LANSI UNDER ATTACK

Taking a small pot from the fire, the old lady added the last of the fruits and leaves from her herbs to the bubbling mixture. Grinding everything to a thick paste, the dull smell, a combination of rotting fruit and mint spread through the hut.

After letting the mixture cool, she gently spooned it onto her hand and arm.

Breathing deeply, she relaxed into her chair, staring numbly at the fire while the warmth of the elixir seeped into her skin.

The wound was healing nicely.

It had been a deep bite.

She didn't know how long she'd passed out. Waking sometime the next morning, she'd found herself covered in blood.

Looking at the wound once more, she smiled grimly.

While her treatments had been able to stop the bleeding and stave off infection, as she opened and closed her hand, wincing in pain at the point where her muscles simply refused to move any further, she knew she'd never have full use of her hand again.

The wolf lay sleeping beside her, unaware of what it had done.

Leaning towards it, she looked at its wound once more.

Still a lot of festering, gooey blood and pus.

Its condition hadn't improved since she'd taken it in. It had eaten the small pieces of meat she'd offered, but it was still very weak.

In the time since her first attempt to treat the wound, she hadn't been able to get close enough to try again. Whenever she'd reached towards it, she'd met angry growls, and despite its weakened condition, it had turned itself away from her.

As much as her wounds hurt, she knew something had to be done.

'I can't let you die,' she said quietly.

Kneeling, she reached for the small pot and spoon.

Crawling slowly to the wolf's side, she gently patted its face.

When she saw no reaction, she steeled herself, gathering some of the pasty medicine onto a spoon.

Gently, she spooned it onto the wolf's fur, a small amount at first, and after seeing no reaction, spreading it more liberally and deeply.

'Very good,' she whispered. 'Perhaps this will –'

With an ear-splitting yelp, the wolf convulsed, its head thrashing from side to side, its body twisting awkwardly, the force of its movements sending the old lady tumbling to the ground.

A moment later, the wolf came to rest on top of her, its body-weight trapping her beneath it.

Lansi lay quiet.

With ten of the regiment remaining at Stanthorpe, the remainder had split into three among the other provinces. Norwood had gone with the group to Delfar; Montcreath, his second in command, to Kordeit; leaving Dane and Will in charge at Lansi.

As the gates closed behind him, Dane took in his first sights of the province.

Ringed by a tall wooden fence, they made their way towards the first group of homes; a variety of wooden dwellings with thatched rooves lining the street in front of them. In the distance were a couple of larger, stone buildings, Beasley's residence among them.

The streets were empty, the only noise coming from within the confines of the homes, where people waited anxiously, not wanting to venture outside.

'This way,' said Beasley.

Arriving in a large, open area, Dane guessed it to be the site of the market.

Looking around, the entire place was deserted. Carts that would normally be full of merchandise were empty, and there wasn't a trader or buyer anywhere to be seen.

'This may do nicely,' said Beasley, wiping his brow in the hot sun. 'It's empty and open, away from the flocks, and there are plenty of places for the knights to take shelter.'

'You may be right,' said Dane. 'But I think there may be somewhere more suitable.'

A group of knights in Lansi colours approached.

'Allow me,' said Beasley. 'Royal Knights Thorburn and Hevenshire, I present Raymond Illings, Commander of Lansi.'

'Pleased to meet you both,' said Illings, a knight slightly taller and several years older than Dane, nodding to them both in turn.

'I'd be grateful if you could show us around,' said Dane. 'So, we can decide the best location to set our trap.'

'You don't think we should set it here?' asked Illings.

'Perhaps,' said Dane. 'But I'd like to see the rest of the province. I'm particularly interested to see where the girl was taken.'

Beasley and Illings looked at each other knowingly.

'Is something wrong?' asked Dane.

'No,' said Beasley. 'We'll take you there. But it may be a little … awkward.'

'Why is that?' said Dane.

'It's no matter,' said Beasley. 'We'll show you.'

Making their way through the streets, Dane took in the silence and lack of activity, together with the looks on the faces of the people they passed.

'They don't appear pleased to see us,' he said to Will.

Will nodded.

'I know. But I don't know why.'

'I think I have an idea,' said Dane, motioning to a man he saw ahead.

Upon reaching the man, Beasley drew his horse to a stop.

'Charles,' he said.

Dane saw the man made no move to acknowledge the Governor. Judging by his dishevelled appearance — clothes loose and untidy, hair messy and unkempt, his unshaven face with tired, heavy eyes, and his mouth set in a look of anger and pain — Dane knew who this had to be.

To Dane and Will, Beasley said, 'this is Charles Wardsworth.'

With a nod, Dane said, 'On behalf of the King, I'm sorry for your loss.'

Wardsworth spat on the ground.

'Your words mean nothing,' he said. 'They're not going to bring my daughter back.'

Glancing behind Wardsworth, Dane spotted a woman and a small child cowering in the doorway of the house.

'We're sorry for the loss of your daughter,' Dane said to the woman.

'Don't you dare speak to my wife!' Wardsworth yelled, his face red-hot with rage.

Dane saw the woman shrink further at her husband's words.

'You come here, with your empty words, your pomp and bravado, and expect us to feel better?' said Wardsworth. 'My wife and I have lost our daughter. My son has lost his sister. Nothing you say will bring her back. So, go back to Brindabeare, and you tell your King he can rot in the ruins of Nadensa, for all I care.'

'Charles,' said Beasley, 'you need to be careful what you say, or –'

'Or what?' said Wardsworth. 'You'll have me arrested? You'll hang me for treason? Well, why don't you go right ahead? Hang the lot of us. At least, we'll be reunited with my daughter.'

'I'm warning you,' said Beasley.

'And I'm telling you,' said Wardsworth, 'I don't care.'

'Please,' said Dane. 'We're here to help.'

'Help?' said Wardsworth. 'You'll help me get my daughter back?'

Dane sat motionless, looking into Wardsworth's despairing eyes.

'I didn't think so,' said Wardsworth, spitting in Dane's face. 'That's what I think of your help.'

In the next moment, Beasley and Illings had their swords drawn, pointing at Wardsworth.

Wiping his face, Dane gently grabbed Beasley's arm.

'It's all right,' he said. 'The words of a grieving man aren't enough to have him arrested.'

Hesitating for a moment, Beasley sheathed his sword. Illings did the same.

With a final nod to Wardsworth, Dane eased Thunder forward.

To Will, Beasley and Illings, Dane said, 'I know exactly where I want the trap set.'

'How is she?' asked the King.

'Sleeping,' said Marilena.

'That's not what I asked,' said the King.

Marilena nodded.

'She's in the same condition as yesterday. In all honesty, I'd say she's weaker.'

'I don't understand,' said the Queen, turning away, tears welling in her eyes. 'Why don't we know what's wrong with her?'

'We are still examining her, my Queen,' said Lord Frederick.

'You've been examining her for days,' said the Queen. 'And she's getting worse, not better.'

'We won't rest until we know,' said Lord Frederick.

Dragging the last of some freshly killed sheep to the hunting ground, Dane and Will kept a watchful eye on the sky.

'This could take days, maybe weeks,' said Will.

'I know,' said Dane. 'But there's no doubt it's hunting. All these attacks in recent days.'

'I don't understand it,' said Will. 'After one large kill, you would think it would be satisfied for a while.'

'We're dealing with something we've never seen before,' said Dane. 'Who knows what would satisfy a creature like this.'

Adding their sheep to the pile, they made their way to where Beasley and the others were hiding.

The site they had chosen had been simple enough. After touring the province, much to Wardsworth's disgust, they had placed the sheep in the same place where Charlotte had been taken.

'My daughter's blood is on your hands!' Wardsworth had yelled when he saw what they were doing. 'If you kill it here, where my daughter was taken, her blood is on your hands!'

Glancing to his left, Dane saw Warsdworth now, standing alone in his yard about twenty feet away, his face a picture of despair and roiling anger.

Turning away, Dane looked at Will and the others.

'That's the last of it,' he said. 'There's nothing more to do, except wait.'

A noise distracted him, breaking the prevailing silence around them.

A moment later, Dane heard a familiar squawk overhead.

Looking skyward, he saw Blaze circling towards him. Walking away from the others, he held his arm out, allowing her to land for a moment, before, having removed the message in her claws, launching her into the sky once more.

As Will walked towards him, Dane read the note twice to be sure of its contents.

'Don't say a word,' he said under his breath, handing Will the note and walking to the rest of the group.

'From Norwood at Delfar. The kestrel attacked in the late hours of yesterday. Despite the efforts of all who were lying in wait, it escaped, and several knights were injured.'

'How could it escape?' asked Illings. 'If knights were there to kill it, how did it get away?'

'The message doesn't say anything about that,' said Dane.

'If it escaped, then what we've got here is useless,' said Illings. 'We're defenceless.'

'We don't know that for sure,' said Will. 'Without knowing what happened, there's no way to know if we have reason to be concerned. They may have simply been unlucky.'

'You have some of your best archers in that group,' said Illings.

Dane nodded.

'And more here,' he said.

'As do we,' said Illings. 'If we can't kill it with arrows, we have no chance of killing it.'

'Until we know more, there's nothing to take from what we have, other than knowing there's been an attack. We have to believe that between everyone here, we can defeat it.'

'Very well,' said Illings.

'Let the first group wait as we've planned,' said Dane. 'And the second group will relieve them in three hours.'

'We have to do something!' said the King. 'We can't just sit and do nothing!'

'Rest assured –'

'I don't want to hear it!' said the King. 'I don't want to hear another word about all the signs being normal, the herbs and remedies you've tried, that there's nothing you can see that suggests there's anything wrong with her – when she's lying here, clearly unwell – I don't want to hear it. I want answers!'

Lord Frederick looked at the other faces in the room.

The Queen and Marilena were distraught; the Queen crying silently.

Vanessa lay sleeping, her face pale and withdrawn, a bead of sweat on her forehead.

'You've found nothing in the *Annals* and other records?' asked the King.

'No, Sire,' said Lord Frederick. 'I'm afraid not. There are records of sickness, but nothing that resembles her condition.'

A knock at the door drew their attention away from Vanessa.

Carruthers entered, a note in his hand.

Reading the message, the King turned his attention to Vanessa without response.

'Sire?' asked Carruthers.

'It can wait,' said the King.

Bowing himself from the chamber, Carruthers closed the door after himself.

The King passed the note to Lord Frederick.

'Another attack,' said Lord Frederick, a quizzical tone in his voice as he looked to the King. 'The message says it breathes fire.'

'We will deal with the kestrel when my daughter has recovered,' said the King.

'Very well,' said Lord Frederick.

'She is the future Queen of this land,' said the King, taking Vanessa's hand. 'We must do all we can to help her.'

Looking towards the Xerin Mountains in the distance, Dane thought his mind was playing tricks on him. Sitting in the same place for nearly three hours, with the same mind-numbing view, it had been hard to stay alert and focused on the task at hand.

A tiny, dark spot emerged, growing larger and larger as it came closer.

A few moments later, it filled the top of his vision, growing larger still, so big it ...

'It comes!' a voice yelled.

'Get ready to attack!' said another.

Snapping his thoughts to the present, Dane saw the image for what it was for the first time.

The kestrel!

Larger than any bird he'd ever seen, for a moment he stood in dumbstruck awe at the sheer size and majesty of it. Its wingspan was at least forty feet from end to end; its claws large enough to seize a grown man; its beak a giant, cleaving hook, strong enough to tear a person to shreds.

Gods have mercy ...

Flying on an unwavering course, zooming and gliding at the same time, it swooped towards the now rotting sheep that lay about twenty feet from where Dane had hidden.

A volley of arrows loosed.

'Not yet!' yelled Dane. 'Wait until it's closer!'

In the next moment, a lone man leapt into the clearing, running straight at the pile of sheep, an arrow nocked and drawn back.

'Who is –'

'Come and get me!' yelled Wardsworth, jumping to the top of the pile, loosing his arrow at the kestrel.

'Come and get me!' he yelled again, nocking another.

With a deafening screech, the kestrel zeroed in on its target, its mouth opening wide ...

'No!' Dane yelled, sprinting from his hiding place.

With no thought for either the kestrel or his own well-being, Dane launched himself at Wardsworth, knocking him out of the way, sending them both rolling off the pile of carcasses as the kestrel loosed a ball of fire, right over the top of the place where Wardsworth had been standing.

A scorched pile of sheep remained.

Swooping past, the strength of the undercurrent from its wings creating a shroud of dust, it screeched again, lifting itself higher into the sky and turning in a wide arc to attack once more.

Running to Wardsworth, Dane collared him, dragging him away from the bait.

'Leave me be!' said Wardsworth. 'I have to kill it!'

'You need to stay out of the way!' said Dane. 'It would have killed you, right then and there!'

Continuing to struggle, Wardsworth yelled, 'I don't care! I don't care!'

Now on the other side of the path from where he'd hidden with the others, Dane kept his grip on Wardsworth.

'Let me go!' Wardsworth screamed again.

The kestrel's scream pierced the air as it started to zoom in on its prey again.

'It's coming again!' said Dane, a bead of sweat dripping down his back. 'I have to -'

With an elbow to the face, Wardsworth broke free of Dane's grip, running to the pile of sheep once more.

Stunned for a moment, Dane could do nothing but watch as Wardsworth stood among the pile of burning sheep, fumbling an arrow onto his bow as the kestrel zeroed in.

Unleashing another ball of flame, Wardsworth screamed as he burned, collapsing into the pile of carcasses around him.

Cursing, Dane saw Will running towards him as the kestrel took to the sky once more, circling for another attack.

'No one wanted to shoot at it while he was there,' said Will, crouching beside him.

'Look at the size of it,' said Dane, wiping the trail of dust it created out of his eyes.

'How do we get close enough without being burned?' asked Will.

Thinking quickly, Dane struggled for an answer.

As the kestrel screeched again, he saw it.

Pointing to a bench, he and Will ran towards it, upending it and dragging it towards the sheep. They were only halfway there when the kestrel unleashed another ball of flame.

With a scream of agony from someone to his right, Dane saw a knight lifted into the air, before falling to the ground as the kestrel veered away from a volley of arrows.

'We have to hurry,' he said, dragging the bench behind the pile of smouldering sheep.

Two knights ran to their stricken colleague, dragging him out of the way.

'The arrows!' yelled Illings from nearby. 'They're no use! We can't kill it!'

'Take cover!' yelled Dane.

Bewildered, Illings retreated to his hiding place.

With the bench in position, Dane and Will squeezed themselves behind it, the horrible smell of burnt mutton around them.

'We won't be able to see it,' said Will, reaching for an arrow. 'We're going to have to react to its sound.'

Dane nodded.

'If it doesn't work, we're dead.'

Looking on, Beasley and his knights, and others drawn towards the sound and flame couldn't believe what they were seeing.

Rising on a gust of wind, in a wide, sweeping turn, the kestrel rose vertically, spreading its wings to their full span. All who saw it were unanimous in their retelling – this was no myth – in its momentary pose at the top of its turn, the kestrel was so large it blocked the sight of the sun, a dark shadow falling on all beneath it.

Stopping for the slightest moment, pivoting at its apex, dipping slightly and allowing itself to fall under its own weight, turning towards its smouldering prey in the street below, it breathed the intoxicating smell once more, using its weight to gather speed as it swivelled towards the ground, leaning forward and launching itself like a loosed arrow towards its target.

Screeching constantly, gaining speed all the while, it flew towards them, claws stretching as it came closer and closer to its prey.

Behind the bench, Dane and Will heard the kestrel's cries; distant at first, then louder and louder as it came closer.

Swooping down, the kestrel let loose another fire ball; earlier than in its previous sweeps, seeking to clear the path in front of its prey as it swept past.

Waiting until the last possible moment, Dane and Will rolled out from behind the bench.

Springing to their feet, arrows nocked and drawn, they fired straight into the kestrel's neck, diving to the ground as it passed them.

In what appeared to be slow motion, with an agonising scream, the kestrel banked to its right and rose upwards, before stopping in mid-flight and falling to the ground, landing on its back and bursting into flames.

As Dane, Will and the others made their way to the site of the dead bird, its body turned to ash, moments before the wind swept it away to nothing ...

... and with a shriek, Vanessa woke with a jolt; wide-eyed, disoriented and confused, looking at the stunned faces around her.

Chapter 10
STRANGE EVOLUTIONS

People bustled their way around the market, hurrying from stall to stall, eager to get their trading done before the best of the food sold out. The fine weather attracted those wanting to buy and trade, and others wanting somewhere to spend a nice warm day.

A popular place to meet, greet and talk, the marketplace's recent conversations were clouded by talk of *the serpent* – the mysterious creature seen by more with each passing day; the tales of its exploits growing as time went on, making it difficult to sort the truth from the lies.

'What do you mean it flies?' asked one.

'I saw it with my own eyes,' said the other.

'First you tell me it breathes fire, and now you tell me it flies? Serpents can't do either of those things.'

'Well, this one can. We moved the herd to higher ground, well away from the trees. I thought they'd be out of its path and safe. It made no difference. We were out there the following morning, and we saw something in the sky, heading towards us, and the next thing we knew –'

Screams cut him off before he could finish.

People ran in all directions, clamouring to get away, baskets and food scattering everywhere, a large emptiness emerging in the middle of the market.

The serpent landed with a thud, slithering on its belly for a moment before rising off the ground and folding its wings. It stood on its hind legs; becoming harder to see as it blended with its surroundings, swishing its head from side to side, scenting the air and absorbing the sensations it smelled for the first time.

Knights ran into the square, swords and arrows drawn.

Unconcerned, the serpent continued looking around.

A knight ran up from behind, slashing with his sword.

The sword bounced harmlessly off the serpent's skin, leaving not so much as a scratch.

In the next instant it turned, seemingly amused to find the bewildered knight standing there.

Another ran from the side, swinging as hard as his colleague had done, with the same effect.

Yet another approached with an arrow, shooting from point-blank range, only to see it fall harmlessly to the ground.

With confused looks on their faces, the knights stood trans-fixed, unsure of what to do.

Turning to the first attacker, the serpent loosed a ball of flame, striking him in the face.

With a terrified scream, the knight fell to the ground.

Screaming as one, the onlookers scattered further.

The serpent's head sprang from its body, latching onto the stricken knight. Dropping to the ground, it dragged the knight to its body, wrapping its middle in coils around its prey, and with a final loud hiss, took flight over the wall, carrying its meal away.

'I swear, it was the bravest thing I've ever seen,' said Beasley.

Beckoning to Dane and Will, he said, 'If not for these Royal Knights, I don't know how we would have survived.'

'Yes, yes,' said Kavendish. 'We're grateful it's dead. They were in the right place at the right time. If your knights were there, they would have killed it.'

Glancing at each other, Dane and Will said nothing.

All the patrols deployed through the Stanthorpe region, including the one despatched to the Xerin Mountains were on their way back to Brindabeare, and having arrived over the last few days, were debriefing the governors at Stanthorpe.

'I disagree,' said Beasley. 'My knights *were* there and tried to kill it. Their arrows bounced away and had no effect. These two were brave enough to get right up close to it, and that's why they killed it.'

'So, *dragonslayer,*' said Kavendish, looking at Dane with his now-familiar, overgrown toad-like smile, 'your legend grows further. It seems we add *"kestrel-killer"* to your list of titles.'

'If it's all the same to you, Governor,' said Dane, 'we did what was required. There's nothing noteworthy about it.'

'On the contrary,' said Kavendish. 'Governor Beasley has just told us his knights were unable to kill it. You obviously possess a special talent, given you killed it with nothing more than an arrow – something Governor Beasley's trained knights failed to do.'

'It's not something I can explain,' said Dane, 'other than to say, as Governor Beasley reported, a couple of us managed to get close enough to shoot it at very close range. It's skin and feathers looked to be more like scales, which are harder to penetrate.'

'Are you sure about that?' asked Kavendish.

'What does it matter?' asked Beasley, saving Dane from a reply. 'The kestrel is dead, and the threat is no more. We should be grateful for everything they did to help us.'

Others in the room nodded, including Norwood and Governors Cooper and Moore.

'It attacked us, and we weren't able to kill it,' said Moore. 'Having seen it up close, I'm relieved it's dead. And I pray there isn't another one out there somewhere.'

'I agree,' said Cooper. 'We can all sleep easier, knowing it's no longer a threat.'

With a nod to Dane and Will, he said, 'I thank you on behalf of all in my province.'

'The Leader's Convention will be held soon,' said Kavendish with a wide grin. 'There may be more that can be shared then.'

'I don't know what more will need to be said about it,' said Dane. 'But we'll give details if needed.'

'If you're not out slaying some other creature,' said Kavendish. 'Or guarding your Princess.'

Dane bristled.

Something's not right about this.

'Governor, what are –'

'You mean, *our* Princess,' said Beasley.

'Of course,' said Kavendish smoothly.

'We need to be on our way,' said Norwood. 'We won't take any more of your time.'

'Please,' said Kavendish. 'You won't stay for the night? I have some of the finest Wandabyne ales in my cellar. After your travels and ordeals, surely an evening of relaxation and revelry is in order?'

'Thank you, Governor, but we need to get back to Brindabeare,' said Norwood. 'The sooner we depart, the better.'

'Very well,' said Kavendish. 'Please pass my thanks to the King. And my best wishes to the Princess in her recovery. I would be most disappointed if she were unable to attend the convention.'

Taking their leave, Dane, Will, Norwood and the other governors made their way to the horses.

'Thank you again,' said Beasley, shaking hands with Dane and Will. 'Despite what Governor Kavendish said, you have my gratitude for what you did for us.'

'We're glad we were able to help,' said Dane.

'And do pass on my best to the King, the Princess and Lord Frederick,' said Beasley as they parted.

'What is it with Governor Kavendish?' Will asked Dane as they checked their saddles.

'I don't know,' said Dane. 'But I don't think it's the last we'll hear of him.'

Yet another who doesn't want to trust me ...

'Well?' said the King.

Removing his hand from Vanessa's forehead, Lord Frederick looked at the King, Queen, Marilena, Salsbury and Patrice.

'Sire, I can't explain it,' he said.

Filled with hope at what seemed signs of recovery a couple of days ago, Vanessa had fainted again, helped to bed under the watchful eye of Marilena. Lord Frederick, the King and Queen had been summoned to her chamber.

The King's face contorted with despair.

'It makes no *sense!*' he said. 'This mystery illness that no one can solve. I won't stand for it. There has to be something we're doing, or not doing that's causing this.'

'I understand, Sire,' said Lord Frederick. 'And we are doing all we can to find a remedy.'

'Well, you're obviously not working fast enough!'

'Father, please,' said Vanessa, propping herself up among the pillows around her. 'Lord Frederick is not to blame.'

Pacing anxiously around the chamber, the King ran his hand through his hair, shaking his head in disgust.

'It all started when she started those, those *fighting lessons,*' said the Queen.

'And Dane's not to blame either,' said Vanessa.

'But, dear,' said the Queen, 'don't you see? You were well until –'

'No,' said Vanessa. 'You never liked the fact I wanted to do it, and you're using this as a reason to say it was a bad thing. It has nothing to do with it.'

'Well, what else have you done that's not part of your normal routine?' said the Queen.

'I started those sessions not long after I came home. Things were fine until the dragon attacked the castle. My sessions with Dane have nothing to do with it.'

'Well, is it possible, in your current condition, you're not thinking about this with a clear mind?'

'A clear mind?' said Vanessa. 'You think I'm insane?'

'That's not what I meant,' said the Queen.

'That's *exactly* what you meant!' said Vanessa. 'My poor, sick, helpless daughter, who let herself be talked into those "unseemly training sessions." And now she's unwell, she doesn't have the sense to see right from wrong.'

'Now dear, that's not fair,' said the Queen.

'Fair?' said Vanessa, her anger rising. 'You dare talk about what's fair? I'm the one who is ill. And while you're happy to offer your own opinion and listen to everyone else, you choose not to listen to me, and put anything I offer against you down to the fact I've lost my senses.'

'Vanessa, please,' said the Queen.

'I hate to disappoint you,' said Vanessa, ignoring her reply, 'but my mind is very clear, and I'm telling you my condition has nothing to do with how I feel from a physical point of view. It's something else. And if you don't want to accept that, if you don't want to believe what I say, then –'

'Vanessa,' said the King. 'That's enough.'

'No, it's –'

'I said *that's enough.*'

Turning away from her mother and father, Vanessa lapsed into a brooding silence.

'Perhaps we should leave you for a while,' said Lord Frederick. 'Let you get some rest.'

'I don't want rest,' said Vanessa. 'I want to get out of this room.'

'But we can't have you wandering the castle in this condition,' said the Queen.

'And I'm not going to stay holed up in here,' said Vanessa, throwing off the bedsheets and stepping out of the bed.

'Princess,' said Lord Frederick, 'the Queen is right.'

'No, she's not!' said Vanessa. 'Marilena. Help me dress.'

'Are you sure?' said Marilena, looking at the others.

'Yes, I'm sure,' said Vanessa, standing and walking towards the dressing room.

She made it a few steps before being struck with dizziness, stumbling another couple of steps, before turning and staggering back to the bed.

'You see,' said the Queen. 'You're in no condition –'

'*Get out!*' Vanessa screamed. *'Just get out!'*

Approaching the Great Forest clearing, the road to the Borsan River Bridge leading to Brindabeare ahead, Dane hesitated, waiting for Norwood to ride up to him.

'A scuttler wishes to speak with me,' he said.

'A scuttler?' said Norwood. 'Where?'

'Beyond a thicket over there,' said Dane, pointing past a mid-sized elm to the right of the trail.

'I can't see anything,' said Norwood.

'Trust me,' said Dane. 'He's there. You have to know how to find them.'

Will nodded.

'He's done it before. I can't see them either; but he finds them.'

'Very well,' said Norwood. 'Make it quick.'

Dismounting, Dane walked about twenty yards to his right.

'Greetings, Reuben,' he said, handing the empty vial that had contained Vanessa's blood to the little creature waiting for him, its grey fur covered in the latest collection of rags and other materials foraged from its travels.

'Thank you, Master Dane,' said Reuben, looking reverently at the vial, beckoning Dane into his cave.

Crouching to fit through the opening, Dane made his way inside.

The cave looked slightly larger than when he'd last been here. To his right, he saw what looked to be a recently hollowed out section, no doubt to store more of Reuben's forest treasures.

'What do you wish to tell me?' asked Dane.

'Creatures,' said Reuben. 'New creatures. Never seen before.'

'I know,' said Dane. 'The dragon and the kestrel. They're both dead. We killed them.'

Reuben nodded.

'The kestrel attacked Kelvin near Lansi.'

'Angus told me,' said Dane. 'We've just come back from Lansi. We killed it.'

'There are others,' said Reuben.

Dane's eyes widened.

'Other kestrels?'

'No,' said Reuben, shaking his head. 'Other creatures.'

Dane's mind started spinning.

'What creatures?' he managed to say.

'One looks like a serpent,' said Reuben. 'The other is a sarkoe that runs as fast as a horse.'

'*What?*'

'A few of us have seen them. At Mundool and Rhondo, and other settlements in that area. The sarkoe is heading towards Candahorn.'

Dane hesitated.

Raegan's provinces ...

Are they linked to the dragon and the kestrel?

To Vanessa?

'Tell me about them,' said Dane.

Once Reuben had finished, Dane felt his mind racing.

The whole land is in trouble!

'Thank you, Reuben,' said Dane, striding from the cave, before breaking into a run as he raced to Thunder.

Will didn't need to look twice to know something was wrong.

'There's more,' said Dane.

'More kestrels?'

'No. *More creatures.*'

'Lord Frederick?' Dane asked Laidlaw, having stabled Thunder and made his way into the castle.

'I believe he's with the Princess,' said Laidlaw. 'And he says he's not to be disturbed.'

'Thank you,' said Dane. 'He'll want to hear this.'

Making his way along the hallways and up the stairs, he found Marilena guarding the door leading to Vanessa's chamber.

'What are you doing here?' asked Dane.

'It's nice to see you, too,' said Marilena.

'I have to see Lord Frederick,' said Dane.

'He's inside,' said Marilena, stepping in front of Dane as he moved to walk past her, 'and gave strict instructions not to be disturbed. I'm here to make sure of it.'

'Mother,' said Dane. 'It's urgent.'

'He said there were to be –'

'It's *urgent!*' Dane hissed. 'I need to see him *right now.*'

Seeing the look on his face, Marilena hesitated.

'If you won't let me in,' said Dane. 'Then tell him I have news that affects the entire land.'

Marilena's eyes widened.

When Dane gave a forceful nod of confirmation, she reached for the door, looking at him for a moment, before knocking gently and disappearing inside.

Moments later, she reappeared, motioning him inside, before closing the door behind her.

Dane found Vanessa propped up in bed, with Lord Frederick seated next to her.

'How are you feeling?' Dane asked as he approached them.

'No better than when you left,' said Vanessa.

'It may be nothing more than a lingering fever,' said Dane, trying to sound convincing.

Vanessa looked at him desperately.

'No lies,' she said. 'Remember?'

'I hear you killed the kestrel,' said Lord Frederick.

'Yes,' said Dane, turning to face him. 'But that's not why I rushed in here. There's more.'

'More kestrels?' said Lord Frederick.

'No,' said Dane. 'More creatures.'

Dane saw Vanessa's eyes widen at the news.

'There are two creatures loose in the land around the Candahorn provinces.'

'That means –' said Vanessa.

'Raegan's not involved,' said Dane, finishing her sentence. 'He wouldn't set them on his own provinces.'

'What creatures?' asked Lord Frederick.

'One is apparently a serpent than can walk, fly and breathe fire,' said Dane. 'And the other is a sarkoe that can breathe fire and run on land as fast as a horse.'

Vanessa's jaw dropped in shock.

Lord Frederick raised a concerned eyebrow.

'Have you received reports like this?' asked Dane.

'We've received a few messages,' said Lord Frederick. 'And we weren't sure what to make of them – whether they were nothing more than wild rumour. And yet, until recently, we'd never seen a dragon emerge from the Highland Mountains, nor had we heard of a fire-breathing kestrel – and both were real.'

'Everything about the kestrel is true,' said Dane. 'We passed a couple of settlements on our way to Lansi, and there were scorch marks on the ground. When it attacked us, I saw it with my own eyes.'

Lord Frederick nodded, considering.

'What's unusual, is the initial reports made no mention of it breathing fire.'

'You're right,' said Dane. 'The first we heard about it was when we arrived at the settlements. It's as though it found a new ability; a way to do something you'd never expect a kestrel to do. It made killing it that much harder.'

'I've never heard of something like this before,' said Lord Frederick.

'It's all true,' said Dane.

'I don't doubt you,' said Lord Frederick. 'What I find unusual is the kestrel evolving, becoming more than itself, acquiring new abilities as time goes on.'

'But this isn't like any other kestrel,' said Dane. 'So perhaps it's another thing about this particular creature that was unusual.'

'Perhaps,' said Lord Frederick. 'But tell me more about the serpent and sarkoe. You say they can breathe fire.'

'That's what Reuben told me,' said Dane. 'The serpent was first seen at Mundool. It's been attacking their flocks, and it can stand as though it has legs, and blend with its surroundings. It shoots its head at its prey and reels it in. And now, Reuben says it can breathe fire and fly.'

'Are you sure?' asked Vanessa.

'That's what he told me,' said Dane. 'And what his friends saw. Just yesterday, it attacked a market. It breathed fire on a knight who was trying to kill it and flew away with him.'

'What kind of creature is that?' asked Vanessa.

Lord Frederick said nothing, a curious look on his face as he considered what Dane had said.

'What?' said Dane.

Standing and pacing the chamber, Lord Frederick started piecing everything together.

'First a dragon,' he said. 'Then a kestrel, and now, these other creatures. We killed the dragon; and despite no mention of it in earlier reports, we hear the kestrel and these other creatures can breathe fire.

'And now, the kestrel has been killed, and despite hearing nothing beforehand, we hear the other creatures can fly.'

'Only the serpent,' said Dane. 'Reuben didn't say the sarkoe could fly.'

'I wouldn't be surprised if those reports change.'

'A sarkoe that can fly?' said Vanessa. 'How is that even possible?'

'It's as unlikely as it being able to breathe fire,' said Lord Frederick. 'But it appears a pattern is emerging.'

'What pattern?' asked Dane. 'What does it mean?'

'It means we're dealing with a most peculiar set of circumstances regarding the Elements of Nature,' said Lord Frederick.

'Go on,' said Vanessa.

'Let's think of the creatures themselves,' said Lord Frederick.

'The dragon is Fire-sourced,' said Dane.

'And the kestrel is Air-sourced,' said Vanessa.

'Yes,' said Lord Frederick. 'The serpent is Earth-sourced and the sarkoe is Water-sourced.'

'One from each element,' said Dane.

'Yes,' said Lord Frederick. 'But that's not the issue.'

'Then what is it?' said Dane.

'Once the dragon was killed, the other creatures could breathe fire,' said Lord Frederick. 'And once you killed the kestrel –'

'The serpent could fly, and you think the sarkoe will be able to fly,' said Dane, the enormity of it hitting him.

Vanessa gasped.

'Yes,' said Lord Frederick. 'It would appear these creatures are somehow connected; and when one dies, the others evolve, attaining attributes from their dead comrades.'

'Vrenin's fire,' said Dane. 'What in the name of the Gods are the elements doing to us?'

'I'm afraid that may not be all,' said Lord Frederick.

'Why not?' said Vanessa.

'How was the kestrel killed?' said Lord Frederick.

'With an arrow,' said Dane, nodding towards Vanessa, his voice dropping to little more than a whisper as the realisation dawned on him.

'An arrow with your blood on it.'

Chapter 11

NATURE'S REVENGE

It came soaring over the outer wall – *a sarkoe* – a sarkoe that in no way resembled those seen anywhere throughout the entire history of the land. What it was doing here, out of water, no one could guess.

Feared water creatures seen mostly around the Osa River – sarkoe are giant crocodilians, growing between thirty to forty feet in length, their jaws strong enough to snap their prey in two with a single bite. While there had been occasional sightings along the Astuvius River, no one had heard of sarkoe being seen so far inland.

Why it had come here, into Candahorn itself, no one could understand.

Initially there had been rumours of what was thought to be a large dog, wolf, or panther terrorising Rhondo and the surrounding settlements; there was no other way to explain the remains of the stock it plundered – pigs, goats and sheep literally torn in half – no other animal could have done it.

Those rumours had soon turned to something else.

Recent reports talked of it being strong enough to burst through stone; then they said it could breathe fire, burning everything around it while it plundered.

And now, to the horror of all who bore witness, it stood in front of them, having soared over the wall, landing among the herds, litters and flocks on the outskirts of the city.

Those tending the animals scattered in all directions.

Easily thirty feet long, it stood to the height of a large wolf, but with the skin of its crocodilian origin.

Swishing its shorter, land-running tail and swivelling its head from side to side, it scented its prey immediately, somewhere to its left.

Without hesitation it ran, breaking through the fence and into a litter of pigs. With reckless abandon, it tore its way from one end to the other, gorging itself by taking single bites out of several, tossing the remains away like loose rubbish.

Reaching the end of the pen, it smashed its way through the fence on the other side, turning and unleashing a ball of flame, drowning out some of the panicked squeals from the remaining litter.

Trotting ahead, it came to a small, single-roomed wooden house, the home of the family tending the pigs. Hearing the anguished screams of the litter, the man had watched anxiously from the rear window, and now he and his family huddled behind the beds in a corner, trembling with fear as the sarkoe approached them.

Making its way inside, it stopped, standing in strange, unfamiliar surroundings, searching for a sign of movement.

A stray pig squealed. Turning towards the noise, it unleashed another ball of flame, blanketing the doorway for a moment.

The family crouched further into their small corner; the man shielding his wife and child, the woman covering her daughter's mouth in the hope she wouldn't scream and make the creature aware of their presence.

Unperturbed, it looked around the room, bumping past the table and cooking pot in the centre, before bursting through a wall and running through the front yard, out on to the street.

Except for the duty knights guarding the animals, the street was empty.

Those nearest the sarkoe fanned out; one behind and two in front. They had what they thought a simple and effective plan – those in front would cause a distraction, allowing their colleague to sneak up and kill it.

Careful to be far enough away to avoid its flame, the two knights drew their swords, waving them cautiously.

Whether or not the sarkoe saw a threat, it stood still for several moments, looking at them with no movement apart from its swishing tail.

Seizing his chance, the knight raced up from the rear, sword raised, slamming it down behind the sarkoe's head.

To his surprise and horror, instead of a killing stroke, his sword struck as though it had hit solid stone. Sliding harmlessly away, his momentum tilted him to the right, knocking him off balance as he fell to the ground.

Angered at the attack, the sarkoe turned, pouncing on the stricken knight, who screamed in agony as the sarkoe's massive jaws snapped shut, every one of its razor-sharp teeth sinking deep into his body.

Seeming to understand the connection with the two who stood before it, the sarkoe swished its head around, leaping forward in a movement faster than either expected, unleashing bursts of flame with deadly force. The two knights slumped to the ground.

The sarkoe wandered along the dirt road, crossing a large open area and making its way towards the large stone wall protecting the centre of the city. Watched by all at the gate-house and the patrol on the ramparts, perhaps sensing the hostility ahead, it broke into a run, reaching its full speed in a few strides.

Running with the relaxed ease of a wolf a fraction of its size, at a distance of about forty yards from the gatehouse it launched into the air, clearing the wall with a mighty leap, landing in a grassy field on the other side.

Surprised yells greeted it on all sides, none expecting such a creature to do what they had just seen.

Arrows flew everywhere, many falling short, those managing to strike bouncing away like twigs.

Unleashing an angry ball of fire in the direction of the gate-house, the sarkoe turned away, trotting towards the road ahead.

Horses emerged from the gatehouse.

Taking separate routes to the invader, they carried their riders into the surrounding streets as they made their way towards the castle.

'Off the streets!' one rider yelled.

'Clear the roads!' yelled another.

People hesitated, unsure of the reason for the panicked looks on the face of the knights who were shouting at them.

In the distance, some saw what appeared to be a burst of flame from the road near the gatehouse.

From the main street?

What would –

In the next moment, out of nowhere, something soared through the sky, landing with a loud thud, the ground trembling under the force of its weight for a moment before it gathered itself and started walking towards them.

Screams broke out as another burst of flame erupted from the creature and it broke into a run. An older man wasn't fast enough; the sarkoe butting him in the back, sucking the breath out of him and knocking him off his feet, before biting down with a loud crunching sound as its teeth tore through his body.

Running towards the nearest building, it burst into an armoury, clanging against swords, mail, armour and shields, knocking over anvils and shaping plates, unruffled by the intense heat in the forge at the rear. The two apprentices had but a single moment to dive behind it and take cover.

The sarkoe emerged onto the street once more. There were frantic screams as people rushed away, ducking inside the nearest building or behind whatever they could find to hide themselves.

Wandering from one of the taverns, a couple of men found themselves face-to-face with what they thought was some kind of large wolf – no, a stray horse – no, a ...

Trying to make sense of the blurred image in front of them, a wall of fire filled their vision, a moment before they felt a burst of intense heat on their faces. Slumping to the ground, neither felt anything as the sarkoe took a bite from each of them.

Desperate knights approached on horses, their hooves clattering softly on the road underneath them.

'We need to get it off the streets,' said one.

'Easier said than done,' said another.

'Down there,' said the first. 'If we can guide it down there, we may be able to lead it out the west gate.'

Leaving the two men, the sarkoe trotted away, along what were now empty streets: the only sound those of the knights behind it.

Keeping their distance, the knights carefully spread to the sides, watching it carefully.

With no further distractions, it slunk slowly through the streets, the Candahorn castle looming about a hundred yards ahead.

At the castle itself, the gates had been closed and every platform on the ramparts had at least two knights at the ready.

'One would think we were under siege,' said a knight manning the gatehouse.

'This creature has been running through the city, killing everything in its path,' said another. 'And nothing can kill it. We may as well be under siege.'

'Look!' said the first.

Following his gaze, both saw a distant flame, followed by a dark shape that soared through the air and over the western wall. Moments later they saw a section of the outer city wall crumble as the sarkoe broke through it and into the open land beyond the city.

'Thank the Gods for that,' said the second knight.

His colleague gave a relieved nod.

'Let's get word to the Governor.'

Vanessa looked at Dane and Lord Frederick.

'My blood?' she said.

Dane nodded.

'Like the dragon,' said the King, now present with Salsbury in Vanessa's chamber.

'Yes,' said Dane. 'I only shared it with Will at the time, but Norwood's message from Delfar said they shot it cleanly, and the arrows had no effect.'

'What does this mean?' said the King, glancing to Lord Frederick and back to Dane. 'Are you saying the only way these creatures can be killed is if the weapon has my daughter's blood on it?'

'I don't know, Sire,' said Dane. 'But it's the only thing common in both instances.'

'Apart from you,' said the King. 'You killed both of them.'

'Will – Royal Knight Hevenshire –'

'What about him?' said the King.

'We both killed the kestrel,' said Dane.

'His arrow?'

'Yes, Sire,' said Lord Frederick. 'Both had weapons fused with the Princess's blood.'

'I still don't understand it,' said the King. 'And what does it mean for these other creatures?'

'It's hard to say,' said Lord Frederick. 'But if we piece everything together, we can see a pattern. From what we know, the creatures emerged at the same time. One from each element – the dragon from the Highland Mountains, the kestrel from the Xerin Mountains – and if I were to guess, the serpent emerged from Harlanwood, and the sarkoe from somewhere near the Astuvius Falls.'

'Are you saying the Gods unleashed these creatures?' asked Vanessa, her eyes wide-eyed with shock.

Although they had never been seen, Lord Frederick had just named the rumoured residences of the Gods of the Ruling Elements of Nature.

Dane's mind exploded with questions.

Why would the Gods unleash these creatures?

What does that mean?

What do they have to do with Vanessa?

'I wouldn't be so bold as to say the Gods created these creatures,' said Lord Frederick. 'But if two emerged from what legend says are the birthplaces of Fire and Air, it's a fair assumption as to where the serpent and sarkoe may have come from.'

'Very well,' said the King. 'How sure are you about how to kill them?'

'We know others have tried without success,' said Lord Frederick. 'And we had no success against the dragon or the kestrel until they were struck with weapons with traces of the Princess's blood on them. Without the blood, it's likely they would still be alive.'

'And who knows what they would still be doing,' said Vanessa.

'So, no matter how unlikely,' said Lord Frederick, 'there appears to be a connection between these creatures and the Princess. But, at the moment –'

'Wait!' said Dane, a bolt of realisation hitting him.

The others looked at him, wondering what he was about to say.

'The City of Lost Souls,' he said.

'What about it?' said Vanessa.

Looking at Lord Frederick, Dane continued.

'You said there was a change – a disruption in the balance of the Ruling Elements when we escaped?'

'I did,' said Lord Frederick.

'And you said the disruption was large enough to have caused the disturbance that occurred, and the city may have been destroyed.'

'Yes,' said Lord Frederick.

'Is it possible, because we escaped the disturbance, the balance wasn't restored?'

'There's no way to know for sure,' said Lord Frederick. 'There's always an imbalance in the elements; a constant shifting and movement between them. There would rarely, if ever, be a time when one could say they were in perfect balance.'

'But if I'm right?' said Dane.

'Yes,' said Lord Frederick. 'It's possible.'

'Then isn't it possible another disturbance created these creatures, whether by the Gods or something else, to try and restore this balance?'

A collective gasp filled the chamber.

'Are you saying these creatures are trying to kill us?' said Vanessa.

'Not us,' said Dane. '*You.*'

Vanessa gasped, her face a mixture of shock and fear.

The King was at a complete loss as to what to say.

Lord Frederick stroked his chin, deep in thought.

'But we both escaped,' said Vanessa.

'Not really,' said Dane.

'What?' said Vanessa. 'We *both* escaped. *Together.*'

Dane shook his head slightly.

'I entered the city with Blaze,' he said. 'And I came out with Blaze. Both times it was by my choice and in the same manner. You entered the city with the wolves, against your will, as all prisoners do, and escaped with Blaze.'

'That doesn't mean anything,' said Vanessa.

'He may have a point,' said Lord Frederick, thinking it over.

'What point?' asked Vanessa.

'There's one more thing,' said Dane. 'Do you remember what happened as we approached the portal?'

'I do,' said Vanessa nervously. 'Blaze needed to land, and she perched on your shoulder.'

'And?' asked Dane.

'And what?' said Vanessa.

'There was a moment when you suddenly felt some sort of shiver, like a convulsion. You were unsettled for a moment, and I asked if you were all right.'

'Yes,' said Vanessa, replaying it in her mind. 'I do remember that.'

'Perhaps that was the moment,' said Dane.

'The moment what?'

'The moment the Gods, the elements, nature itself, or whatever it is, marked you. You were marked and those creatures were created; one from each element. The creatures were to restore the balance by –'

'*Killing me?*'

Dane bowed his head in silent acknowledgement.

'That's absurd!' said the King.

'Sire,' said Lord Frederick. 'He may be right.'

'*What?*'

'It would explain some of what has, until now, been a mystery,' said Lord Frederick.

'How?' said the King, glancing between Salsbury and Lord Frederick, his eyes wide in disbelief.

'Every living thing is made up of a combination of the Ruling Elements of Nature,' said Lord Frederick. 'You, me, every person, every *thing* you see around you. While some possess more of one element or elements than the others, everything you see is created from a combination of all of them. When there is a disruption in the elements, as we know, nature seeks to restore that balance.'

'What does that have to do with this?' said the King.

'When a prisoner is placed in the City of Lost Souls, they are banished forever, never to return,' said Lord Frederick. 'The parallel existence between the rest of the land and the city keeps the evil elements contained within the city, allowing the rest of the land to exist in its own state of balance.'

'And?' said the King.

'In the case of the Princess,' said Lord Frederick, 'as Dane said, she is the only person ever to escape. It would appear that nature itself sensed this, which is why she felt the sensation she did as she approached the portal, why we experienced the disruption in the Gargaun Ranges, and why these creatures have been created.'

'This is still speculation,' said the King.

'It is,' said Lord Frederick. 'But it's plausible. It's possible that nature itself is seeking to restore balance in the Ruling Elements and all living things by creating these creatures in response to the Princess's escape. One from each element, to take the Princess's place. In effect, it's nature's attempt to exact revenge for her escape – to restore its balance by seeking to kill her.'

'But why?' said Vanessa. 'I was never a prisoner. Raegan controlled the wolves – he had them take me into the city.'

'While we know you were not a prisoner, it's unlikely nature would understand it,' said Lord Frederick. 'There would appear to be a sense in the elements that anyone led into the city by a Gargaun wolf is to remain for the rest of their lives. The emotions you displayed as you were led into the city would have been similar to others sentenced there.'

'But –'

'If this is all correct, it's the only explanation we have that makes sense,' said Lord Frederick.

'What were we supposed to do?' said Dane. 'We couldn't leave her to die – nature's revenge be damned.'

'We're not questioning the rescue and escape,' said Lord Frederick. 'We're trying to understand why this is all happening. It appears, however unpleasant, and however wrong, that this is the consequence.'

'Why aren't the creatures attacking us?' said the King. 'The only one to attack us is the dragon.'

'For the moment, that's true,' said Lord Frederick. 'The dragon emerged from the Highland Mountains and sensed the Princess directly. I suggest the other creatures have been too far away to sense her at this point. I think it's only a matter of time before they do, and once that happens, they will move towards Brindabeare.'

'How do we know any of this is true?' said the King, still trying to make sense of it all.

'At this point, we don't,' said Lord Frederick. 'But it has a sense of logic to it, and it offers an explanation as to why the Princess is ill.'

Dane, Vanessa and the King looked at each other, then to Lord Frederick, stunned.

'Yes,' said Lord Frederick to the gaping mouths around the room. 'The Princess first became ill when the creatures emerged.'

Thinking on this, Dane realised Lord Frederick was right.

'The dragon was close enough to sense your presence and attacked the castle,' said Lord Frederick, looking at Vanessa. 'When it was killed, you showed signs of recovery, before falling ill at the same time we heard the kestrel was breathing fire.'

Vanessa nodded.

'And the same has happened since the kestrel was killed,' said Lord Frederick.

'What are you saying?' said the King.

'I think I understand,' said Dane. 'As each creature grows and changes, it takes more and more elements from Vanessa. That's why she didn't feel anything at first – they were too small. But as they grow and change, they take more and more elements from her, which is why she keeps falling ill.'

Lord Frederick nodded.

'Mother of Gods,' Vanessa said quietly. 'It all makes sense. No one can find anything wrong with me, and I keep saying it's like a part of me is missing.'

Nodding in recognition, Dane saw it as he watched Vanessa now – her eyes lacking their usual clear, azure blue, her facial expressions less vibrant.

The King stared blankly ahead, lost in thought, trying to understand.

'We have to kill them,' said Dane. 'If they're all dead, the balance will be restored; their elements will disappear, and Vanessa's elements will be restored. We have to kill them, before –'

'Before they take all my elements,' said Vanessa. 'And I die.'

Chapter 12
PLOTS AND PLANS

The old lady knew it didn't have long to live.

Lying prone in front of the fire, its breathing shallow and laboured, its tongue lolling on the ground, it looked utterly helpless.

She'd tried everything she could think of to save it, and the results had been the same each time – howls of pain from the patient, and injuries to herself for her trouble.

Now, as the rain pounded and the wind lashed outside, there was little more she could do, other than sit silently and give it some comfort at the end.

Despite what many said about wolves, she knew differently.

They weren't savage beasts who ravaged flocks, attacking anyone who dared to stop them, a pest to be rid of and a menace to all.

No – they were lords of the forest; the strength of a wolf pack stronger than any other creature in the land. A co-ordinated pack could kill a beast many times its size, using its combined guile and strength to trap and outsmart its prey.

How this one had come to be alone, padding aimlessly along the road, miles from a food source, she didn't know. All she knew was she couldn't let it die. Sensing a sudden purpose after all these years of isolation and solitude, she had to help it in what-ever way she could.

She'd taken it in, trying to nurse it back to health, but no mat-ter what she tried, the wound refused to heal. Water and herbs, various combinations of her sticky paste, all the remedies she used for her own ailments and afflictions had only caused more pain.

Kneeling next to it, she spooned some water into its mouth and onto its tongue.

It had no effect, puddling around its head.

'Please,' she begged. 'You must live. You must live.'

Sitting now, cradling its head in her lap, stroking it gently, she continued muttering to herself.

The rain pelted harder, and she could hear the wind swirling among the trees outside.

She paid it no heed, knowing she was safe in here ...

With a loud *crack!* she heard above the noise of the rain, her world unravelled as a huge tree collapsed on the tiny hut, crash-ing through the roof, slamming into the ground and splitting the room in half.

Stretching across the room, one end of the tree crashed into the fire, loose branches and leaves catching alight, throwing up sparks as they came to rest.

Startled, the old lady jumped back, swiping embers away as they landed in her hair and on her clothes, creating a ring of char-coal around her as they settled on the ground.

With a forlorn glance at the hole in the roof, she knew the dam-age lay beyond repair, and with no one else within miles, there would be no way to fix it. Content to live a solitary life since her husband died, she hadn't laid eyes on another soul for at least ten years.

Once the storm abated, she would have to salvage what she could and find somewhere else to live. Where that may be - at this point she had no idea.

The only thing to do now was ride it out. The fire still burned, offering little against the cold now sweeping in through the hole in the roof.

Glancing to the wolf, she hoped it hadn't been injured, and yet a small part of her hoped the falling tree may have put the poor beast out of its misery.

She certainly didn't expect to see the vision in front of her.

Glowing with an intense heat, stronger than all the fire in the room, she saw an ember sizzling against the wound in the wolf's neck.

Expecting to hear howls of pain, instead the beast was calm, its breathing slower and more relaxed than she'd seen in days.

Not wanting to approach it, she watched in wonder as it reached out with its paw, drawing more embers into a pile, before leaning over so its wounded neck smothered the embers on the ground.

She heard a sizzling sound from under the wolf, and saw smoke seeping out from under its body, drifting into the air.

Spellbound, she watched the wolf lean further into the ground, seemingly trying to crush the embers against itself.

After a minute or so, the wolf lifted its head off the ground, laying on its stomach once more. The embers were nowhere to be seen, seemingly absorbed into its body through the open wound.

It lay still for a few moments, its eyes closed.

Gathering herself, she started crawling cautiously towards it, not wanting to create a distraction or disturbance.

As she leaned in to look at the wound, her vision blurred.

Reaching up to rub her eyes, a hot flash of light filled the room, blinding her completely, and for several moments she saw nothing but black.

In a momentary panic, blinking frantically, she saw small splotches of light dotting the background of the darkness around her, before her eyes came back into focus, allowing her to see clearly once more.

Looking in front of her, she jumped back in shock.

'*Mother mercy,*' she said.

Lying in front of her, where the wolf should have been, was a man.

'You lied to us!' said Norton, leaning across the table and pointing a stubby finger at Mortensen.

'Be careful what you say,' Mortensen replied.

'You told us Lord Raegan created the dragon!' said Norton, ignoring the warning and trying to lean closer. 'You told us he went into the Highland Mountains and sent the dragon to Brindabeare!'

'Are you saying the dragon did not attack Brindabeare?' asked Mortensen.

'But he didn't send another one!' said Norton. 'And nothing has attacked Brindabeare since.'

'Be that as it may,' said Mortensen. 'We have to trust Lord Raegan is doing whatever is required to aid his quest to become the Supreme Ruler of the land. It is our duty to be patient and wait for his orders.'

'Have you seen him?' said Hazelwood. 'Have you spoken to him? You are his High Commander. Have you seen him at all, in the entire time since the girl escaped the City of Lost Souls?'

'That is not for me to say,' said Mortensen.

'Is he alive?' asked Farrington. 'There are rumours he's dead. I don't want to believe them, but the more time that passes before he shows himself, the more others are inclined to believe it.'

'And the more who believe it, the more his power – *our power*, weakens,' said Norton as he resumed his seat. 'We can't tell our people to follow someone who is invisible. Over time, they will rise against us.'

'Gentlemen,' said Mortensen, standing and walking calmly around the table. 'I assure you, our Lord is alive and well, and will reveal himself when it is appropriate to do so.'

'So, in the meantime,' said Maynard, 'we do nothing?'

'We will remain ready to respond to Lord Raegan's orders, whenever he chooses to issue them.'

'There is still no trace of the pulse,' said Norton. 'Surely that means something?'

The others looked at Mortensen expectantly.

'We've been over this,' said Mortensen. 'It is not for us to question.'

'What do we do about the creatures?' said Norton. 'The serpent that's attacked my flocks? The sarkoe, or whatever it is that's been attacking everything around here?'

'We will find a way to deal with them,' said Mortensen.

'They can't be killed!' yelled Norton. 'I've lost countless numbers of my flocks, and knights have been killed. No weapon can kill them – I've seen it with my own eyes.'

'Every creature has a weakness,' said Mortensen. 'We simply have to manage, until a way is found to stop them.'

'Are you not listening?' said Norton. 'Nothing can kill them!'

'I am aware of the reports,' said Mortensen. 'And yet there were similar tales about a giant kestrel in the Stanthorpe region – a creature unlike any that had ever been seen before; said to breathe fire, no less – and yet the Brindabeare Knights found a way to kill it.'

'Be that as it may,' said Norton.

'*Be that as it may,*' said Mortensen, his temper flaring at last. '*They found a way to kill it.* Now, I am sure they have weapons no greater than ours. A sword is a sword, an arrow is an arrow, and they found a way to kill it.'

'Maybe, Lord Frederick helped them,' said Maynard.

'Not according to the reports,' said Mortensen. 'As with the dragon, Lord Frederick did not kill the kestrel. They say he wasn't even there. The kestrel was said to be killed by Dane Thorburn and another Royal Knight named Hevenshire.'

'Governor, I assure you,' said Norton, 'my knights are as capable as any in the land, and they cannot kill this serpent. They have shot arrows from close range; they have slashed it with swords, and they have no effect at all. It's as though its skin is made of stone.'

'I am aware of that,' said Mortensen. 'Candahorn has been victim to the sarkoe, and the efforts of my knights were met with similar results.'

'So, we stand and watch while these creatures plunder their way through our lands?' asked Hazelwood. 'And hope there are enough of us left when Lord Raegan finally reveals himself to carry out his grand plans of conquest?'

'Be careful,' said Mortensen. 'What you are saying is close to treason.'

'Don't you –'

'Not another word,' said Mortensen.

Nodding to the guards at the doorway, a couple stepped forward, hands on swords.

'Very well,' said Hazelwood. 'Very well.'

'Perhaps we can trap them,' suggested Maynard.

'Impossible,' said Norton. 'The serpent can breathe fire and fly. No one would be able to get close enough to trap it.'

'Although these creatures are troublesome, all is not lost,' said Mortensen.

'What do you mean?' asked Norton.

'We can use the situation to our advantage,' said Mortensen.

The others looked at him, confused.

'There are ways we can take advantage of this,' he said when there was no response.

'How?' asked Farrington.

'We've sent word,' said Mortensen.

'What word?' asked Farrington.

'Word that Lord Frederick created these creatures as retribution for the dragon he's accused Lord Raegan of sending to attack Brindabeare.'

'That will do little to ease the continued losses in my flocks,' said Norton.

'It will create anger among our people,' said Mortensen. 'While at the same time, removing the focus of discussion away from Lord Raegan. And it will create discord and doubt among Brindabeare's allies. We've sent reports saying Lord Frederick sent the kestrel to the Stanthorpe region.'

'Why would that help?' asked Maynard. 'Everyone will know it's not true.'

'Stanthorpe has been a region of mixed loyalties,' said Mortensen. 'There were times throughout history when they allied with us. It was only after the Great War that Stanthorpe declared its current allegiance to Brindabeare.'

'You're trying to create unrest in the Stanthorpe region?' asked Farrington.

'Indeed,' said Mortensen.

'There's only one thing wrong with that,' said Hazelwood.

'Which is?' said Mortensen.

'As you said,' Hazelwood replied. 'The Brindabeare Knights killed it.'

'This is why you are a great Commander, but not a great thinker,' said Mortensen. 'We say Lord Frederick created the kestrel, sent it to plunder the Stanthorpe region, and sent his own knights to kill it, so he could have Brindabeare claim the glory for killing a creature of his own creation.'

Hazelwood and the others nodded thoughtfully.

'And when the Brindabeare Knights debriefed at Stanthorpe, Governor Kavendish was already suspicious.'

'That's all very well,' said Norton. 'I think it will take more than that to turn them against Brindabeare.'

'Don't be so sure,' said Mortensen. 'You would be surprised how quickly the seeds of discord can be sowed with the right tending. Not just among the Stanthorpe region, but perhaps in Wandabyne as well.'

'It might work,' said Maynard.

'The Leader's Convention will be held shortly,' said Mortensen. 'With more of these reports, we may find that, not only the convention, but perhaps the Valentaland Charter itself will collapse.'

'Nothing we've discussed is to be shared beyond this room,' said the King, looking to each in turn.

The Council were present, as were General Silvers and Hindmarsh, together with Dane and Will.

All nodded their agreement as the King continued.

'And by no one, I mean *no one*,' he said. 'Even the Queen is unaware of this. We will shortly have the Leader's Convention, with representatives across the land as our guests, and I will not have it torn apart by discussion and rumour about my daughter and her connection – if indeed there is a connection – to these creatures.'

Again, there were nods around the table.

'What we need to discuss now, is what action to take.'

'If I may, Sire,' said Marilena. 'I would like to take the Princess back to her chamber.'

The King nodded.

Rising slowly from her chair, Vanessa stood on wobbling legs until she felt Marilena's hand at her side.

'Thank you,' she said to all in the room. 'Thank you all.'

Looking on as Marilena shuffled Vanessa from the chamber, Dane felt his stomach tighten.

Wherever these creatures are, we will find them.

Find them and kill them.

'Sire?' said Fairbrother. 'If I may?'

The King nodded.

'Forgive me, but I didn't want to ask in front of the Princess. Even if these creatures can be found and killed, how do we know it will restore her to full health? A lot of this appears to be no more than conjecture.'

'That's true,' said Lord Frederick. 'And while we will do whatever else we can to cure her, what we have been able to piece together is as credible as anything else we know about what may be causing her illness.'

'Conjecture or not,' said the King. 'I want it resolved, which means we kill them.'

'And, if I may be so bold,' said Fairbrother, looking at Lord Frederick, 'now you have this information, are you able to find a new remedy?'

'Indeed,' said Lord Frederick. 'In consultation with the healers, I have made some new elixirs in the last few hours. We will see over the next day or so if they have the desired effect.'

'Very well,' said Fairbrother.

'And we're sure, absolutely sure,' asked Medhurst, 'that the dragon and the kestrel had traces of the Princess's blood on them?'

'Yes,' said Dane. 'I know it for certain.'

Lord Frederick and Will nodded.

'How do we find these creatures?' asked Silvers.

'Can you track them?' Hindmarsh asked Lord Frederick.

'Possibly,' said Lord Frederick. 'But –'

'For the moment, Lord Frederick will remain here, tending to my daughter,' said the King, the finality in his voice snuffing out any chance for argument.

'Current reports place both creatures in the Candahorn Region,' said the King. 'That is where we will start.'

'That's unfriendly territory,' said Silvers. 'We can't go waltzing in and asking them to get out of our way.'

'That may not be as difficult as it seems,' said Lord Frederick.

'What do you mean?' asked Silvers.

'These creatures have caused destruction among them,' said Lord Frederick. 'Destroying property, killing their flocks and herds. Knights and others have died trying to stop them. Were we to offer assistance, they may well allow it. We'd be helping to rid them of creatures they have not been able to kill.'

Silvers nodded thoughtfully.

'And once we're inside, they could trap and kill us,' said Dane.

'He's right,' said Lindstrom. 'We've all heard the reports coming from Candahorn. They're saying Lord Frederick created the kestrel and sent knights to kill the very creature he created. They can't be trusted.'

'If these creatures are causing as much devastation as we hear, it may be a way to restore peace,' said Fairbrother.

'It's also possible Raegan created these creatures,' said Medhurst.

'Raegan hasn't been sighted for months,' said Lindstrom. 'None of our spies have seen him, and there's been no sightings of Black Knights. He could be dead.'

Dane felt his stomach twist.

If only I killed that wolf!

'But it's possible he's done this to lure us there,' said Medhurst. 'That he's having the creatures attack his own forces to draw suspicion away from himself.'

'We're well aware of the situation with Raegan,' said the King. 'Every day those creatures are alive, my daughter remains ill, and unless Lord Frederick's latest elixirs have the cure, she grows weaker. I want those creatures killed – by any means necessary.

Whether we have the co-operation of the Candahorn provinces or not.'

'Could we ... trap them?' asked Will.

'How?' asked Hindmarsh.

Will shrugged.

'I'm not sure,' he said anxiously, staring at the wall behind Hindmarsh. 'It just occurred to me.'

'May I suggest you think more before you speak,' said Hindmarsh. 'Especially in such company as this.'

'Well ...,' said Will, his mind racing, 'if they're going to make their way here at some point ... then perhaps we can lay some traps. Then we'd be sure to kill them.'

'It's a good suggestion,' said Lord Frederick.

Breathing a sigh of relief, Will nodded gratefully in the wizard's direction.

'What would attract them?' said Medhurst.

'The bait worked well enough for the kestrel,' said Dane, eager to support Will's suggestion. 'Apart from the dragon, they're randomly attacking for food.'

'If they're heading towards Brindabeare, they're after more than food,' said Lindstrom.

'Surely,' said Fairbrother, 'you don't mean –'

'We would not offer the Princess as bait,' said Lord Frederick. 'But we could put something in the traps that would make them think she was there. Some clothing, perhaps perfumed, with drops of blood on them.'

'We can't afford a delay while we wait for traps to be set,' said the King. 'And it may be some time before they reach them. Time my daughter may not have.'

A knock was heard at the entrance to the chamber.

'I said we were not to be disturbed,' said the King.

Striding the length of the room, Lindstrom disappeared behind the door, emerging moments later, accompanied by Carruthers.

'What is it?' said the King when Carruthers reached them.

Handing over a note, Carruthers said nothing, waiting patiently.

The King looked up, nodding to Carruthers, who left the chamber.

'Sire?' asked Lord Frederick.

'From Governor Mortensen,' said the King. 'He requests a meeting.'

✦

Chapter 13
PARLEY

'**F**ather is going to parley?' asked Vanessa. 'With Candahorn?'

Dane nodded.

'Terms have been agreed,' he said. 'Angus has been beside himself with the number of messages he's had to despatch over the last day or so. At one point he thought he would have to send Blaze.'

'When?'

'We leave at dawn,' said Dane.

'You're going?'

'Yes,' said Dane. 'A full Royal Entourage will travel.'

Shifting herself straighter against the pillows, Vanessa yawned, before looking at Dane thoughtfully.

'Where?'

'Delgan,' said Dane. 'Your father refuses to travel to Candahorn, and Mortensen refuses to come here. Delgan's about the same distance from both cities. Word has already been sent, and a return message has been received from Governor Wilkens, agreeing to conduct the parley.'

'Will Lord Frederick be there?'

'Not exactly,' said Dane.

'What do you mean?' asked Vanessa.

'Both have agreed that neither wizard will attend.'

'Raegan's alive?' said Vanessa.

'We don't know,' Dane replied through gritted teeth. 'Mortensen's message insisted Lord Frederick not attend, and your father made the same demand of Raegan.'

'Then what does "not exactly" mean?'

'Lord Frederick will be there,' said Dane. 'Mortensen won't be able to see him, and he won't make himself known, unless it's absolutely necessary.'

'And we're assuming the same with Raegan?'

'Yes,' said Dane, momentary anger on his face once more.

'The exchange?' asked Vanessa.

'Fairbrother and Laidlaw,' said Dane. 'Mortensen will send his counterparts to us. Each party will be hosted half an hour's ride from Delgan by six of the other, with a Delgan guard assigned to each group. They will be released once the delegation from the parley return.'

Nodding thoughtfully for a moment, Vanessa took a sip from her goblet.

Dane watched as she appeared to labour over such a simple task.

She's getting weaker.

Reaching to take the goblet when she'd finished, Dane saw her eyes flash with anger.

'Don't.'

Dropping his hand, Dane said nothing, waiting for the moment to pass.

Vanessa hesitated, her face uncertain, before Dane saw the tension seeping away; her tired, withdrawn look returning.

'This is all a risk,' she said, moving back to the matter at hand. 'Why would father agree to such a thing?'

'It's an opportunity to bring everything into the open,' said Dane. 'Mortensen's message says he wants to discuss having Brindabeare rid his territories of the serpent and sarkoe. He says as the ruling city of the land, we have an obligation to assist.'

'How convenient,' said Vanessa. 'He didn't hesitate to defy us when he abandoned the charter to serve Reagan. He didn't hesitate to help in my capture, even if we couldn't pin it on him. But when he finds himself in a spot of trouble, and his master is unable to assist, we're "the ruling city of the land," and he expects us to come to his aid.'

'Council talked about that,' said Dane.

'It can't be his only reason,' said Vanessa.

'Your father said the same,' said Dane. 'But we won't know until the parley takes place.'

'Agreeing to do anything to help them could be a trap,' said Vanessa.

'We talked about that,' said Dane. 'Your father wants the serpent and sarkoe killed, no matter the cost. Restoring your health is what matters.'

Looking away, Vanessa stared out the window into the night sky.

Dane said nothing, waiting for her to gather herself.

'I just feel so helpless,' she said.

Sitting on the edge of the bed, Dane took her hands in his.

'Vanessa, listen,' he said.

With a tear rolling down her cheek, she turned towards Dane.

'You're innocent in all of this. It's all Raegan's doing. You were kidnapped and left to die in the City of Lost Souls. We found you and brought you back. You are the future Queen and ruler of the land.

'Apart from your father, no life matters more than yours. We will do whatever we have to do to cure you of this illness. It doesn't matter how many creatures we have to kill; how many lives we lose; whether we have to deal with Raegan, Candahorn, or anyone else – we will do whatever it takes.'

'But –'

'No,' said Dane. 'There are no "buts". You can be sure I won't hesitate to do whatever I need to do to defend you, your father and the city. Every knight feels the same. The entire city feels the same.'

'I know,' said Vanessa quietly, her mouth quivering. 'But I feel so helpless.'

Leaning towards Dane, she rested her head against him.

Dane sat silently, an arm around her, consumed by his own thoughts.

I will put an end to this.

I'll find whoever, or whatever is responsible for it and put an end to it.

Mortensen ... Raegan ... Vrenin ... Arclos ... Emilene ... Seruza.

Whoever you are.

I will find you, and when I do, I will kill you.

To Brindabeare's west, Delgan lay near the northern tip of the Strivett Mountains, near the coast. Smaller than a city, but one of the larger provinces in the land, Delganites lived happily in their isolation, the nearest settlement at least three days away.

Governor Wilkens had followed the parley procedures to the letter.

Dane saw the small pavilion serving as the holding area for the Candahorn exchange as he rode past, the entourage leaving six behind, and the Delgan Knights guarding the pavilion in place. He stole a quick glance at the Candahorn delegates, seemingly comfortable in their surroundings, hoping Fairbrother and Laidlaw were similarly accommodated at their location on the other side of Delgan.

Approaching the province proper, he saw the large pavilion that had been set up to host the meeting. Not wanting to risk entrapment inside the fortifications of any location, Mortensen had insisted the meeting take place outside the province.

It would seat everyone comfortably, with areas erected to each side where horses were to be held and tended until they were ready to depart.

Ten from Brindabeare would attend the meeting, with the remainder of the entourage behind them, about fifty yards away. Another twenty or so yards further away, Dane saw a ring of what looked to be at least three times that number of Delgan Knights.

Dismounting, the King led Medhurst, Salsbury, Silvers, Hindmarsh, Dane, Will, and three others into the pavilion: a large open tent-like structure about twenty feet square. Nodding them to their seats, he let them take their places and strode to the centre of the enclosure, where he greeted Governor Wilkens for a minute or so, before returning and taking his seat in the middle of the group.

'The Candahorn delegation will arrive shortly,' said the King.

Fresh skins of water were offered while they waited.

'I don't feel right about this,' Will whispered to Dane.

'Neither do I,' said Dane. 'If they attacked us now, we'd be hopelessly outmatched.'

'We should have waited for them to arrive before we dismounted.'

'You're right,' said Dane. 'But we have to follow the lead of the King and the General. And remember, Lord Frederick is here, too.'

Will nodded.

'All the same,' he said, 'it would have been better if –'

Before he could finish, the sound of horses distracted their attention.

Looking ahead through the Candahorn side of the pavilion, Dane saw a group of perhaps sixty to seventy riders in Candahorn colours arriving.

'There's the first breach,' said Will. 'Their group is clearly larger than ours.'

Glancing to the King, Silvers and Hindmarsh, Dane saw nothing in their faces that gave an indication they either noticed or cared.

The Candahorn riders dismounted, a group of ten approaching the pavilion.

Dane had never seen Mortensen before, and as the Candahorn Governor walked to the centre of the pavilion, his first impressions were of a man similar in stature to Silvers, carrying himself with the confidence and arrogance of a seasoned leader. Mortensen stood at a similar height to the General, with the same steely look in his eyes. With neatly trimmed light brown hair and a thin beard, unlike many of the governors in the land, he, like the King, was clearly of soldierly substance, dressed in the armoured, gold-black uniform of a Candahorn Knight.

Striding to the middle of the enclosure once more, the King shook hands with his adversary, before both returned to their seats, a distance of about ten feet between them. At one end of the pavilion, in the centre of the space between the two parties, Governor Wilkens sat sweating under his thick argent-azure overcoat, his eyes darting towards the knights he had stationed in each corner.

'We are here at your request,' the King said to Mortensen. 'Please state your business.'

Dane saw Mortensen sit more boldly in his seat, clearly insulted by the way the King had spoken to him.

'Candahorn has been attacked by a sarkoe,' said Mortensen. 'Or at least, something resembling a sarkoe. This creature runs on land, breathes fire, and leaps through the air. It leaped over the walls of my city, and has caused considerable damage, destroying buildings, killing livestock, and taking innocent lives. We have been unable to kill it.'

'Disturbing,' said the King thoughtfully. 'How many times has it attacked you?'

'Several,' said Mortensen. 'We were attacked a little over two weeks ago, and on our journey here, I've been informed it continues to attack other places nearby.'

The King nodded, considering the information.

'It appears to be evolving,' Mortensen added.

'How so?' asked the King.

'Not only is it growing, it's becoming more powerful. When we first sighted it, it looked no larger than a dog. It now stands to the height of a small horse. When it was first sighted, it wasn't said to breathe fire. Now it not only breathes fire, it can leap considerable distances.'

'I see,' said the King. 'And the other?'

'Serpent-like,' said Mortensen. 'It has also evolved since it first attacked. It can breathe fire and fly. While it hasn't attacked Candahorn directly, it has attacked several of my territories. We seek your assistance in getting rid of them.'

The King did not respond immediately, content to take his time.

'I question the territories you refer to,' he said. 'You have no authority over any territory, other than your own city.'

Mortensen didn't flinch.

'On that point we disagree,' he said. 'You know that Hezabar, Pardosta, Rhondo and Mundool are loyal to me.'

'I am not aware of that,' said the King.

'If I have come here, only to be insulted –'

'I am not insulting anyone,' said the King. 'I'm simply saying I'm not aware of the loyalty of those provinces to you. It is my understanding they declared their loyalty to Raegan – unless you're saying Raegan is dead and have assumed leadership of the rebel alliance in his place.'

Dane saw Mortensen flinch for a moment, his face turning a dark shade of red, angry he'd been trapped so easily.

'Lord Raegan remains our Supreme Ruler,' said Mortensen.

'Then we are not talking about creatures attacking your territories, but creatures attacking Raegan's territories,' said the King.

'Candahorn, Hezabar, Pardosta, Rhondo and Mundool have all been attacked by these creatures,' said Mortensen. 'As the ruling city of the land, you have an obligation to assist in getting rid of them.'

'Then you are prepared to acknowledge Brindabeare as the ruling city of the land?' said the King.

'No,' said Mortensen. 'I am not saying that.'

'Then why am I under any obligation to assist?' said the King, ready to ask the killer question. 'Why hasn't Raegan killed them?'

Dane saw Mortensen doing his best to remain composed, struggling to control his rage. It had taken less time than expected for the King to have him cornered.

'Lord Raegan has not been able to kill these creatures,' said Mortensen.

'That's interesting,' said the King. 'As we have heard no reports of any sightings of Raegan since my daughter was rescued from the City of Lost Souls.'

'Despite your reports, Lord Raegan is alive and well,' said Mortensen.

'And yet, he hasn't been able to rid you of these creatures?' said the King.

Again, Dane saw Mortensen struggling to contain himself. In the next instant he saw Mortensen's hand subtly move towards his sword.

'Don't even think about it,' said Silvers.

The King placed a placating hand on the General's arm.

'I'm sure he wasn't about to draw his weapon,' said the King. 'Perhaps he finds the temperature in here a touch uncomfortable.'

Shifting in his seat, Mortensen took a couple of calming breaths.

'Raegan has not been able to defeat these creatures?' the King asked again.

'No,' Mortensen replied, his voice barely audible.

'Then perhaps you've declared your allegiance to the wrong wizard?' said the King.

'Lord Raegan has not been able to defeat these creatures because they were created by Lord Frederick,' said Mortensen.

The King looked at Silvers and then Mortensen in surprise.

'You think Lord Frederick created these creatures?'

'I do,' said Mortensen, his arrogance returning. 'Lord Frederick created these creatures in response to baseless accusations that we kidnapped your daughter.'

The King raised an eyebrow.

'As well as the kestrel that attacked the Stanthorpe Region, and the dragon,' Mortensen added.

Dane sat upright in his seat.

The dragon?

'You are aware the dragon attacked Brindabeare?' said the King. 'You're saying Lord Frederick created a creature that attacked my own city?'

'A ruse,' said Mortensen, thinking he was gaining the upper hand. 'The dragon and the kestrel were created so you could claim credit for killing them. To let everyone in the land believe you can defeat whatever the elements throw at you.'

'You think Lord Frederick is able to create such creatures?' asked the King.

'He has created them,' said Mortensen. 'And we demand you remove them from our territory.'

Sitting proudly in his seat, Mortensen beamed, believing he'd turned the tables.

'You must be bitterly disappointed,' said the King.

'How so?' said Mortensen, surprised at the question.

'To have aligned yourself with a wizard that cannot help you. Who can't create or kill these creatures?'

Mortensen shifted angrily in his seat.

'Raegan's quest for power has failed on all fronts,' said the King. 'First, a botched attempt to seize my castle, followed by a failed attempt to kidnap my daughter.'

Seeing Mortensen continuing to squirm uncomfortably, the King smiled.

'Come now,' he said as Mortensen was about to interrupt. 'Are you going say it wasn't your men who attacked the castle? Three separate envoys in Candahorn uniforms who transformed into Black Knights?'

'This is not about –'

'This is *exactly* about that,' said the King. 'On two occasions you aided Raegan's attempts to seize power, and despite the failure of both, you remain loyal to him, while at the same time demanding I offer assistance to rid your city and other rebel provinces of creatures you can't take care of yourself?'

'That's not –'

'Do you realise the stupidity of what you are asking?' said the King. 'You come here, seeking our assistance, without offering a reason why we should help you.'

'There are creatures on the loose, destroying and terrorising my city,' said Mortensen. 'As the ruling city of the land, you have an obligation to assist.'

'And you're certain Raegan can't help you?' said the King.

'As I have told you,' said Mortensen. 'He says Lord Frederick has created these creatures, and on this occasion, has outsmarted him.'

The King shook his head slowly.

'You are a terrible liar,' he said. 'Raegan served me for many years, and one thing I know for certain is he would never admit to you or anyone, that Lord Frederick had gotten the better of him.'

With nowhere left to turn, Mortensen said nothing for a few moments, gathering his thoughts.

'We don't know where he is,' he said.

Dane sat bolt upright.

They don't know where he is.

They don't know where he is!

Did I really kill him?

'Who?' said the King calmly.

'Lord Raegan,' said Mortensen. 'He's disappeared.'

'I see,' said the King. 'You're sure?'

Mortensen nodded.

'And you have no knowledge of his whereabouts?'

'I don't,' said Mortensen.

'As interesting as it is to hear this, I'm struggling to believe you,' said the King. 'After all, you have done nothing but lie to me since we started. How am I to know you're not lying to me now?'

Mortensen said nothing.

'And why should I help you?' said the King. 'Why should I not be content to see an enemy weakened by these creatures?'

'You have provinces that are vulnerable,' said Mortensen. 'They could attack Grelfan or Feryndale.'

'They might,' said the King, scratching his chin. 'Then again, perhaps not. I could send forces there. I could send Lord Frederick, if necessary, to ensure these creatures don't attack those provinces, and ensure they continue to attack and weaken you further.'

'It could lead to a return to peace,' said Mortensen.

The King raised an eyebrow.

'Go on,' he said.

'If you help us kill these creatures, we will consider a return to the Valentaland Charter.'

'Consider it?' said the King.

Mortensen nodded.

Dane sat forward, watching intently, knowing the King wouldn't give in so easily.

'I'm afraid that's not enough,' said the King.

'You don't want a return to peace?' said Mortensen.

'Oh, I do,' said the King. 'But all you have offered is to *consider* returning to the charter. That guarantees nothing. You ask me to offer assistance, and in return you will *consider* a return to peace. I'm afraid it would have to be conditional.'

'I don't have the authority to agree to that,' Mortensen stammered. 'I would have to consult with my council.'

'You're the Governor,' said the King. 'Surely you can agree to this. After all, if you offered the possibility of returning to the charter, you must have the authority to negotiate on behalf of all. Why would you offer this if you were not able to commit?'

'I would need to talk with the other governors,' said Mortensen.

'I thought they were answerable to you?' said the King.

'Well, yes,' said Mortensen. 'But they would still need to be consulted.'

'I see,' said the King. 'And there is one last detail you would need to share with them.'

'And that is?' said Mortensen.

'They would have to surrender,' said the King.

'But we would be returning to the charter and declaring our loyalty to you,' said Mortensen.

'You would,' said the King. 'But I'm afraid it would be up to the new governors to do that.'

Mortensen looked puzzled.

'Indeed,' said the King. 'You and Governors Maynard, Farrington, Norton and Hazelwood would surrender and stand trial for treason. It would be those appointed in your place who would sign the charter declaring their loyalty to me.'

'I ... what ... you mean –'

'You and your fellow governors would stand trial for treason, and all of you, if you wanted an outcome other than to be hanged, would hand over every last Black Knight among you.'

'Out of the question!' said Mortensen.

'But you offered peace,' said the King in mock surprise. 'You must realise there can't be peace as long as Black Knights are present. Surely you can see they would have to be handed over?'

'Enough!' yelled Mortensen, finally losing his temper. 'This meeting is over! There will be no peace! There will be no surrender!'

Standing, he pointed directly at the King.

'Know that I came here in the spirit of peaceful negotiation, seeking to rid the land of a common enemy. I see I have been met by nothing more than hostility and contempt.'

The rest of Mortensen's delegation stood.

As one, turning on their heel, they left the pavilion without a word.

The King remained seated, watching them leave.

Dane and Will glanced at each other, wondering what would happen next.

Once the Candahorn delegation left, Governor Wilkens approached the King.

'That did not appear to go very well, Sire,' he said.

'On the contrary,' said the King, 'it went better than I expected.'

'Very well,' said Wilkens uncertainly.

'Thank you for your hospitality,' said the King.

'The riders have been sent,' said Wilkens. 'The exchanges will take place shortly.'

'Thank you,' said the King.

Leaving the pavilion, Dane and Will shared their thoughts as they made their way to the horses.

'I think the King succeeded,' said Dane.

'I'm not sure I agree,' said Will. 'I don't know about Raegan.'

'I don't think Mortensen knows where he is,' said Dane. 'He may be dead after all.'

'Or it may have been a lie, to give us false hope,' said Will.

'Maybe,' said Dane. 'But I think Mortensen was serious. He doesn't know where Raegan is, even if he's not ready to concede he's dead. That's why he wasn't more willing to negotiate. If he were serious about it, he would have been a lot more persuasive in asking the King for help.'

'You may be right,' said Will. 'But if the serpent and sarkoe are in the Candahorn Region, it will be harder to kill them without coming under attack ourselves.'

'That's true,' said Dane. 'But the King couldn't let Mortensen know his position.'

'Why do you think Mortensen called the meeting?' asked Will. 'He achieved nothing.'

'I think he really wanted the King to help him,' said Dane. 'He's worried about the serpent and sarkoe, and there's no sign of Raegan. I think he was appealing to the King's sense of duty, and once the King agreed, he'd use us to get rid of the creatures, then kill us.'

'Then why did he leave so soon?'

'The King was too smart,' said Dane. 'He laid his traps perfectly, and Mortensen fell into every one of them. I don't think it was his intention to tell us about Raegan or lose his temper the way he did, but the King got the better of him.'

After giving Thunder a quick rub-down, Dane climbed into his saddle, joining the rest of the entourage as they turned towards Brindabeare. Heading to the exchange point, they arrived after a ride of about half an hour.

As Dane reined in, he saw the Candahorn men riding away.

With some time before Fairbrother and Laidlaw were due to join them, the group dismounted and waited in the shade of the holding pavilion, exchanging pleasantries with the Delgan Knights.

Lord Frederick appeared in a flash of light and a *BANG!* joining the King, Silvers and Medhurst as they continued their debrief.

After waiting another half an hour, Dane saw a group of Delgan Knights approaching.

Fairbrother and Laidlaw were not with them.

As they came closer, Dane could see something was wrong.

One of the knights was hunched forward, sitting awkwardly in the saddle. When they pulled up, the stricken rider fell to the ground.

All three were cut and bleeding.

Emerging from the pavilion, the King approached the nearest one.

'You're the exchange patrol?' he said.

'Yes,' said the stricken knight, reaching behind him.

'Where are my men?'

Gasping for breath, the knight struggled to speak.

'Dead,' he said, slowly rising and stepping towards the King.

Dane reacted in an instant.

As the knight drew a small blade from his armour, a knife sizzled from Dane's gauntlet, striking the knight squarely in the back of the neck.

In the next moment Dane and Will grabbed the other riders, wrenching them from their saddles as they tried to draw their swords.

In a matter of moments, both foes were dead.

Turning the bodies over, Lord Frederick said to all, 'Candahorn Knights. They've killed Fairbrother and Laidlaw, and the Delgan Knights assigned to them.'

'They broke the parley!' Medhurst yelled. 'We can't let them get away with it!'

'Do you wish to send riders after them?' Hindmarsh asked the King.

'They will be a long way gone by now,' said Silvers. 'I doubt it would serve any purpose, other than getting more men killed.'

Dane could barely contain his anger.

They were innocent!

How could Mortensen do this?

'The General is right,' said Lord Frederick. 'There's no value sending riders after them.'

With a grunt of agreement, and a grateful nod to Dane and Will, the King turned away, walking towards the horses.

'This will not go unpunished,' he seethed. 'There is nothing more to do here.'

Chapter 14
DISCUSSIONS AND DOUBTS

'How is she?' asked Dane as he arrived at Vanessa's chambers.

'Better,' said Marilena. 'Lord Frederick's latest remedy appears to be working.'

'Really?' said Dane, his voice full of hope.

'She's feeling better than she has for the last few days, but she's still not well.'

'What are you doing here?' said Dane.

'Keeping unwanted visitors out,' said Marilena.

'But you sent for me. Do I need to come back later?'

'No. She's awake and asked to speak to you alone. But please –'

'I know,' said Dane, pushing past and closing the door before Marilena could say anything more.

Seated at a chair by the window, Vanessa turned as Dane approached.

'You look better,' he said, noticing a slightly darker, more natural colour in her face.

Vanessa smiled.

'I do feel a little better.'

'That's good,' said Dane. 'Perhaps this remedy will work, and we don't need to worry about the serpent and sarkoe after all. We can let them get their fill in the Candahorn Region until you're better, then Lord Frederick can help us kill them.'

'We're not sure it's working yet,' said Vanessa. 'I've had episodes like this before, only to lapse again.'

'Maybe it's different this time.'

'We'll see,' said Vanessa.

'We will,' said Dane. 'Has Lord Frederick taken any more blood?'

'No,' said Vanessa. 'He doesn't want anything interfering with the elixir.'

Dane nodded.

'I haven't heard a lot about the parley,' said Vanessa, changing the subject.

Dane noticed her eyes flash a momentary annoyance, as though something was bothering her.

'It was interesting,' said Dane. 'But you know what happened with your father, Fairbrother and Laidlaw, so there's not much more to say.'

'No,' said Vanessa, shaking her head. 'I don't.'

'Really?' said Dane.

'Father has barely spoken to me since he came back.'

'Well, even though he returned safely, this will shock you,' said Dane. 'After the parley was over, while we were waiting at the exchange point, three Candahorn Knights, posing as Delgan Knights tried to kill him.'

Vanessa gasped, rocking back in her chair.

Dane nodded.

'They killed Fairbrother and Laidlaw, and the Delgan Knights guarding them, then they tried to kill your father.'

Vanessa's eyes widened as Dane continued.

'We think that was the reason Mortensen called the parley. He knew your father would never agree to help him. He wanted to draw him into the open, where he'd be more vulnerable and exposed, where we wouldn't be expecting anything like this to happen.'

'Even with a full entourage?'

'No one expected it,' said Dane. 'It was a bold move, and it nearly worked.'

'But you stopped them,' said Vanessa, a smouldering anger on her face.

'It wasn't foolproof,' said Dane. 'Arriving without Fairbrother and Laidlaw made me watch them more closely, even though they appeared to be bleeding, as though they'd escaped an attack.

'When the first one fell to the ground and got to his knees so easily, I knew something wasn't right. Then he reached for a knife.'

'How did they do it?' asked Vanessa. 'How did they replace the Delgan Knights that were supposed to be guarding them?'

'Fairbrother and Laidlaw were found somewhere past Delgan,' said Dane. 'They must have had men lying in wait for them.'

Her face flushing with anger, Vanessa said sternly, 'they have to pay for this. Two innocent men, who did nothing more than play their part in a parley.'

'Yes,' said Dane, angry himself at the memory. 'I always liked Laidlaw, and apart from when he thought I was involved in your kidnapping, Fairbrother always supported me. It's not right that they had to die in something like this. They wouldn't have had a chance to defend themselves.'

'At least the plan failed,' said Vanessa, a little too angrily.

Dane watched her for a moment, wondering what was wrong.

Vanessa took a sip of her goblet, slamming it down on the table, water sloshing over the rim and on to the floor.

'What's wrong?' said Dane. 'He's safe. Once the Candahorn Knights were killed, he was never in danger, and Lord Frederick brought him straight to the castle.'

'It's not that,' said Vanessa.

'Then what?' asked Dane.

'You've told me more since you've been here than father or anyone else. It appears I'm too ill to hear of such things. Things I have every right to know.'

'I'm sure they're not wanting to upset you,' said Dane. 'They don't want you to worry about it.'

'That's the point!' said Vanessa. 'I *should* be concerned about something like this. It doesn't matter how ill they think I am. They're not letting me come to council, and I'm completely in the dark about things I should be involved with.'

'But –'

'*No!*' said Vanessa. 'I don't want you talking like everyone else. Even Marilena's been sworn to secrecy.'

With an angry glance towards the chamber door, she said, 'and she thinks I don't know.'

Letting out a sigh, she said nothing for a moment, staring straight ahead.

'All these rules and protocols,' she said, shaking her head slowly. 'What I can do; what I can't do. It's maddening. Sometimes ...'

'What?' said Dane.

Vanessa hesitated, lowering her gaze and staring at the floor.

'Sometimes I wish ... I could just be a common maid,' she said. 'And not have to deal with all of this. I wonder what it would be like just to be ... *normal.*'

Dane's eyes widened in surprise for a moment, but in seeing the despair on her face, he said nothing.

'I know it sounds silly, but it's true,' said Vanessa, now looking slightly embarrassed. 'I think about what it would be like not having guards and attendants watching my every move. To just be simple and common. I wouldn't have to put up with any of it – I could just cook in the kitchen or tend the hens ... I wouldn't have this mysterious illness and be cooped up here.'

'Vanessa –'

'No!' she said. 'I feel like a prisoner, being here and not being allowed to do anything, or hear anything that might *"upset me."* And who knows what's planned for the Leader's Convention? They'll probably want to keep me hidden away from everyone.'

'That may be the right thing to do,' said Dane.

'*No, it's not!*' said Vanessa, thumping her chair. 'I'm *not* some sick little piglet they can coddle and keep out of sight until it gets better.'

The door opened and Marilena came rushing into the chamber.

'What's wrong?' she asked, leaning over Vanessa, placing a calming hand on her shoulder.

'Nothing,' said Vanessa, calming herself in an instant.

'What did you say to her?' said Marilena, turning an accusing eye to Dane.

'Nothing –'

'Nothing,' said Vanessa. 'It wasn't Dane. I'm just a little tired.'

'Dane was just leaving,' said Marilena firmly, standing and looking angrily into her son's eyes.

'No,' said Vanessa. 'I want him to stay. Just for a moment.'

'Very well,' said Marilena, staring daggers at Dane.

'Alone,' said Vanessa.

Making no move to leave, Marilena stood defiantly between them.

'Please,' said Vanessa.

Looking angrily at each of them in turn, with a loud huff, Marilena strode from the chamber, not quite closing the door.

Standing slowly, Vanessa took Dane's hand in hers.

'I'm asking you, no matter what others may say, not to hide anything from me.'

Dane nodded.

'*Anything.*'

'You know I wouldn't do that,' said Dane.

'Thank you.'

'All in the line of duty.'

Vanessa smiled weakly.

'I'd better go,' said Dane.

Releasing her hand from his, Vanessa settled back into her chair.

'Here,' said Dane, grabbing a loose blanket and folding it neatly in her lap.

'Thank you,' said Vanessa with a gentle smile.

For a moment they looked silently at each other, lost in thought, the crackling fire the only sound in the chamber.

'We're waiting for information on the location of the serpent and sarkoe,' said Dane eventually. 'As soon as we know, I'll be leaving.'

Vanessa nodded.

'It may be before the convention is over.'

With a gentle smile, Dane turned and left the room.

As he opened the door, he felt the momentary resistance of someone leaning and listening on the other side, before it let go, allowing him to open the door completely.

'What do you think you're doing?' hissed Marilena, as she closed the door.

'What do you mean?' asked Dane.

'You know how ill she is! You shouldn't be saying things to upset her. You're only making things worse.'

'Really?' said Dane.

'*Yes, really!*' said Marilena, grabbing his arm tightly. 'You should know better!'

'I know what I'm doing,' said Dane. 'And I know exactly where my loyalties lie.'

Dane felt Marilena tighten her grip on his arm.

'And you would do well to do the same,' he said, pulling himself free and walking away.

Mortensen looked at the other governors.

None made a move to speak.

'So,' said Norton eventually, 'you weren't expecting Meriwether to help rid us of these creatures?'

'Not in the least,' said Mortensen. 'He sat there, pompously thinking he'd outsmarted me, questioning why he would aid an enemy. At no stage did I think he would offer anything.'

'Then we still have no answer as to how to kill these creatures,' said Norton.

'Not at this time,' said Mortensen.

Norton bristled, his lips clenching, clearly displeased.

'Even if you knew he wouldn't send help, you could have asked how they killed the other creatures. How long do we have to continue to tolerate this?'

Maynard and Farrington shifted uneasily, sharing Norton's views but reluctant to speak. Hazelwood stared blankly ahead.

'My knights guided the sarkoe out of the city,' said Mortensen. 'We haven't sighted it for some time.'

'That's because it attacked me,' said Maynard. 'And it's caused a lot of damage. My people were terrified for hours.'

'The serpent attacked me,' said Farrington.

'And me,' said Hazelwood.

'These attacks are unfortunate,' said Mortensen. 'But –'

'But you don't seem to care,' said Norton. 'As long as they're not attacking you.'

'That's not what I'm saying,' said Mortensen.

'With all due respect,' said Farrington, 'we don't seem to be doing anything at all. These creatures attack at random, where they like, when they like, and we're powerless to stop them. They're evolving and becoming more and more dangerous, and our best hope is they attack someone else.'

'And,' said Norton, 'we had an opportunity to parley with our enemy, who to this point has killed two of them, and instead of agreeing to some kind of truce and using it as an opportunity to get them to help us, we try and fail to kill their leader, thereby removing any chance of it.'

'As I have told you, there is no way he would have agreed,' said Mortensen.

'You don't know that,' said Norton.

'Gentlemen,' said Mortensen, doing his best to maintain control of the meeting. 'Which is the greater goal – killing a few meddlesome creatures, or vanquishing our enemy?'

'Even if you killed Meriwether, you would have brought Lord Frederick down on us,' said Maynard.

'Lord Raegan will take care of Lord Frederick,' said Mortensen. 'Are there any among us who doubt this?'

'Governor, may I ask a question?' said Hazelwood.

Mortensen nodded his assent.

'Was the parley ordered by Lord Raegan?'

'There are times when decisive action is required,' said Mortensen. 'As Lord Raegan's High Commander, I took it upon myself to take action in his absence. Had the plan succeeded, and against considerable obstacles it almost did, Brindabeare would now be in a considerably weaker position.'

'But it didn't succeed,' said Norton. 'We still have these creatures to contend with, and Meriwether is still alive.'

'That may be how it appears at the moment,' said Mortensen. 'But –'

'You failed,' said Hazelwood.

'I don't believe I failed at all,' said Mortensen. 'Meriwether knows I am a force to be reckoned with.'

'With our combined force and Lord Raegan, he already knows that,' said Hazelwood, nodding to his fellow governors. 'If you succeeded as you'd planned, he wouldn't be worried about that – he'd be dead.'

'As I told you, there was a risk it would fail,' said Mortensen. 'Even after killing the exchange party, we were outnumbered, sending three against a Royal Entourage. It was a gamble, and from reports, one that nearly succeeded.'

'But you've done nothing more than put Brindabeare on higher alert,' said Hazelwood. 'Do you think Lord Raegan will be pleased about that?'

'You do not need to concern yourself with Lord Raegan,' said Mortensen.

'I believe I do,' said Hazelwood. 'I believe we all do.'

Nervous looks from the other governors greeted this comment.

'You have yet to show us anything that proves you have control of the situation,' said Hazelwood, standing and staring down the Candahorn Governor. 'Or that you've been in contact with Lord Raegan at all. We don't even know he's alive.'

Hazelwood leaned closer.

'Tell me,' he said. 'Exactly what have we gained from this alliance? We were promised power and rule. I was promised Feryndale. I lost a considerable number of knights in the attack in the Gargaun Ranges, and since that time, there has been no sight or sound from Lord Raegan, and everything has turned against us.'

Standing and gesturing to the others, he continued.

'Our power has weakened considerably, there are new and unknown creatures wreaking havoc among us, leaving trails of destruction behind them. While at the same time, Brindabeare has further expanded its power and influence.

'And your response to all of this? To send a few birds, trying to blame the creatures on Lord Frederick, and a botched effort to kill the King. And despite all of this, you think we're going to continue to listen to you?

'Well, I for one won't –'

Before Hazelwood could continue, a knife thrust upward, through his back, and he dropped lifelessly to the floor.

The Candahorn Knight who had approached on Mortensen's silent command retrieved his weapon, wiped the blade on the dead man, and resumed his place at the chamber's entrance.

'Now then,' said Mortensen. 'Is there anyone else who wishes to raise an objection?'

'They're attacking at random,' said Hindmarsh. 'Our scouts can't get a reading on where they might be at any time, and from what the Falconer tells us, the spies are faring no better.'

'That makes tracking them all the more difficult,' said Silvers.

Looking around the chamber, Dane saw all the commanders were present, Royal and Regimental alike, along with a few Senior Knights, such as Will and himself.

While there were only four in the group who knew what was believed to be the secret to killing the creatures, they needed as many ideas as possible about how to find them.

'We can't send search parties,' said Tristan Sandford, a Royal Knight a couple of years older than Dane.

Silvers nodded.

'After the parley, I doubt any of the Candahorn Alliance would let us in,' he said.

'And they could use it as a way to trap us,' said Symkin Bedcroft, the new Commander of the Advance Regiment.

'Indeed,' said Silvers. 'It would be difficult to justify sending sufficient number into the larger provinces, and particularly to Candahorn itself, without it being seen as an invasion.'

'Given they're attacking at random,' said Hindmarsh, 'there's no way to know they would be in the province if they allowed a search. The governors could make it appear as though they were under attack, then ambush us.'

'That's well thought –' Silvers began.

'Perhaps we can try –' said Will, speaking at the same time.

Silvers stopped mid-sentence, and all eyes in the room turned to Will.

'Perhaps we can, what?' said Silvers.

Will hesitated under the General's glare, a bead of sweat trickling down his neck.

'If you have something to say, then say it,' said Silvers.

'Can we ... try and trap them?' said Will. 'Lord Frederick thinks we could.'

'No,' said Silvers without hesitation. 'Finding them is difficult enough. To think we could trap them is ridiculous.'

Will shrank back in his chair.

'Lord Frederick?' asked Travis Henderway, Commander of the First Regiment.

'We can't assume Lord Frederick will join us,' said Silvers. 'For the moment, he is doing what he can to find a remedy for the Princess's illness.'

As the conversation went back and forth, Dane let his mind wander.

We can't trap them.

We can't find them.

Even if we find them, they can easily elude us.

What can we do?

There has to be something ...

'Do we have to do anything?' asked Bedcroft, jolting Dane from his thoughts.

Everyone turned to look at him.

'Why do anything?' asked Bedcroft. 'These creatures are attacking our enemies. Isn't that a good thing? Why should we be concerned?'

Dane and Will glanced at each other, and Dane saw Silvers and Hindmarsh exchange a look.

'Feryndale and Grelfan are at risk,' said Silvers. 'The King wishes to protect them.'

'Very well,' said Bedcroft. 'Then why don't we send forces to Feryndale and Grelfan for as long as these creatures are loose, and aid them if they're attacked? Isn't that what we did when the kestrel was attacking in the Stanthorpe Region?'

'The King wants these creatures killed,' said Silvers.

'But, why –'

'The King wants these creatures killed, and that is what we will do,' said Silvers. 'It is not our place to reason why.'

'But, without Lord Frederick's help –'

'Be careful,' said Silvers. 'Unless you wish me to relieve you of your command and find someone more capable of listening to orders.'

Bedcroft nodded.

'Your pardon, General.'

Silvers nodded sternly.

'But the idea of sending forces to Feryndale and Grelfan is sound,' he said. 'I will recommend it at the next council meeting. Perhaps the solution for the moment is to send forces to both, and from there, link with our spies and be ready to attack once the creatures are sighted.'

'I think we're spreading ourselves too thin,' Will whispered to Dane when Silvers turned away. 'Hoping we'll somehow be in the right place at the right time.'

'You're right,' said Dane.

'And with a small amount of blood available, it's even harder,' said Will.

'The more we think about this, the more complicated it becomes,' said Dane.

'And there's the Leader's Convention,' said Will. 'They're already arriving. I'm sure the King was hoping we'd have resolved this by now. They're going to want answers.'

'How soon do we depart?' asked Bedcroft, drawing Dane and Will back to the main conversation.

'As soon as the Leader's Convention is over,' said Silvers. 'With all the visiting dignitaries, the King wants the entire army here until it's over.'

Heads nodded in affirmation.

With another glance to Dane, Will and Hindmarsh, Silvers said to all present, 'We need to make sure we have all the provisions we need, and liaise with Feryndale and Grelfan before we depart.'

Nodding in understanding, Dane and Will left the chamber.

'You have to attend the convention?' asked Will over their morning meal.

'Yes,' said Dane between bites.

'Why?'

'They want an account of what happened in the City of Lost Souls.'

Will nodded.

'Better you than me,' he said. 'I hate talking in front of crowds.'

'Are you going to be able to say your vows then?' asked Dane, grinning at Genevieve. 'Or are you going to pass out with anxiety?'

'He will be able to say his vows just fine,' said Genevieve, giving Will's arm an encouraging squeeze with both hands and leaning her head on his shoulder.

Will said nothing, rolling his eyes as he picked up his goblet.

Dane laughed, standing and handing his tray to an attendant.

'I'll see you later,' he said, nodding with a smile to a group of giggling maids as he left.

Held every year, the Leader's Convention brought all city and provincial governors to Brindabeare for a week of talks, giving them a chance to meet in one location and discuss pertinent matters. Principal to the convention was the annual signing of the Valentaland Charter, a document confirming their ongoing loyalty to the King as their ruler and Brindabeare as the ruling city.

Created at the end of the Great War, the charter served as a means of ensuring an enduring peace throughout the land. Apart from pockets of trouble, which had been resolved in relatively short spaces of time, the charter had been largely successful, until a few years ago, when the Candahorn delegation declared its intent to set up its own rule and stormed out of the convention.

Dane had inadvertently played a part in this, interrupting proceedings to inform the Brindabeare Council of his sighting of Raegan in the Great Forest, the closest confirmed sighting to Brindabeare since being in exile after killing Dane's father during his first attempt to seize control of the castle. The unexplained halt to the convention had given the Candahorn delegation what they saw as reasonable justification to storm out and break away.

Having been defeated in the Great War, along with Firelord Edan, who, like all wizards with the exception of Lord Frederick and Raegan, was said to have been killed by Vrenin, Candahorn had always been a reluctant participant in signing the charter.

The convention had already commenced by the time Dane found himself walking into the main hall, which had been converted to suit the occasion.

The Brindabeare Council, minus Vanessa and Fairbrother, were seated at one end, with a row of tables along each side, where the governors, outfitted in their official dress armour, were seated. Their entourages sat at smaller tables behind them.

Dane recognised those from the Stanthorpe Region, seated to his left. Kavendish gave him a stony, frog-faced look that roused the annoyance and uneasiness he'd felt when they last spoke; while Cooper, Moore and Beasley gave respectful nods as he walked past.

He also recognised Governors Levensworth and Wilkens from Grelfan and Delgan. By the colour of their outfits, he recognised Governors Finchley, Ingles, Harris and Chipperfield from Wandabyne, Wedlan, Cramden and Lordale for the first time; as well as Governor Werrington from Feryndale.

'The resemblance is uncanny,' he heard one say.

'I'd swear it was Gil Thorburn himself,' said another.

Walking a shade taller, Dane came to the end of the hall, stopping and bowing to the King and Council.

'Royal Knight Thorburn,' said Lord Frederick, seated to the King's right, 'please recount your time in the City of Lost Souls, from the time you entered the city, until you escaped with the Princess.'

Briefed by Lord Frederick and the King before the convention that he would be asked to do this, Dane began his story.

The room sat silent, hanging on every word.

'Blaze – our eagle – found her, and led me into the city. I still don't know how it worked – one moment I was walking towards a lake, and in the next it all changed, and I was somewhere else. There were caves and rock mounds everywhere, and no trace of the ranges.

'I started searching for the Princess, and after some time passed, I was captured by a group of exiled wizards.'

A collective gasp echoed through the hall.

'I don't know how old they were, or how long they'd been there, but they looked ancient,' said Dane.

A ripple of laughter spread among everyone present.

'They'd also captured the Princess. Which meant I no longer had to find her. If I could escape, I'd be able to get her out. But it wasn't that simple. Once I escaped the wizards, we became separated, and I lost her again.'

'If I may?' interrupted Kavendish, standing as he spoke. 'Can I ask how you managed to escape from a group of exiled wizards? How many were there?'

'Four,' said Dane, turning to face the Stanthorpe Governor.

'You escaped from four exiled wizards?' said Kavendish in disbelief. 'From what we've been told, they were the most evil and wicked wizards in the history of the land – doers of the most horrible things imaginable. And you – nothing more than a knight.'

'They'd lost their power,' said Dane, ignoring the insult. 'The pulsing sound of the otterlings – creatures that dig the caves and tunnels in the city – drained them of their power. They thought I was a wizard – they thought we were both wizards, and one of them told me they lost their power in a matter of days.'

Kavendish looked unconvinced.

'And how did you escape?' he asked.

'They had a ritual. They thought the Princess was an Earthlord, and they pitted her in a battle with the other Earthlord in their group. Their leader, Medwin, wanted to create what he called a coterie – one wizard from each element and a Masterlord. He believed this group would be able to pool their resources in another ritual and restore their power, so they could escape and seek their revenge on the wizards who exiled them.'

'They didn't know Nadensa was destroyed?' said Kavendish.

'No,' said Dane. 'And I didn't tell them.'

'How noble,' said Kavendish, his voice dripping with contempt. 'You still haven't told us how you escaped.'

'You haven't let me,' said Dane, keeping his voice and emotions calm.

With a curt nod and an angry grunt, Kavendish sat down.

'They were distracted during the ritual,' said Dane. 'And while they weren't looking, I was able to free myself from the stake I was tied to, retrieve my sword, and kill three of them.'

'And the fourth?' asked Kavendish.

'The woman helped me escape,' said Dane. 'I wounded Medwin, and she crushed his skull with a rock.'

'How convenient,' said Kavendish, his voice dripping with contempt. 'And why would this evil, exiled wizard help you in such a way?'

'Retribution,' said Dane. 'She said Medwin arranged to have her husband killed during the same ritual, and she never forgave him for it.'

'Did you kill her?' asked Kavendish.

'No,' said Dane. 'As I said, the Princess and I became separated, and I had to find her again.'

'And you left a killer behind?'

'I did,' said Dane. 'Finding the Princess was more important. I trusted that she wouldn't come after me. She was so happy with all the food she had to eat.'

'Food?' asked Kavendish.

'The dead wizards,' said Dane. 'She was going to eat them.'

There was a collective intake of breath from all except the Brindabeare Council.

'Disgusting!' Dane heard Beasley say.

'Horrid!' he heard from a voice he didn't recognise.

'All the same,' said Kavendish, with his toad-like smile, 'you left a killer behind.'

'As I said, finding the Princess was more important,' said Dane.

'Quite right,' said Levensworth.

'And how did you escape the city?' asked Kavendish.

'I found the Princess, and once she recovered enough to under-stand where she was, Blaze led us towards the portal where I'd entered the city.'

'What do you mean *"recovered enough"*?' asked Kavendish.

'The noise of the otterlings,' said Dane. 'It's a constant scraping sound – you'd have to hear it to understand it. It fills your mind; constant and never-ending. It disorients you, so you don't know where you are, or what you're doing.'

Kavendish looked at Dane as though he hadn't believed a word he'd said.

'I don't know how long the Princess had been in the city before I found her,' said Dane. 'And she didn't have the protection I had. Blaze's squawking numbed the sound. When I could hear Blaze, I didn't hear the scraping. She'd had nothing to counteract it until I found her, so she was somewhat dazed and confused until the effect of the scraping sound wore off.'

'Nothing else attacked you?' asked Kavendish. 'No other wizards or mysterious creatures?'

'There were no other wizards,' said Dane, maintaining his sense of calm. 'But there were Gargaun wolves. Four of them found us as we were escaping.'

'You defeated four Gargaun wolves on your own?' asked Kavendish in that same contemptuous and disbelieving tone of voice.

'Blaze attacked one,' said Dane, maintaining his self-control. 'And I struck two more, like this.'

With a flash of movement, the knives from his leggings embedded themselves in the side of the long table, right in front of Kavendish.

Rocking back, hands to his mouth and eyes wide with shock, Kavendish shrank into his chair.

'After those two were wounded, I chased the last one away,' said Dane, casually approaching the table and wrenching out his knives.

Others in the room looked on with awe as he restored his weapons, turning to face the King, Lord Frederick and the council once more.

Chapter 15
ACCUSATIONS

'On behalf of all in the Wandabyne Region, I commend you and all who rescued the Princess,' said Governor Finchley, speaking for the first time; his tone of voice and demeanour leaving Dane in no doubt he was a man to be respected.

All but Kavendish nodded their agreement.

'While we are pleased the Princess is safe,' said Kavendish, recovering his composure, 'I can't help but wonder how much of what has been reported really happened.'

A collective gasp filled the room.

Everyone was aghast.

Cooper, Moore and Beasley stared at Kavendish in disbelief.

'Explain yourself,' said the King, his face as hard as stone.

Standing once again, Kavendish addressed the chamber.

'Until the Princess disappeared, none of us had heard of this place, this *"City of Lost Souls."* And given none of us know where it is, I have to say I doubt the truth of its existence.'

'What are you trying to say?' asked Finchley. 'That it's a lie?'

'That's outrageous!' yelled Governor Wilkens, knocking his chair over as he stood.

'Hear, hear!' said Governor Werrington, his hair flaying across his face as he sprang to his feet.

'I'd be more than happy to take you there,' said Dane, with an uncertain glance to Lord Frederick. 'It's about thirty days from here ... although, it may no longer exist.'

'No longer exist?' said Kavendish with relish. 'You confess this place doesn't exist?'

'No,' said Dane, glancing at Lord Frederick for a hint of guidance.

'Then what *are* you saying?'

'Once the Princess escaped, there was a major disturbance, a quake of some kind. Trees were uprooted, rocks rained down from the ranges, the lake shot plumes of hot water into the air. For a moment, it looked as though it was going to swallow us all.

'Thankfully, Lord Frederick arrived and helped us.'

Glancing to Lord Frederick once more, Dane said, 'Once it stopped, we thought the reaction was caused by a disruption in the Elements of Nature, and the city may have been destroyed.'

'Did you investigate?' asked Kavendish.

'Of course not,' said Dane, stunned at the question. 'We'd just escaped. Why would we want to go back?'

'How convenient,' sneered Kavendish. 'You rescue the Princess from a place nobody can find, and that you say may no longer exist.'

'Governor,' said the King. 'In the time after my daughter was kidnapped, Raegan appeared to my council and stated he was taking her to the City of Lost Souls. All were present, as was Royal Knight Thorburn. Are you suggesting this is not the truth?'

'Well, Sire,' said Kavendish, choosing his words carefully, 'I'm suggesting it seems a rather unlikely story.'

'Governor,' said Lord Frederick. 'There are many things about the land that are unknown, that were lost when Nadensa was destroyed and the wizards apart from my brother and myself were killed.

'The Great War changed everything, and while we've been fortunate to have lived in a time of enduring peace since that time, we now have a rebel faction, led by a powerful wizard, seeking to rule the land, and some of what has been dormant for centuries or thought to have been destroyed altogether is being rediscovered; some of which are unpleasant.

'Until Raegan and his rebels are dealt with, we face a time of uncertainty, and we have to deal with whatever happens along the way.'

'I agree with you,' said Kavendish. 'We do face uncertain times. Which leads me to my next point of discussion.'

'I think we've heard quite enough from you,' said Finchley.

'Are you saying I don't have the right to be heard?' said Kavendish.

'Only if the King allows it,' said Finchley.

Both looked to the King.

Unruffled, the King nodded for Kavendish to continue.

'Thank you,' said Kavendish with a curt bow. 'As I was saying, we do indeed face uncertain times. Most recently, as I am sure you know, my region was subjected to attack by a giant kestrel; the likes of which has never been seen. For weeks, the entire region was unsafe. People and livestock were killed.'

'And thanks to the knight who stands before you,' said Beasley, motioning to Dane, 'the kestrel is no more.'

'Yes,' said Kavendish, with a condescending smile. 'Once again, our gallant Royal Knight came to the rescue.'

Dane's mouth dropped.

'What are you trying to say?' said Finchley, asking the very question on Dane's mind.

'It seems that wherever there's trouble, Dane Thorburn arrives to save the day – just as his father did,' said Kavendish, the tone of his voice dripping with mock awe. 'First, he rescues the Princess from a city none of us have heard of, that even now, may not exist; then it's a dragon that supposedly attacked this very castle, and finally, the kestrel that terrorised my region.'

Dane couldn't believe what he was hearing.

I killed the kestrel and he's unhappy?

'In every instance, when it seems no one else is capable,' said Kavendish, pointing to Dane as he spoke, 'you miraculously appear and save the day.'

The rest of the chamber looked at Kavendish, stunned.

'Would you prefer he didn't?' asked Lord Frederick. 'I didn't see the kestrel, but from what we were told, it caused a great deal of destruction; yet you appear displeased it's been killed.'

'Quite the contrary,' said Kavendish. 'I and my fellow governors are relieved it's no longer a menace to our people.'

Cooper, Moore and Beasley nodded hesitantly, agreeing with the comment, but not wanting to be part of everything else Kavendish was saying.

'What I want to know,' said Kavendish, looking directly at Dane, 'is how you were able to kill it when no one else could; with exactly the same weapon, and how you were able to kill the dragon, when our esteemed Lord Frederick, with all his power, and the mighty Scarafuse, could not.'

Keeping his voice steady and his eyes on Kavendish, much less he raise suspicion, Dane responded.

'Royal Knight Hevenshire and I were much closer to the kestrel than the other knights and shot it under its throat. Lord Frederick and I attacked the dragon together. Lord Frederick struck from above and I attacked its throat. The dragon's top-jaw is stronger than the outer skin of its throat, which is why my sword cut through and killed it.'

Quickly scanning the room, he saw everyone nodding in agreement, some with admiration, at what they'd heard.

Only Kavendish remained unconvinced.

'A most commendable tale,' he said, his voice dripping with contempt.

'What do you mean?' asked Dane. 'Everything I've told you is the truth.'

'He's right,' said Beasley. 'I saw them kill the kestrel. They hid under a bench, right on top of the bait we planted. No one else thought to do that, and I doubt whether many would have had the courage.'

Kavendish gave the chamber a contemptuous nod.

'Yes, yes,' he said softly. 'Indeed, it was both ingenious and brave. But you haven't told us the entire story. Have you?'

'I don't know what you're saying,' said Dane.

'Oh, I'm afraid you do,' said Kavendish.

'Governor,' said Lord Frederick. 'Should you have something to say, please, share it with us all.'

Kavendish nodded, a look of triumph on his face.

'Very well,' he said, his eyes gleaming with pleasure. 'Royal Knight Thorburn, please tell the convention what it was that really enabled you to kill the dragon and the kestrel.'

Dane's mind raced.

He knows!

'I've already told you,' he said.

'And as convincing as that was,' said Kavendish, 'it's time to hear the truth.'

'Governor,' said Lord Frederick.

'As commendable as Royal Knight Thorburn's skills with a sword and an arrow are,' said Kavendish, his voice rising, 'the reason he was able to kill the creatures is because his weapons had traces of the Princess's blood on them!'

The room was silent for a moment, stunned at what they'd heard.

Dane, Lord Frederick, the King and council didn't move a muscle, their faces icy calm despite hearing what only they knew being shared by someone who had no business knowing.

The rest of the chamber shared wide eyes and gaping mouths; confused and bewildered at what they'd heard.

Kavendish lorded over them all, a look of devilish glee on his face.

Roars of protest drowned out the room.

'That's outrageous!' said Finchley.

'Absurd!' said Wilkens.

'Preposterous!' said Ingles.

'Impossible!' said Beasley.

'*No!*' Kavendish boomed over all the other voices. '*Very possible indeed!*'

More shouts of protest filled the chamber.

'*Enough!*' said the King.

The room fell silent.

Looking directly at Kavendish, the King responded.

'It's an interesting claim you make,' he said calmly. 'Indeed, when the dragon attacked the castle, my daughter was wounded and bleeding. In seeing her to safety, Royal Knight Thorburn may have had some of her blood smeared on him. He may have also been injured himself.'

Dane nodded.

'As to what her blood had to do with killing the dragon?' said the King. 'I say nothing at all.'

'It had everything to do with it!' said Kavendish.

'Outrageous!' said Finchley.

Raising his hand, the King quieted others who were about to offer their support.

'Governor Kavendish,' he said. 'What you saying is nonsensical. How can the presence of blood, whether it be from my daughter or anyone else, have anything to do with killing the dragon?'

'The presence of the Princess's blood has everything to do with being able to kill the dragon,' said Kavendish, *'because Lord Frederick used her blood to create it!'*

Stunned silence filled the chamber.

For a moment, everyone seemed frozen to the spot, unable to move as they took in what Kavendish had just said. He'd shocked them already, but this latest outburst seemed to have floored them completely.

Lord Frederick spoke first.

'Governor,' he said. 'No wizard has the capability to create another creature. Some were known to be able to transform into other creatures, but being able to create one is simply not possible.'

'Hear, hear!' said several voices at once.

'What about Edan?' said Kavendish.

Mouths stopped half open.

'Yes!' said Kavendish, the toad-face triumphant. 'Edan created the Fire-Walkers!'

'And Vrenin killed him!' said Finchley.

'Be that as it may,' Lord Frederick said to Kavendish. 'You're suggesting I created a dragon that attacked this castle. *This castle?* Why would I do such a thing?'

'A diversion!' said Kavendish. 'You created the dragon, the kestrel, and no doubt the other creatures, so you could come to the rescue and show you're stronger than Raegan – to ensure everyone remains loyal to you and the King!'

Dane stood stunned at all he'd heard.

He thinks Lord Frederick created these creatures?

'Governor, that is an outrageous and unfounded claim,' said the King. 'Were it to be true, such action on Lord Frederick's part would amount to treason.'

Others in the chamber nodded, aghast at the absurdity of Kavendish's claim.

'Besides,' said the King, 'why would there be any reason for Lord Frederick to do such a thing? All present have been loyal to Brindabeare since the end of the Great War.'

'*Hear, hear!*' shouted many in the chamber.

'You forget the Stanthorpe Region has not always been an ally of Brindabeare,' said Kavendish.

'I do not,' said the King. 'I am well aware of the times before the Great War when Stanthorpe was aligned with Candahorn. Are you saying you wish to change your allegiance?'

'*No!*' yelled Beasley.

'*Never!*' screamed Cooper.

'*Not me!*' yelled Moore.

Kavendish glanced around the chamber, struggling to keep himself under control.

'I am not suggesting anything of the kind,' he replied. *'Yet.'*

Incredulous looks greeted the response.

'You have thought of not signing the Charter?' asked the King, seemingly untroubled at the prospect.

'Well, I –'

'If you have, it seems your fellow governors don't share your position,' said the King.

Beasley, Moore and Cooper nodded dutifully, looking at Kavendish as though they'd never laid eyes on him before.

'I pledge my loyalty to you, Sire,' said Beasley.

'As do I,' said Cooper.

'And I,' said Moore.

'What say you?' said the King, his eyes locked on Kavendish.

'Until I get satisfaction,' said Kavendish, standing to his full height and puffing out his chest, 'I will not be signing anything.'

'You have accused Lord Frederick of creating the dragon,' said the King.

'And the kestrel, and the creatures currently in the Candahorn Region,' said Kavendish.

'And your evidence?' said the King. 'My daughter's blood on the sword used by Royal Knight Thorburn when he killed the dragon.'

'And on the arrows he used to kill the kestrel.'

'For now, let's concentrate on the dragon,' said the King. 'What evidence do you have that my daughter's blood killed the dragon?'

'I have said that already,' said Kavendish, pointing to Dane as he continued. 'He killed it when Lord Frederick couldn't. His sword had the Princess's blood on it and Scarafuse did not.'

'You're saying Lord Frederick created the dragon but was unable to kill it?' said the King.

Kavendish hesitated, suddenly unsure of himself.

'Well, I –'

Dane saw Kavendish's face shifting from confusion to anger and back again as he pondered the question.

'It's simply not possible,' said the King.

Kavendish's expression became more and more uncertain.

'Governor?' said the King.

'Well ... but,' stammered Kavendish.

Dane now saw embarrassment mixing with the other expressions on Kavendish's face.

'Governor,' said the King. 'Do you see what you're suggesting?'

'Well ... but, I still think ... the kestrel – well, if they weren't created by Lord Frederick, then they were created when the Princess escaped from the City of Lost Souls.'

'That may be true,' said the King. 'And if it were the case, are you suggesting we should not have rescued my daughter?'

'Well, no,' said Kavendish, stumbling over his words. 'Only, that, perhaps we should have known it would happen. And taken steps to prevent it. To kill them sooner.'

'Hindsight is a wonderful thing,' said the King. 'And were it known these creatures would emerge as a result of my daughter escaping, I'm sure we would have been better prepared to deal with them. But at the moment, that theory is unproven, and we may never know if it's right or wrong.'

The King raised a calming hand as Kavendish was about to protest.

'Unlike your claim about Lord Frederick, it is a possibility we have considered.'

'And what has been done about it?' asked Kavendish, trying to recover his poise.

'As you know, the dragon and kestrel have been killed,' said the King. 'The other creatures remain at large, and from last reports, are somewhere in the Candahorn Region. A parley with Governor Mortensen failed to resolve what may have been a joint effort to kill them.'

'So, what is to be done?'

'We are still deliberating. Once we agree on a course of action, we will share it with everyone here.'

There was a series of nods of agreement throughout the chamber.

'Was Governor Mortensen asked about Raegan?' said Kavendish.

'He was,' said the King. 'And if you choose to believe what he told us, he said Raegan has nothing to do with how these creatures came to exist and cannot kill them. For the same reason Lord Frederick would not create a dragon and have it attack my castle, Mortensen said Raegan would not create a creature and have it attack his own region.'

'Is it true Raegan is missing?' asked Kavendish.

'We don't have an answer for that at this time,' said the King. 'All we can say is he hasn't been seen since he left my daughter in the City of Lost Souls.'

Kavendish nodded thoughtfully.

'Have you seen him?' he asked Dane.

'No,' Dane replied without hesitation.

'Are you sure about that?' said Kavendish.

'Of course,' said Dane.

'You didn't see him while you were in the City of Lost Souls?'

'I didn't,' said Dane.

'I think you're being very modest,' said Kavendish. 'I hear there's a possibility you killed him.'

With the shock of hearing what Kavendish had said combining with his own feelings about whether he'd killed Raegan or not, it took all Dane's self-control not to react. Apart from a single bead of sweat running down his neck, there was no hint about how he was feeling.

'Let me ask you again,' said Kavendish, his eyes bulging at Dane as he spoke. 'Did you see Raegan in the City of Lost Souls?'

'No,' said Dane.

'Not even when he was a Gargaun wolf?' asked Kavendish, his face bursting with satisfaction.

His heart skipping a beat, Dane kept his voice steady.

'I don't know what you're referring to,' he said.

'Yes, you do!' screamed Kavendish. 'You know exactly what I'm talking about!'

'I did not see Raegan in the City of Lost Souls,' said Dane.

'But you saw a Gargaun wolf you *thought* was Raegan! Didn't you?'

Dane hesitated.

How does he know?

'I had to get past a group of wolves when we were escaping. I injured a couple of them. But I didn't see Raegan.'

'But did you not say, after you escaped, that one of the wolves looked like a man?' said Kavendish.

The chamber drew a collective breath.

'Lord Frederick has told us wizards can transform into creatures,' said Kavendish. 'Creatures like a wolf. So, I ask again, did you see Raegan in the City of Lost Souls? Did you perhaps even kill him?'

'If Royal Knight Thorburn had killed Raegan, don't you think word of that would have been shouted across the land by now?' said Lord Frederick, saving Dane from an immediate response.

'It explains why Raegan has been unseen for such a long time,' said Kavendish. 'Your gallant knight has at worst injured him; at best killed him. And you have withheld this information from the convention!'

Some of the governors gasped in horror.

'Governor,' said the King. 'You need to be very careful about what you're saying. To accuse me of withholding information is a very serious matter. You should not make such a claim unless you are prepared to support it. Such a claim, if unfounded, would also amount to treason.'

Kavendish hesitated.

'However, I'm prepared to give you the benefit of the doubt,' said the King. 'We don't deal in speculation and rumour. I don't know where you claim to have heard this information, or who you heard it from.

'The land abounds with unfounded reports on many things. What you have said is merely one of them. Regardless of what you claim Royal Knight Thorburn saw in the City of Lost Souls, he has not reported it in an official capacity. Perhaps the information you heard has been embellished from the reports about my daughter's rescue.'

Dane let out a deep breath, relieved and at the same time admiring the way the King and Lord Frederick handled themselves.

He saw Kavendish shifting nervously on the spot, wearing a look of angry defiance despite all the King had said.

'It could be true,' said Kavendish. 'And you wish to keep it from us to keep us living in fear.'

'You keep coming back to ruling by fear,' said Lord Frederick. 'Why would we seek to do that when there is no need for it?'

'To ensure everyone signs the Charter,' said Kavendish.

'And I ask again,' said the King. 'Are you considering not doing so? We've heard your fellow governors intend to sign, which would make you the only settlement in your region that is not loyal to us. If that were the case, we would have to put measures in place to protect the others.'

'Are you threatening me?' asked Kavendish.

'Not at all,' said the King. 'I'm merely stating that, as in any other instance where I am made aware of a threat to the safety of cities, provinces and settlements under my protection, I would take the required action to ensure their continued safety.

'Your city is considerably larger than the provinces and settlements in your region. Were you to cause unrest or try to enlist others by force, I would have an obligation to respond in kind.'

Beasley, Cooper and Moore gave appreciative nods in response.

'Are you suggesting I'm not capable of governing my region?'

'Governor, please,' said the King. 'Must we continue to have to cover this matter?'

Dane wondered what the King was talking about.

'Each year, you claim to rule all provinces and settlements in what is known as the Stanthorpe Region. Your city, the provinces and settlements around you are known as the Stanthorpe Region because you are the largest settlement in the area. Indeed, you are the only city, and by association, you have the largest army of knights, which also means - the incident with the kestrel notwithstanding – the greatest capability to ensure not only your own safety, but the safety of all in the region.'

Dane saw Kavendish's face turning a dark shade of red as the King continued.

'Let me remind you again,' said the King. 'In the same manner as Governor Finchley's position in Wandabyne, and, despite his alliance with Raegan, Governor Mortensen's position in Candahorn – you have no ruling authority over any province or settlement.'

The King raised his hand as Kavendish, his face now a beetroot-red, made as though he was about to interrupt.

'And despite your continued claims to the contrary,' said the King, 'you have no claim on Lordale, as it is part of the Wandabyne Region.'

Both Finchley and Governor Chipperfield gave approving nods on hearing this.

'Very well,' Kavendish conceded with a deep exhaling breath, his face twitching as he sought to control himself. 'I see there is nothing to gain from continuing this line of discussion.'

'Have we addressed your concerns?' asked the King. 'Is there anything else you wish to discuss before you commit to the Charter?'

'The Princess,' said Kavendish. 'She is unwell?'

The slightly condescending tone of voice had Dane immediately on guard.

'She is,' said the King.

'What exactly ails her?' asked Kavendish.

'At this time, we're not exactly sure,' said the King. 'Although Lord Frederick's latest remedy appears to be helping.'

'Strange,' said Kavendish, scratching his chin as though concentrating on something. 'Very strange.'

'Indeed,' said the King. 'It's been a mystery and source of frustration to all concerned, including the Princess herself. It's unlike her to be ill for any period of time, let alone something like this, which has afflicted her for months, for no apparent reason at all.'

'It's as though something in the Elements of Nature themselves is having an effect on her,' said Kavendish, the swagger and contemptuous tone in his voice again.

Dane glanced at Lord Frederick, who, although not showing it, must have been thinking the same thing.

How does he know everything we've been talking about as well as we do?

'At this time, we don't know what the reason is,' said the King, calmly glossing over Kavendish's heightened knowledge of the matter. 'We can only hope this latest elixir works and everything can get back to normal.'

'Indeed,' said Kavendish. 'But before I pledge to sign the Charter, I would like to see her.'

'I'm afraid that's out of the question,' said the King. 'As we told you at the commencement of the convention, she is too ill to attend.'

'If you wish me to sign the Charter, then I insist,' said Kavendish.

'Why?' said Dane. 'Why does it matter to you whether she's here or not? If she's unwell, she's unwell.'

'You would do well to mind your place,' said Kavendish with a condescending sneer. 'I do not answer to common knights. Especially those who threaten me, as you did only a short time ago.'

'What –'

'Then you can answer Royal Knight Thorburn's question directly to me,' said the King.

Kavendish made a sweeping gesture with his hand as he replied, as though he was speaking for all present.

'I, as I am sure all here, would like to see our future Queen. To lay our eyes on her beauty, even if, due to her illness, it may not be shining as brightly as we have come to know.'

Dane swallowed the feeling of bile building in his throat as he looked at Kavendish, standing straight and tall, his arm stretched to his right, the look of smug arrogance on his face, his lip curled in a malicious smile, as though he was daring anyone to question or contradict him.

How can he hold the entire convention to ransom?

Question after question – statement after statement?

'Governor,' the King said strongly, shifting in his seat, his face hardening as he showed signs of increasing frustration. 'We have given more than enough time to your concerns. The Princess is ill and will not be attending the convention in any capacity.'

'I am not asking for her to attend in any formal capacity,' said Kavendish. 'Only that you allow us to lay our eyes on her. Surely you will not deny us that?'

With a short nod to Lord Frederick, the King beckoned Salsbury to him and whispered in his ear. With a bow, Salsbury left the chamber.

'Very well,' said the King. 'The Princess will join us briefly to greet you all.'

Kavendish resumed his seat, his stature and arrogance restored.

The image of a bloated toad who'd just swallowed a bug drifted into Dane's mind as he turned away from Kavendish, casting his eyes at Lord Frederick.

With the slightest hint of recognition between them, Dane knew Lord Frederick shared his concerns about what Kavendish knew.

'If I may, Sire,' said Governor Werrington, gesturing towards his counterpart from Grelfan. 'Governor Levensworth and I would like to know when you plan to send assistance to our provinces?'

'We are discussing this within council,' said the King. 'At this time, I suggest it will be as soon as the convention concludes.'

Both governors nodded thoughtfully.

'I've been fortunate until now,' said Levensworth, his soft voice making him hard to see and hear from the end of the chamber. 'We have yet to be attacked by either creature. When I heard they were attacking at random, I was quite concerned, and I remain nervous about the possibility.'

'As do I,' said Werrington. 'I have knights on patrol at all hours. But if one were to attack, from all reports, we would be powerless to do anything to stop it.'

'We will do whatever we can to assist you,' said the King. 'We wish to be rid of these creatures as much as you.'

'Thank you, Sire,' said Werrington.

The King gave an acknowledging nod to both.

With a temporary lull in proceedings, a few of the governors chatted amongst themselves, others spoke to their entourages, some talking about the feast to take place in the main hall in the evening.

Dane was pleased to hear snippets of conversation that were critical of Kavendish, who seemed to sit contentedly, that same condescending smile on his face.

Feeling a hand on his shoulder, Dane turned to see Governor Finchley, his dark auburn hair matching the gules-maroon colour of the tunic he wore under his armour, standing before him.

'I commend you on all you have done,' he said, shaking Dane's hand warmly.

'Thank you, Governor,' said Dane.

'I hope you will find your way to Wandabyne in the future,' said Finchley.

'I hope so, too,' said Dane.

With a parting nod, Finchley made his way back to his delegation.

With a knock, a side door opened, and Salsbury entered, with Vanessa walking slowly behind him, flanked by Marilena and Lady Madeline, with Genevieve behind them. Carrying herself with all the grace she could muster, Vanessa took her place beside the King.

The ladies stood anxiously to the side, Marilena looking at Dane in a way that suggested she felt he was responsible for Vanessa being there.

'Princess,' said Kavendish, standing and gesturing to all as he spoke, 'it is indeed an honour and pleasure to see you. We can see you are not well and thank you for taking time from your recovery to meet with us.'

'Thank you,' Vanessa replied.

Dane could feel his anger rising.

If he says one word that upsets her ...

'We were most relieved to hear you were saved from the City of Lost Souls,' said Kavendish in a tone of voice that suggested to Dane he meant nothing of the sort.

Vanessa gave Kavendish a gentle nod.

'It distresses me that I can't take a more formal part in the convention,' she said, with a fleeting glance at the King and Lord Frederick. 'But I will be informed of all that transpires and thank you for your attendance.'

The chamber erupted in enthusiastic applause.

'Bravo!' said some.

As Dane watched Kavendish, he saw the clapping of a man looking as though he was forced to do so under threat of stabbing if he did otherwise.

As the applause died down, Vanessa stood, ready to take her leave.

She'd almost reached her escort when Dane saw her stagger ...

In an instant he was rushing forward ...

Like a stone, she dropped to the floor ...

The ladies screamed ...

Lord Frederick and the King rushed to her side as Dane reached her.

'Space,' said Lord Frederick.

Dane, the King and the ladies retreated.

Lord Frederick lifted Vanessa off the floor, and with a flash of light and a *BANG!* they were gone. The ladies rushed out, Marilena giving Dane a despairing glance as she left the chamber.

'I guess she really is ill,' said a voice behind Dane.

Whirling around, he saw the toadlike face of Kavendish staring at him.

Grabbing him by the collar under his chest plate and leaning in close, Dane spoke so only the two could hear.

'Get away from here, *right now*, or I'll kill you where you stand.'

Chapter 16
CONSEQUENCES

The rumour spread like wildfire.

'Raegan's dead!'

'Dead?'

'Yes! Dane Thorburn killed him when he saved the Princess!'

'How?'

'Raegan turned into a wolf, and he killed him!'

'How do you know?'

'The convention! He told everyone at the Leader's Convention!'

'Why didn't we know this before?'

'They weren't sure at first, but now they know! He's dead! He's dead! Thank the Gods, he's dead!'

Dane felt every eye in the city on him.

In the hallways.

In the stables.

In the armoury.

Indoors and outdoors.

Knights, servants, maids.

Men, women and children.

If he didn't know better, he would have said even the eagles and ravens were watching him.

Making his way towards the dining hall, he saw people gawking and pointing at him as he walked past. Others slunk away in awe, as though they were scared he'd look at them.

'This is getting out of hand,' he said to Will. 'The dragon was bad enough, but this is madness.'

As he took his meal, others at the serving tables stood aside, clearing a path for the one who'd saved them from the evil wizard and restored peace to all, closing ranks again as he and Will walked away.

'Let's find somewhere quiet,' he said, eyeing an empty bench.

Nodding at a group of knights as he sat down, he saw them hesitate for a moment, before resuming their meal.

'This is wrong,' said Dane. 'Everyone thinks he's dead. They're acting as though there's nothing to fear – that it's finished.'

Will nodded.

'Have the King and Lord Frederick said anything?'

'I don't know,' said Dane. 'I haven't spoken with either of them since I left the convention.'

'Until it's over, they may not know how far it's spread,' said Will. 'Or maybe they think it will die down in a couple of days.'

'Does it look to you as though it's going to die down in a couple of days?' said Dane, scanning the hall again.

The volume of talk had quieted since they'd arrived, everyone speaking in hushed tones, as though they were afraid he might take offence at their conversation.

'Give it time,' said Will. 'The truth will be known soon enough.'

'And when it is, they're going to think I'm a liar.'

'You haven't said anything,' said Will. 'You can't be responsible for rumour.'

'That's not how those like Fenwick will see it,' said Dane, eyeing him a couple of tables away with Winslow and Harrop, a look of deep loathing on his face as their eyes met for a moment.

Harvey and Donovan joined them.

'So, how does it feel to have killed a wizard?' Harvey boomed, a huge smile on his face as he slapped Dane on the shoulder and sat down.

Dane heard the entire hall go quiet.

Mouths were half-open, goblets half-raised, some stood frozen in mid-stride; everyone hanging in suspense as they waited for the answer to the question they'd all wanted to ask.

Turning back towards his friends, he leaned towards Will, Donovan and Harvey, bringing them in close, so only they would hear what he had to say.

'Don't ask me that again,' he hissed.

About to interrupt, Harvey hesitated when Will grabbed his arm.

'What?'

'I don't *know* if I killed Reagan,' said Dane.

'What do you –'

'Be *quiet!*' said Will.

Dane nodded.

'Look,' he said. 'I badly wounded a wolf in the ranges. And to me, it looked as though it staggered like a man.'

Harvey and Donovan's eyes widened.

'But I *don't* know if I killed it,' said Dane. 'And I *don't* know if it was Raegan.'

Harvey and Donovan looked at Dane, then Will, who nodded slowly.

'Then why is everyone saying it?' asked Harvey. 'You told them at the convention.'

'I didn't,' said Dane. 'It was Governor Kavendish from Stanthorpe.'

'How would he know?' said Donovan.

'We don't know,' said Dane. 'I've only told council what happened, and that's always in the strictest of confidence.'

'That means –' said Harvey.

'There's a traitor among them,' said Dane, finishing the sentence.

'So, we don't know if Raegan is dead?' said Donovan.

'No,' said Dane.

'You didn't think to kill it?' said Donovan. 'The wolf?'

'All I was thinking about was the Princess,' said Dane, a knot of frustration and anger twisting in his stomach. 'Once it went away, it was no threat. All I wanted to do was escape. I didn't realise what I'd seen until Lord Frederick told us wizards could transform into other creatures. Even now, I can't say for sure what I saw.'

'What are you going to do?' asked Donovan.

'I don't know,' said Dane, with a glance at all the eyes in the room looking on. 'But it can't go on like this.'

'I don't think you should do anything,' said Will.

'If he's not dead, people are going to blame you,' said Harvey, suddenly relieved he wasn't sitting in Dane's shoes.

'For what?' said Dane.

'For not killing him when you had the chance.'

'Exactly,' said Dane through gritted teeth. 'That's why we – I – can't let it get out of hand.'

'No one will be able to fault what you did,' said Donovan. 'And General Silvers and Commander Hindmarsh will set the army straight.'

'It may turn out to be a good thing,' said Will. 'He could be dead, or at least badly injured. If you didn't kill him, you may have weakened him – which would explain why there's been no Black Knights except the four we killed when we returned.'

A couple of knights shuffled past, making their way to a bench behind them.

'S-sorry,' said one.

'Y-your pardon,' said the other.

Seeing the nervous embarrassment on their faces, and every head in the room looking at him once more, Dane snapped, slamming his goblet on the bench and jumping to his feet.

'*Enough!*' he yelled. 'All of you!'

Everyone in the hall stared at him in stunned silence.

'You all think Raegan's dead?' he said, walking towards the middle of the hall. '*Do you?*'

Nobody moved.

'Well, *he's not!*' Dane yelled, glaring defiantly to his left and right.

Mouths dropped open around him.

'The truth is, *we don't know!* Make of that what you will; believe what you choose to believe – I really don't care!'

Breathing heavily, his face hot with anger, he turned to his left, barging past a couple of frozen, open-mouthed knights, and stormed out of the hall.

'*You lied to us!*' said Norton, thumping a fist on the table.

Maynard, Farrington, and Simeon Everidge, the new governor of Hezabar, watched anxiously.

'*He's dead!*' said Norton. '*Dead!* Where does that leave us now?'

Mortensen looked at the others, his face icy calm.

'Let me assure you,' he said slowly, 'any talk of Lord Raegan's death is nothing more than rumour and gossip.'

'You've seen him?' said Norton. 'Tell us you've seen him, and perhaps we'll believe you.'

'You dare to question me?' said Mortensen.

'I'm asking for the truth,' said Norton. 'Have you, or have you not seen Lord Raegan since the girl was rescued from the City of Lost Souls?'

'You forget your place,' said Mortensen. 'You are part of this alliance by my doing. I can just as easily undo it.'

'You threaten me?' said Norton.

The others shifted nervously in their seats.

With a glance to Everidge, who, although slightly shorter, was equally as imposing as his predecessor, Norton said, 'are you going to kill me as you killed Hazelwood? You can only do that so many times before you lose the support of the others. And where will that leave your alliance?'

Everidge looked at Mortensen nervously.

'You wish to go crawling back to Brindabeare?' said Mortensen. 'How do you think they will respond?'

Norton said nothing.

'Allow me to enlighten you as to exactly what would happen, as Meriwether told me at our parley. While he would welcome Mundool back under his control as the ruler of the land, he would demand your surrender and likely hanging for treason and install a new governor in your place.'

Norton shifted in his seat.

'Is that what you want?' asked Mortensen.

'Well, I –'

'Governor,' said Maynard, interrupting. 'You can be assured the loyalty of Pardosta to our cause remains steadfast. However, it has been some time since we have heard from Lord Raegan, and I wish to understand what it is he wants us to do.

'These rumours will have an effect, no matter how small, until something happens to change their minds. The simplest way to do that would be for Lord Raegan to appear, whether to you or any number of us. In doing so, the reports of his death will be seen for what they are – nothing more than malicious lies.'

'Gentlemen,' said Mortensen, looking at each in turn. 'We do not question Lord Raegan's motives. We wait for his orders and respond when they are given.'

'So, you haven't seen him?' asked Farrington.

Mortensen took a deep breath, then slowly shook his head.

'I have not,' he said.

Norton and Maynard gasped.

'*You lied to us!*' said Norton. '*All this time!*'

'No,' said Mortensen.

'You told us you'd seen –'

'I told you no such thing,' said Mortensen, standing and looking directly at Norton. 'At no time have I said I have seen Lord Raegan. What I have said is we wait until we hear from him, and then we will act on his command.'

'What if he *is* dead?' said Norton.

'There has been no proclamation from Meriwether or Lord Frederick,' said Mortensen. 'That alone gives me comfort they don't know any more of Lord Raegan's whereabouts than we do.'

'But –'

'Don't you think, if they knew of Lord Raegan's death, they would have announced it by now? Why would they wait for it to be raised by an outsider at their convention?'

The governors nodded thoughtfully.

'However unlikely, it could be true,' said Norton. 'Did you know he could turn into a wolf?'

'Not specifically,' said Mortensen. 'I knew he entered the City of Lost Souls in a manner that ensured he wasn't affected by all he told me of it; so, it stands to reason he did it by turning into a wolf.'

'Then it's possible,' Norton breathed. 'He may have been killed when he was in his wolf's form.'

'I wouldn't be so sure about that,' said Mortensen.

'How so?' asked Maynard.

'You are forgetting one thing,' said Mortensen.

No one replied for a moment.

'What?' said Norton eventually.

'The only way a wizard can be killed is from the sword of another wizard.'

The mouths of the others dropped, their eyes widening in wonderful, stunned surprise and relief as they realised the truth of what they'd heard.

Leaning forward, Norton thumped the table gently in relief, a wide grin spreading across his face.

'Of course,' he said. '*Of course!*'

Maynard, Farrington and Everidge smiled.

Mortensen breathed a sigh of relief.

'I apologise for doubting you,' said Norton.

Mortensen offered a forgiving nod.

'All the same,' said Maynard, 'if Lord Raegan would just show himself, even for the shortest moment, it would set our minds at rest.'

'That is Lord Raegan's decision,' said Mortensen.

Maynard nodded dutifully.

'I'm sure we can quell this rumour within our own region,' said Mortensen. 'As for the rest of the land, if they choose to believe it, it may actually work in our favour.'

'Agreed,' said Norton, all mutinous thought forgotten.

'And there was another revelation from the esteemed Governor Kavendish that will also work in our favour,' said Mortensen.

The others looked at him with puzzled faces.

'What do you mean?' asked Everidge.

'The creatures,' said Mortensen. 'It appears Brindabeare has a more vested interest in getting rid of them than we thought.'

'Really?' said Farrington. 'How so?'

'Governor Kavendish told the convention Dane Thorburn killed the dragon and kestrel because his weapons had the girl's blood on them. He said there's a connection between her and these creatures.'

'Yes,' said Farrington, the memory rekindling in his mind. 'The message said Lord Frederick created them, or they were created in response to her escape from the City of Lost Souls.'

'Indeed,' said Mortensen. 'But how they were created is not the point. From piecing together the messages I've received, they believe the creatures and the girl are connected in some way, through the Elements of Nature, and they're draining her of her energy and strength as they evolve. It's the reason they think she's ill – their existence is slowly killing her.'

'Which is why the dragon attacked their castle,' said Everidge in stunned disbelief.

'Exactly,' said Mortensen. 'Which is why –'

'They have to kill them,' said Maynard maliciously. 'To save her life, they have to kill them.'

'I'd never have thought I'd have reason to be grateful for these creatures,' said Norton, 'but if she dies ...'

'Indeed,' said Mortensen.

'It means they'll be desperate to kill them,' said Farrington.

'Yes, it does,' said Mortensen.

All the governors were smiling now.

'Should we try and trap one?' asked Norton hopefully.

'No,' said Mortensen.

'Why –'

'Given the destruction they've caused so far, an attempt to trap them would be futile,' said Mortensen.

Norton nodded ruefully.

'But all is not lost,' said Mortensen. 'It can still work to our advantage.'

'Agreed,' said Norton, his eyes wide with glee. 'We hold Brindabeare responsible for everything they've done. We demand they rid the land of them and kill them in the process.'

Mortensen nodded.

'Indeed, we do,' he said, a wide smile on his face. 'Indeed, we do.'

'How did he know?' asked Vanessa.

'I have no idea,' said Dane, shaking his head.

'But he knew everything?'

'All of it,' said Dane. 'Everything about Raegan, and everything we know about these creatures.'

'Who would have told him?'

'I don't know,' said Dane. 'They didn't ask him.'

'Yes,' said Vanessa. 'It would have given him credibility.'

'It's only been discussed in council,' said Dane. 'And I know Will wouldn't tell anyone -even Genevieve.'

'You're right,' said Vanessa. 'It has to be one of the councillors.'

'Yes,' said Dane. 'Who do you think it is? Medhurst or Lindstrom?'

'I don't want to believe it's either of them,' said Vanessa.

'If I were to guess, I'd say it's Medhurst,' said Dane.

'Why?'

'In the first instance, he's never liked me,' said Dane. 'From the earliest time I could remember, and even more in the last few years. He's found every reason he can to criticise and belittle me.

'When I was on trial for your kidnapping, he relished it. He was determined to find me guilty, and he was sure he would. Then, once I was cleared, he wouldn't look at me for weeks afterwards.'

'But while he may clash with you, does it mean he's disloyal?' asked Vanessa.

'Well, I think he's more likely than Lindstrom,' said Dane. 'I've never had a reason to doubt him.'

Vanessa nodded.

'It has to be one of them,' said Dane. 'Has your father said anything about what he intends to do to find out?'

'No,' said Vanessa. 'He wasn't telling me much before the convention, and since that episode, he hasn't seen me at all. It's just as I said – I'm a prisoner up here.'

'How do you feel?' asked Dane, taking her goblet and putting it on the table beside her bed.

'It's not too bad at the moment,' said Vanessa. 'Lord Frederick saw me this morning and took some more blood.'

'Is that wise?' said Dane. 'You don't ... you don't look well.'

'I don't feel any worse,' said Vanessa. 'Most of the time it's a dull headache. Not a splitting, thumping headache, like the scraping sound in the City of Lost Souls; but it's constant, and there are times it's overpowering, and I have to rest. Other times, like the convention, if I do too much, I get dizzy and pass out.'

'There really is a connection between you and the creatures,' said Dane. 'Isn't there?'

'It would appear so,' said Vanessa with a grimace. 'There's no other explanation. They grow stronger – and I grow weaker.'

'I can't believe it,' said Dane. 'You're the future Queen of the land. It doesn't make sense.'

'Sometimes nature and the elements work in ways we can't explain,' said Vanessa. 'For whatever reason, I'm deemed a threat to the balance of nature.'

'But it's the creatures who are causing all the damage,' said Dane. 'Surely that's not nature's intention.'

'You saw how the dragon attacked,' said Vanessa. 'It wanted to kill me. I think they all do. Everything the dragon did was because it wanted to kill me. You killed the kestrel before it could sense me, and while the serpent and sarkoe haven't found me, they're connected to me, and they're sapping my strength.'

'And now the whole land knows,' said Dane.

'There's nothing we can do about it,' said Vanessa.

Kneeling beside the bed, Dane took her hand in his.

'I wanted to kill Kavendish,' he said. 'Not just for what he knew; for the way he demanded you come to the convention.'

Vanessa smiled.

'Marilena wasn't pleased either.'

Dane nodded with a wry smile at the memory of how she'd looked at him.

He saw Vanessa stiffen for a moment, shifting uneasily.

'Are you all right?'

'Yes. Just a little sore.'

'Do you need me to get you anything? Do you need Mother's help?'

'No,' said Vanessa, shaking her head. 'I'm fine.'

'Let me,' said Dane, standing and leaning behind her, easing the pillows straighter so she could prop herself up.

'Thank you,' she said, settling herself.

'Perhaps I should go,' said Dane.

'No,' said Vanessa. 'Tell me more. Apart from a brief walk each day, I can't even leave the chamber. You're my only connection to anything that's happening outside this room.'

'I'm leaving soon,' said Dane softly, sensing the regret he saw on Vanessa's face as he spoke.

'How long will you be gone?'

'It's hard to say,' said Dane.

Neither spoke for a moment, lost in their own thoughts.

'Everyone thinks I killed Raegan,' said Dane, breaking the silence and trying to keep his voice steady.

Vanessa reached over, gently placing her hand on his arm.

'And I know what you're thinking,' she said.

Dane said nothing.

'You're thinking all those guilty thoughts,' she said, grasping his arm tighter.

Dane turned away, looking blankly around the chamber.

'Don't!' she said.

'I *should* have killed it!' said Dane, his voice rising, his face burning with anger.

'Dane,' said Vanessa.

Dane gave no response.

'Dane!' she said again.

Slowly, he turned towards her.

'If it weren't for you, I would have died there. Even if Raegan was there – even if he survived, we'll deal with it.'

'If he's alive, everyone will say I'm a liar,' said Dane.

'Father and Lord Frederick will set everyone straight,' said Vanessa. 'Once the convention is over. I'm sure they denied it in front of the governors.'

'They did,' Dane deadpanned in response.

'Then wait until it's over. Word will spread, and all will be restored.'

'It's not that simple,' said Dane, recalling the incident in the dining hall. 'Some will seek to use it against me. No matter what your father and Lord Frederick say, there will be some who say I lied.'

'And they aren't worthy of your concern,' said Vanessa, squeezing his arm. 'You know that.'

Dane sat, staring out the window, stewing in his thoughts.

'If he's alive, they'll blame me for everything he does. All the damage he creates, every life he takes. People like Fenwick will say it was my fault for not killing him in the City of Lost Souls, *and they'll be right!*'

'And anyone who thinks that is not worthy of your time,' said Vanessa. 'Of anyone's time.'

Dane said nothing for a moment, gathering his thoughts and staring out the window.

'The night he killed my father ...,' he said slowly, 'when he wanted to kill me ... I had nightmares – for years. I'd see his face – that twisted, evil smile when he looked at me.'

Vanessa watched him shiver for a moment as the scene replayed itself in his mind.

'Despite all that, I'd always dreamed about killing him – what it would feel like if I ever had the chance. And now, to think I was so close. If only –'

'No!' said Vanessa. 'There is no *"if only."* If everyone thought *"if only,"* we'd all be paralysed with guilt and regret. Nothing is achieved when you think like that. You only get down on yourself; riddle yourself with guilt, and little situations become much worse than they ever should or need to be.'

Dane said nothing for a few moments, before shrugging his shoulders and letting out a deep breath.

'You're a great knight, Dane Thorburn,' said Vanessa. 'Those who should know – my father, Lord Frederick, General Silvers, Commander Hindmarsh. Without fail, they all speak very highly of you, and with the exception of Hindmarsh, who was too young to know, they all say you remind them greatly of your father.'

Despite his anguish, Dane managed a smile; the words soothing him a little.

'We'll find these creatures,' he said, changing the subject. 'We'll find them and kill them.'

Vanessa nodded, squeezing his arm once more.

'I know you will.'

Chapter 17

ATTACK OF THE SERPENT

The afternoon breeze carried through the streets, cooling what had been an unseasonably hot day. People sheltering against the heat ventured outside once more, hoping to finish the day's work before the sun went down, relieved at the change in the weather.

With word the Leader's Convention had finished the night before, Rufus Mortimer felt at ease for the first time since the Governor had left, knowing he and the rest of the party would be back in a few days. A military man, he never liked being in charge of the daily tasks – having to listen to petty squabbles did nothing but give him a headache.

Wandering down the main street, he nodded to those he knew. Some nodded curtly in response, while others, despite his tall, imposing frame, long, scruffy hair and full-length beard, acted as though he was invisible.

Recognising one who'd snubbed him, he couldn't help but chuckle, reliving the dispute over a hen the day before – *a hen!* – both men equally adamant the other had stolen it.

Surely there were more important things ...

Movement to his left distracted him.

What?

It looked as though the roof of one of the buildings was moving – it wasn't ruffling in the breeze, it was *moving*, somewhere near the top.

In the next moment, the entire structure looked as plain and simple as always. Feeling a bead of sweat on his brow, he put the illusion down to the toll of a long day.

Clearing his mind with a quick shake of his head, he followed his line of sight to the right.

Now the wall was moving.

He saw it clearly this time – a definite bulge about half-way down.

'What in the name of –'

He never finished the sentence.

In the next moment, the shape on the wall leapt into the air, the dark brown changing colour as it blended with its surroundings, growing in size as it soared through the sky towards him, landing on the road about fifty feet away.

Uncoiling, the serpent rose to a height of about eight feet, locking its hind legs in place.

Struggling to understand what was happening, Mortimer beheld the swaying shape in front of him, barely visible as it blended perfectly with its surroundings. In the time it took for his eyes and mind to align with what he was seeing, his battle instincts took over, and he had his sword in his hand.

The serpent lashed out, its neck and face shooting forward to his left.

A spray of red splashed into his vision, raining like a fountain on the ground in front of him.

Screams rang out – man and beast, loud and crazed, the loudest right behind him.

Turning again, the serpent shot towards its next target, the force of the attack so strong it knocked the man off his feet, the strength of the bite and recoil tearing the limb completely from the body.

From Mortimer's vantage point, it looked as though the man fell backwards of his own accord.

Scanning the scene in front of him, he saw people screaming and running away.

'Off the road!' he yelled.

With a loud *crack!* a piece of the wall nearby fell away against the force of the body that slammed against it, driven into it by the power of the serpent's strike. The woman fell to the ground, and from Mortimer's point of view, she'd flown through the air and hit the wall of her own accord.

A horse screamed and Mortimer saw it fall to the ground, a large piece of flesh missing from its midsection.

The screams of the injured beast filled his ears as Mortimer saw a long, thin arrow shooting towards him; a face with fangs on the end, the image becoming larger as it came closer.

At the last moment, purely by reflex, he ducked, rolling to his left, avoiding what would have been a killing strike.

Now with its back to him, Mortimer sprang to his feet, running up behind the swaying shape, swinging his sword in a two-handed swipe with every ounce of strength.

The result was unlike anything he'd ever felt before.

His hands and arms from wrist to shoulder screamed in pain as his sword struck what seemed to be solid stone.

How was it possible? Although the serpent's body looked supple and soft, its skin was as strong as a sandstone wall.

With a split-second to react as the serpent lashed out towards him, Mortimer threw himself to the ground. Rolling to his right and springing to his feet in one motion, he threw himself over a fence railing, moments before a section right next to him exploded in fragments and splinters as the serpent's head smashed right through it.

'Inside!' he yelled, jumping to his feet once more. *'Everyone inside!'*

Unabated, the serpent struck again and again, breathing fire now – splintering fences, cratering walls, shooting through doors and windows, appearing to strike at anything and everything in its path.

Other knights were around him now, shocked at what they saw; and after seeing him strike at the air, only to hit what had to be some mysterious, invisible stone surface, their mouths open in terror.

'W-what d-do we do?' asked one.

Mortimer could only stare as the serpent, swivelling and twisting its body, uncoiled and launched itself, whip-like, towards him once more.

As its face arced through the air, its fangs the only visual cue he had, Mortimer had an instant to push his companion sideways, before the head of the serpent snapped towards the ground, spinning to its right in the last moment as it lurched at its prey.

He felt a burst of intense pain for a moment, before falling to the ground.

The fire in his leg was like nothing he'd felt before.

As hot as liquid steel, it shot up his leg, slowing in speed but continuing to spread through his body.

The serpent had only nicked him, and even though it wasn't a clean bite, it had pierced him as though he wore nothing but rags, some of the material hanging loosely where it had torn away, leaving naked, scorched skin behind.

He found his vision starting to blur and heard a dull noise in his ears.

Was someone trying to talk to him?

It was muffled and hard to understand; loud, then soft.

'... all right?'

Turning his head, he saw a face in front of him.

Who?

Adkins?

The voice floated into his mind again.

'Are you ... right?'

Blinking rapidly in an effort to clear his vision, he tried to stand up, the world swimming around him, as his body swung to the right, seemingly of its own accord.

He found himself on his back, staring into a blue sky.

The pain in his leg increased again, and he felt it more and more as it continued to work its way through his body.

Trying to speak, no words came out.

Rolling onto his side, everything tilted once more.

Pushing himself to a sitting position, he took a couple of deep breaths, reaching for the moving object in front of him.

With all his strength, he stood with the help of whoever was supporting him.

'... all right?' came the voice again.

Looking through foggy eyes, he saw the fangs of the serpent about twenty yards away, glinting in the afternoon sun for a moment, before flying through the air towards him.

Raising his hand towards it, he felt the poison in his body flare once more.

With an anguished scream, he wobbled for a moment, before the serpent's head appeared to freeze in mid-flight.

Leaning forward, taking his full weight on his feet, he lumbered a step, thrusting his hand towards the serpent as its head started retracting towards its body.

In his final moments, among the blurring images in front of him, he saw the serpent breathing fire, before launching itself into the sky.

In the same moment the serpent ceased its attack and fled, some distance away, another creature woke from a deep sleep.

Having feasted in Harlanwood the night before, it had had a relaxing swim and spent the day resting on the shore near the Astuvius Falls, digesting its meal.

Despite its full belly, as the scent drifted past on the breeze, its body tensed.

In an instant it was wide awake; its senses more alert than they had ever been before, and despite its indulgences from the previous day, it was ravenously hungry.

Dane and Will were walking their mounts from the stables to meet the King before departing. Hindmarsh and General Silvers were ahead of them, just out of earshot.

'Candahorn's demand arrived this morning?' asked Will.

'Yes,' Dane replied.

'So, they know about the possible connection between the Princess and the creatures?'

'Apparently,' said Dane. 'It appears our traitor has told them everything.'

'Who do you think it is?' asked Will.

'It has to be Medhurst or Lindstrom,' said Dane. 'Vanessa and I were talking about it last evening. Of the two, I would say it's Medhurst. I have plenty of reasons to doubt him and none to doubt Lindstrom.'

'Angus doesn't check the messages before they're sent?'

'No,' said Dane. 'Once they're sealed, they can only be opened by the person they're sent to. Otherwise, it could be seen as having been tampered with. A sealed message means it's genuine.'

'There must be something that can be done.'

'With the creatures causing the panic they have, together with the notes and reports about Raegan, there are a lot more messages than usual,' said Dane. 'Angus and the clerks have a hard time keeping track of them.'

Neither spoke for a moment.

'We could be walking into a trap,' said Will.

'We have no choice,' said Dane. 'Threat or no threat.'

'We have Lord Frederick,' said Will. 'That will help.'

'Only until we get the Feryndale and Grelfan delegations home,' said Dane. 'And if he hears Vanessa's getting worse, we'll be on our own.'

'Let's hope our traitor hasn't shared our plans,' said Will.

Dane cringed.

I hadn't thought of that.

The castle loomed before them, shrouded in late afternoon shadow, an unseasonably strong wind in the air.

As they approached, Dane saw the King and Vanessa standing on the rampart.

What's she doing here?

Did she convince the King to allow it?

In the next moment he had his answer, as the King turned towards her, and after a couple of strong words he wasn't able to hear, he saw Vanessa blanch for a moment, clearly upset, before shrinking into Marilena's arms and being led away.

The Advance Regiment were assembled and waiting for them.

Dane saw Donovan, Albert and Fenwick among them.

To his left he saw the Delgan, Grelfan and Feryndale delegations. With the convention over, they had agreed to travel with the regiment while making their way home.

Also part of the group were several accomplished archers, who, like Dane and Will, had arrows that had been fused with Vanessa's blood.

As everyone formed up below the rampart, Lord Frederick emerged on his mount.

As one, all faced the King.

'I want the serpent and sarkoe killed,' said the King.

The Brindabeare troops stood silently as Silvers removed a ribbon, cut it in two, placing one end inside his armour, tying the other to his sword and raising it towards the King.

Taking the ribbon from the General's sword, the King tied it to the hilt of his own, before raising his sword in the air.

'For the people of our city –' he boomed.

As one, raising their swords, the knights yelled in reply, 'In the name of the King!'

With a flick of his wrists, Dane turned Thunder away from the castle, heading towards the gates and the mission ahead.

'They approach?' asked Mortensen.

'They do,' said Thurman. 'Exactly as the message outlined. Scouts have been sent in advance and will meet with the regiment once they're in the region.'

'Ensure they're found before the regiment arrives,' said Mortensen.

'We have men on alert,' said Thurman. 'If any approach, they will be killed for reason of spying.'

Mortensen nodded.

'Have the creatures been sighted?'

'We have word of a recent attack by the serpent in Grelfan,' said Thurman. 'Of the sarkoe, there has been no sign.'

'I see,' said Mortensen. 'Very well. It appears we are prepared for whatever may come.'

'How will we deal with Lord Frederick?' asked Thurman.

'He will be more concerned with killing the creatures than worrying about us,' said Mortensen. 'There will be casualties on both sides – hopefully more on their side than ours.'

Thurman nodded, dismissing himself from the room.

Mortensen pondered the situation for a moment.

'Perhaps this is when Lord Raegan will reveal himself,' he said quietly, reaching instinctively for the ever-weakening pulse within.

Having farewelled the Delgan delegation after emerging from the Great Forest, the regiment started towards Grelfan.

Via the scuttlers, they'd been informed the serpent had attacked a couple of days earlier, the word putting everyone on alert.

Distraught with worry, Levensworth had been adamant his party travel on immediately, and it took some smooth talking from Lord Frederick and Silvers to convince him otherwise.

Lord Frederick had despatched himself to Grelfan, where he had spoken with several who witnessed the attack.

'There were casualties,' he'd told everyone upon his return. 'People, livestock, dwellings – there was damage everywhere.'

Everyone listened with concern as Lord Frederick continued.

'It's grown to eight feet when it stands, and it appeared to be attacking at random, and from what I heard, more aggressively than before, which is why there was more damage to buildings.'

Dane's mind wandered.

It's getting stronger and more vicious – and Vanessa's getting weaker and weaker.

To Levensworth, Lord Frederick said, 'Your Commander, Mortimer?'

Levensworth nodded.

'I'm sorry to say, he was among those killed.'

Dane saw the Grelfan delegation bow their heads.

Glancing to Werrington, he could see by the looks on their faces that the Governor and his delegation were contemplating a similar fate at Feryndale.

The day's ride had been uneventful, and scouts were sent ahead to find a suitable site for the evening camp.

Dane, Will and Donovan waited for the scouts to return.

'I don't know how we're going to kill these things,' said Donovan. 'And why Lord Frederick can't find them.'

'At the moment he's more concerned about getting the others to safety,' said Dane. 'Once we do that, I expect he will try and track them, but they're powerful creatures. They may be able to hide themselves.'

'Just what we need,' said Donovan morosely.

'He's a Masterlord,' said Will. 'He'll find them sooner or later.'

They heard Blaze's familiar squawk above them, the sound piercing the murmuring among the regiment.

Looking towards the horizon, they saw one of the scouts returning, hunched over his saddle, an arrow in his back.

In the next moment, topping a rise about a hundred yards ahead, a horde of enemy knights emerged, unleashing a volley of flaming arrows at them.

In an instant, the regiment charged as one.

As the two forces converged, Lord Frederick sent a ball of flame into the air. Moments later it slammed into the earth, blasting a large hole in the ground between the two groups.

Anticipating this, the regiment split down the middle, easily avoiding the crater in front of them.

Some of their adversaries were not so lucky, either thrown into the air by the force of the blast or falling helplessly into the hole.

Dane rode hard and true, charging straight into the enemy. Through the dullness of the fading light, he saw the dark vert-sleeved colours of Pardosta.

Striking hard, he cut down his first two adversaries without resistance, before Thunder's momentum was slowed and eventually stopped by the weight of the force attacking them.

Swinging again, he cut across and through his next opponent, wheeling Thunder around and working his way into a gap to his left.

Around him, Will and Donovan were following similar paths with their opponents.

Striking again, his arm jarring for a moment as his opponent parried the blow, Dane reversed his hand, turning his body in the same motion and slashing in the other direction. Cutting through his opponent's armour, he swung a final time, seeking out his next victim and urging Thunder forward as his opponent fell to the ground beside him.

The enemy numbers were greater, but with the combined force of Lord Frederick and the ruthless efficiency of the Advance Regiment, it made little difference.

Dane kept Thunder angling into his next opponent, boring in from one side, slashing down and across, striking from side-on, where his foe had no means to counter.

After another minute or so, some of the regiment had crashed through the Pardostan line, circling around and attacking them from all sides.

Soon it was over, the eerie silence post-battle reigning over the field.

Dane found Will not far to his left.

With nods to each other telling them they were unhurt, Dane looked further afield and among others he saw Silvers, Hindmarsh, Donovan, Albert and Fenwick. All were seemingly unscathed.

To his right, he saw Lord Frederick threading his way towards Silvers.

Waiting for the order to regroup, he had a moment where he heard Blaze squawking again, before another group, this time in Hezabar colours, pounced on them.

Strewn across the battlefield, caught among the debris of the previous battle, the regiment had to go straight on the defensive.

Dane whirled Thunder around, tilting to his left at the last moment, narrowly avoiding the opponent who sought to cut him down from his right, swinging back to a straight-on position in one smooth motion, striking down the rider following immediately behind.

With this success, he forced Thunder forward, standing his ground against the momentum of his attackers, who in their lust for victory, were more intent on breaking through the line and surrounding them as the regiment had done to the Pardostans earlier, rather than methodically working their way through the disjointed regiment's defence.

He found he could avoid most of the attacks by angling Thunder to one side or the other, swivelling on the spot, ducking away and striking only when it was absolutely necessary: giving himself a kill for each slash of his sword.

With a swipe to his right, he claimed one; a backhanded slash to his left claimed another; the next hapless victim fell from a sweeping blow he made behind himself as he turned around, Thunder rearing for a moment before lurching forward – each blow, each swipe stronger than the one before, energy surging through his body as his eyes sought his next target.

After a minute or so, the momentum of the enemy had slowed, and it was man-to-man combat once more.

Now raining blows left and right, Dane pushed Thunder to his left, where he'd seen Will from the corner of his eye. If they could find a way to link up, they'd be more effective.

He worked his way in that direction, taking evasive action when an attacker came at him from the right.

Beating off another with a barrage of blows, he found himself next to Fenwick, who'd just finished off his opponent.

'With me!' said Dane, pushing his way forward and leaning Thunder into Fenwick's horse, guiding them in the same direction.

Ignoring him, Fenwick turned away, seeking an enemy rider a few yards away.

Dane swore under his breath for a moment, before looking past Fenwick and with a shout of, *'Yah!'* launching himself at his next opponent with a renewed burst of adrenaline.

Hacking past this and a few more adversaries, he joined up with Will, and without a word, they worked together, cutting a trail through their foes as they sought to join with others.

To his left, he saw a group of about four Hezabarians working in the same manner as himself and Will. Grunting, he pushed Thunder in that direction, Will following on instinct.

As Dane made to slash at the first opponent, he heard what sounded like a whip flying through the air, before snapping hard against something. In the next instant, the enemy knight in front of him fell, having been wrenched out of his saddle.

Bewildered for a moment, he knocked the empty horse out of the way, seeking the next one.

A moment later, with an anguished scream, the knight he'd sought to kill found himself thrown backwards and torn out of his saddle. As Dane glanced fleetingly at the body as it fell, he saw what looked like a thin, wavy-like form gripping the knight's shoulder for an instant, before it appeared to snap back, disappearing into the background.

What in the name of –

Slashing at the next opponent, he took care of him with a couple of blows, before the last of the four attackers suffered the same fate as the first two.

With a bolt of realisation, he knew.

The serpent!

'Back!' he shouted to Will. 'Back!'

Reaching over with his left hand, he pulled Will's horse violently to the right, nearly knocking him out of the saddle, an instant before the serpent's head shot past, where it would have struck Will squarely in the chest.

Shaken by the sudden movement of his horse and the whizz of air he'd felt as the serpent's head had shot past, Will looked around for a moment.

'Back!' Dane yelled again.

Moving in the direction of Dane's voice, Will looked at him, wondering what was going on.

'The serpent!' said Dane. 'It's here!'

'Where?' said Will, confused.

Keeping his eyes glued on his surroundings, Dane heard the dull *whump!* of the serpent's head snagging its latest catch to his right.

'There!' he said, pointing as he and Will both saw a Brindabeare Knight pulled off his horse.

Watching again, they saw another knight fall in the same manner, then another and another.

By now, others from both sides had seen what was happening.

The enemy force didn't hesitate, fleeing as one.

The regiment remained where they were, for a moment uncertain of what to do.

Dane and Will saw Hindmarsh turning towards them, unsure what he was seeing.

'Commander!' Dane yelled, a moment too late.

Before either could react, the head of the serpent cast itself as straight as an arrow, ripping through the air, embedding itself in Hindmarsh's throat. A moment later, the Commander of the Royal Knights was unceremoniously torn from his saddle.

In a flash of light, Lord Frederick appeared beside them, Scarafuse alight – a blade of liquid fire.

Watching on, Dane saw Lord Frederick walking towards what appeared to be the swaying shape of the serpent's body, raised on what looked to be giant centipede legs.

In the next moment, he saw the neck of the serpent reeling through the air, back to its body in preparation to strike its next victim.

At the precise moment neck and body joined as one, Scarafuse struck, the white-hot sword striking the serpent's body –

... where it bounced off as though it had been nothing more than a twig, falling harmlessly to the ground.

For a moment Dane thought his eyes were playing tricks on him.

Then he saw Scarafuse in Lord Frederick's hand once more.

The serpent's body left the ground, flying directly towards Lord Frederick.

Sheathing his sword, Dane grabbed an arrow from his quiver, nocking and drawing it in one smooth motion.

Following the blurred image as it landed, he let his arrow fly. At the same time, in a flash of light, Lord Frederick disappeared.

The arrow missed by the barest of inches, grazing the outer edge of the serpent's body as it flew past.

In response, the serpent raised itself to its full height, turning in the direction the arrow had come from – looking straight at Dane.

Reaching for another arrow, he knew there wouldn't be enough time before the serpent struck.

Struggling desperately, he fumbled the arrow out of his hands, and it fell helplessly to the ground.

Looking up, eyes wide and his body paralysed with fear, he saw the serpent's head spring forward; its dark eyes blazing and its mouth widening, venom dripping from its fangs, and waited helplessly for the end ...

Chapter 18
LOOKING AHEAD

With a dull *thwack!* an arrow tore through the serpent's body at the point where its head met its neck, and it fell to the ground, dead.

With a glance to his left, Dane saw Will with his bow in hand.

'Thanks,' he said, a wave of relief washing over him.

Will nodded.

'If it weren't for you, we'd both be dead,' he replied with a grin.

Like the dragon and kestrel, the serpent's body burst into flames, leaving behind a pile of ash.

Lord Frederick, Silvers, and others approached.

Raising a finger to his lips, and with a slight shake of his head, Lord Frederick stopped Dane asking the question on his mind.

'Was that the serpent?' asked Donovan.

Dane and Will nodded.

'I saw Ashbury fall, right next to me,' said Donovan, still not believing it. 'But I didn't see anything. I thought it must have been Raegan.'

'It was the serpent,' said Lord Frederick. 'We certainly didn't expect to find it here. It means only one thing – it was heading towards Brindabeare.'

Taking in all that had happened, no one spoke for a moment.

'What do we do now?' asked one.

'We need to take action to protect Grelfan and Feryndale,' said Lord Frederick.

'Agreed,' said Silvers. 'The regiment will divide evenly among both until we arrange permanent postings.'

Having scattered at the height of the fighting, the Grelfan and Feryndale delegations approached cautiously.

Upon hearing the news of the protection they were to receive, Dane saw them looking more relaxed and comfortable.

'Thank you,' said Levensworth.

'Yes, indeed,' said Werrington. 'It's no secret Hezabar wants to rule us, and they outnumber us considerably. It's a relief to know we have extra support.'

To Dane, Will and Silvers, Lord Frederick said, 'We need to return to Brindabeare without delay.'

The parties dispersed.

After a ride of about an hour, Lord Frederick stopped suddenly, scanning the area.

'What's wrong?' said Dane.

'I feel something,' said Lord Frederick. 'A ... presence. Something within the Elements of Nature I haven't felt before.'

Turning Thunder in a slow circle, Dane looked around, his eyes and ears alert for anything unusual.

'It's not here, but I can feel it,' said Lord Frederick after a few moments.

Dane, Will and Silvers waited anxiously.

Dismounting, Lord Frederick handed his horse to Dane.

'Continue to Brindabeare without me. I will either find my way back to you, or I will meet you there.'

With a nod to Silvers, he waved his hand, dematerialising with a flash of light and a *BANG!*

The light of early morning woke the old lady from what had been a restless night.

Physically and mentally exhausted, her aches and pains never quite going away; at the moment she found it a struggle to get through each day.

The damage to the hut had been extensive. Not only had the storm destroyed the roof, the resulting damage to the rest of the structure had resulted in one of the thatched walls collapsing a day or so later.

Forced to find somewhere offering more warmth, she'd ventured out during the days that followed, careful to mark her bearings, lest she lose herself on the way back. Wandering into the woods, about an hour's walk past her traps, she'd found a small, hollowed out and empty cave, large enough to kneel in, about a week after the storm.

Her day now consisted of making her way between the cave and her destroyed hut, tending to her vegetables and traps along the way, before making her way back to the cave for the night.

The daily grind would have been hard enough to endure alone, but there was an added complication.

She had a companion – a man – in a state considerably worse than her own.

She still couldn't believe it.

He'd appeared at the height of the storm, among the embers that had scattered on the floor when her roof caved in.

The wolf she'd been tending had turned into a man.

Dressed in black, pieces of his clothing on his arms, legs, chest and back were torn, with loose strips dangling from his body.

What happened?

Who is he?

His face was pale and gaunt, with dark hair and beard. Strangely, it looked as though it was somehow out of shape – his cheeks were sunken, as though they had been pushed back, and his nose and chin were shaped more like a snout than a man's face.

Checking around his jaw, the wound was in the same place on the man's neck – a dark slit about the width of a knife. It was clearer on the man's skin than the wolf's matted fur, and she saw it had been a very deep, almost fatal cut. Whoever stabbed the wolf-man had come awfully close to killing him.

Since his transformation, he'd remained in a deep fever; eyes closed, as though in some kind of trance; his face hot, his breathing rapid, his skin covered in sweat.

She'd been unable to do anything more than tend the wound, wipe the sweat from his brow and offer occasional sips of water. She'd never seen anyone endure a fever like this. Day to day, sometimes hour to hour, she wondered how long he'd survive.

Nonetheless, if he was to die, it wasn't going to be from lack of effort on her part.

Needing better shelter than the hut, and with the man helpless and unable to move of his own accord, she had spent several days building a makeshift stretcher.

One day a couple of weeks ago, when the weather had been kind, she'd spent most of the day dragging the injured man from the hut to the cave.

Much taller and heavier than she, it had taken an enormous effort to get there. She'd had to stop numerous times to make running repairs as the stretcher sagged and collapsed under the weight it was carrying; at other times she had to rest from sheer exhaustion.

Arriving just as the sun set, she'd breathed a sigh of relief, collapsing into a sleep that lasted until well after dawn the next day.

Turning to her right, she saw the man now, unchanged from how she'd seen him the night before.

Who is he?

How did he end up like this?

Will he live, or will it all be in vain?

Her mind clouded with these and other thoughts, she crawled from the cave, standing and stretching her aching bones, yawning at the sky.

With a final look at the man in his deep, fever-filled stupor, she started ambling towards the hut, a small sack in her hand for the vegetables she'd pick, hoping to find something in her traps to skin and cook with the day's meal.

Silence.

Presence.

Floating along the void, he's here and yet he's not here.

There's a presence ... somewhere ... just beyond his reach.

One moment it's close enough to touch, then it drifts away, calling and teasing.

His mother and brother, laughing as they played together.

'Don't hurt your brother!' ...

The image fades, drifting away on a wisp of wind ...

Silence, emptiness ...

A room ...

Everyone quiet ...

Mother...
Voices...
'You can't stay here'...
Another image ...
Mother ...
Lying still ...
Everyone standing around ...
The room fades ...
Standing in a courtyard ...
The Council watches from the dais ...
'Remember what you've been taught' ...
Another voice – deep and commanding ...
'Focus your mind' ...
'Let yourself go' ...
'Let it draw you to its core' ...
'... to its core' ...
'... to its core' ...

Standing before council, Dane, Will, Lord Frederick and Silvers continued the debrief of their journey.

'You're saying you were attacked twice?' said the King. 'By two separate forces? Before the serpent attacked you?'

'Yes, Sire,' said Silvers. 'The first attackers were Pardosta Knights, and the second group were from Hezabar.'

'Most unusual,' said the King.

'I agree,' said Silvers. 'It would appear the Pardosta Knights were prepared to sacrifice themselves, with the aim of inflicting as much damage as possible, before the Hezabar Knights attacked.'

Nodding thoughtfully, the King pondered the information.

'Even with Raegan unsighted, the rebels remain committed to their cause,' he said. 'I would not have expected a province to sacrifice itself so readily for another – even more so when the other province has a governor who's barely come to power. What do you know of him?'

'Everidge was second in command to Hazelwood,' said Silvers.

'What about Forrester?' said the King.

'Killed after Renshaw reported the impending attack on Feryndale in the days before Raegan attacked the castle.'

The King raised an inquisitive eyebrow.

'Yes, Sire,' said Silvers. 'Someone reported Renshaw's appearance here, and it was traced back to Forrester.'

Dane registered this in his mind.

Our traitor's work again!

He remembered the occasion – the lavish dinner celebrating his and Will's success in the Tournament of Knights, when Renshaw, looking little more than a peasant, burst into the room to warn them. The attack on the castle happened soon after – Black Knights disguised as Candahorn envoys arriving from everywhere; among them, fellow cadet Morgan Hainsley, who was subsequently killed by Vanessa.

Silvers continued.

'Reports to date advise Everidge has remained steadfast in his loyalty to the rebel cause.'

'All the same, it doesn't appear to have been the most organised plan,' said the King. 'It would have been far more effective to attack in one large group.'

'They knew Lord Frederick was with us,' said Silvers. 'I think they were relying on the element of surprise.'

'Unless they were Raegan's orders,' said Dane, his tone a mixture of objective thought and frustration.

'Let's not speculate on that,' said Lord Frederick in a stronger tone than normal – a tone Dane knew was directed at him.

'Regardless of whose orders they were, it appears they were intent on trapping us,' said the King. 'While we suspected something like this might happen, I would have thought it more likely after the creatures were killed.'

'Unless they knew exactly when we'd be coming,' said Dane.

Silence greeted his comment.

'There's a traitor among us,' said Dane when he received no response. 'Someone is sharing information with them. They were waiting for us. It's the only explanation.'

Others nodded as they thought about what Dane had said.

Not only had they been attacked; the scouts had disappeared without trace.

'And the serpent appeared during the battle?' asked the King.

'That's correct,' said Silvers.

Turning to Lord Frederick, the King said, 'You said you were unable to kill it?'

'That's correct, Sire,' Lord Frederick replied. 'On this occasion, I, too, had fused blood on my blade, yet Scarafuse had no effect.'

Scratching his chin, the King looked away for a moment, absorbing what he'd heard.

'What are we to take from this?' he asked.

'There would appear to be another element to these creatures we weren't aware of,' said Lord Frederick. 'Although it requires the Princess's blood to kill them, it appears they are immune to a wizard's weapon.'

'How can that be?' asked Medhurst.

'Like everything we've discovered about these creatures, we can only guess from our own experience,' said Lord Frederick. 'If it's nature's belief a wizard has escaped from the City of Lost Souls, it stands to reason that one of the defences these creatures possess would be immunity from any power a wizard may wield.'

Dane shook his head in wonder, and with a sideways glance at Will, saw him similarly struck by what Lord Frederick was telling them.

'It makes killing them that much harder,' said Medhurst.

A thought burst into Dane's mind – *it doesn't help when you give our secrets to others!*

'Perhaps,' said Lord Frederick. 'But we should not let problems such as this detract from the fact we have killed another.'

'By luck more than anything,' said Medhurst.

Reluctantly, Dane found himself agreeing with Medhurst.

He wanted to add, *'and despite your traitorous ways,'* but remained silent.

'It doesn't matter how they're killed,' said Lord Frederick. 'So long as they are.'

'You heard the reports from Grelfan,' said the King. 'And from what you saw in your encounter, what do you make of the serpent?'

'It was attacking indiscriminately and at random,' said Lord Frederick. 'I suggest it was stronger and more aggressive than it had been when it attacked Grelfan. It struck at will, purely for the sake of it, as though it were possessed by some driving force. I believe the strength and power it displayed would have been stronger than any time in its life.'

The King paused a moment, before turning to Dane and Will.

'Your thoughts?'

'Yes, Sire,' said Dane. 'When it first attacked, it was killing Hezabar Knights. Then it attacked some of ours. I don't think the colours mattered. It was attacking whatever it saw around it. It seemed to be in some kind of blind fury.'

'I agree, Sire,' said Will, a hot flush creeping up the back of his neck. 'At first, I thought it was Lord Frederick ... until I saw our knights being attacked.'

To Lord Frederick, the King said, 'Why do you think it chose to attack in such a barren place?'

'I think it was making its way to Brindabeare,' said Lord Frederick.

'You're saying it has sensed my daughter?'

'Yes, Sire,' said Lord Frederick with a nod. 'We knew the time would come when they would find her and make their way here. It was heading towards Brindabeare and either came across the battle by chance or sensed her blood on our weapons.'

Dane glanced at Will, his mind racing.

No wonder it came after me!

'Then we're fortunate to have killed it before it got here,' said Lindstrom, bringing Dane's mind back to the present.

'We are,' said the King. 'But it leaves the sarkoe unaccounted for. What do we know of its whereabouts?'

'Over the last few days, I have felt traces of something new – something deep in the Elements of Nature; but so far, I've been unable to find it,' said Lord Frederick.

'There haven't been any sightings in over a week, Sire,' said Lindstrom. 'Its last known attack was a settlement near Candahorn; then it was seen somewhere near the Astuvius River.'

'Could it sense my daughter from such a distance?' the King asked.

'I would say it's possible,' said Lord Frederick. 'Everything about them gets stronger every day. It stands to reason it's developed a keener sense of the Princess's whereabouts.

'We don't know where the serpent was when it picked up her scent, or how fast or far it travelled once it did.'

'Perhaps it happened when she was on the rampart,' said Dane. 'She was in the open, and there was a strong wind. That may have been nature's doing – sending her scent into the land.'

'Well thought,' said Lord Frederick with an approving nod.

'And if the serpent picked up her scent, the sarkoe will too,' said the King.

'If it hasn't done so already, I'm sure it will,' said Lord Frederick. 'And I have no doubt the sarkoe is already stronger than the serpent, having absorbed the serpent's elements into its own. It will be more dangerous than anything we've faced so far, being equally strong in all the Elements.'

A flood of thoughts filled Dane's mind.

Each creature is stronger than the last.

Fire passed from the dragon ...

Flight passed from the kestrel ...

What will pass from the serpent?

'If I may?' asked Dane, his thoughts transferring to words.

The King nodded.

'In addition to its own abilities, the sarkoe will be able to breathe fire, fly – or leap through the air, and ... blend with its surroundings.'

All in the chamber took a moment to let this sink in.

'You're right,' said Lord Frederick.

'How in the name of the Gods are we going to be able to stop something like that?' asked Medhurst.

Dane looked at him, trying not to betray his thoughts.

You can start by not sharing this with our enemies.

'I don't care how we do it – it simply has to be done,' said the King. 'My daughter grows weaker by the day.'

Dane turned away, as though he'd been physically struck by the King's words, a deep, roiling anger working its way through him.

'We may yet be fortunate,' said Lord Frederick.

'How so?' said the King, asking the question on everyone's mind.

'Given the serpent was making its way to Brindabeare, we know the sarkoe will do the same.'

'How is that a good thing?' said Medhurst.

Against his better judgement, Dane found himself agreeing with Medhurst once more.

'It means we don't have to search for it,' said Lord Frederick. 'It will come to us.'

'And it could attack and kill the Princess before we're ready,' said Medhurst. 'If it has all these extra abilities, we won't even see it until it's at the gates.'

'We start preparations immediately,' said the King. 'We have to think of every measure we can take to protect my daughter. She needs to be in the most secure place in the castle, where we can have as many knights as possible to protect her.'

'If I may, Sire,' said Lindstrom. 'If it can sense her, it will be able to find her, no matter where she is.'

'Then we put her in the most impregnable place in the castle,' said the King.

'She's already there,' said Medhurst. 'In the tower. There's no safer place in the entire land.'

'No,' said Dane, strongly.

Everyone turned to look at him.

'It's not,' he said with more certainty.

'What do you mean?' asked Medhurst, looking at Dane as though he were a fool. 'What place can be more secure than the tower where she is?'

'You're looking at it from the wrong point of view,' said Dane.

'Have you lost your mind?' asked Medhurst.

Looking to the King, Dane said, 'If I may explain?'

The King nodded.

'The tower is the most secure place in the castle, and I would agree, in the land, from an outside attack.'

'Then, you agree?' said Medhurst, a wide, condescending smile on his face.

'No,' said Dane.

Rocking back in his seat, Medhurst couldn't believe what he was hearing.

'It's not the safest place from the sarkoe,' said Dane. 'It can fly, or at the very least, leap. That takes away the defences that would otherwise make the tower a stronghold. Remember the damage done by the dragon?'

Heads nodded.

Medhurst sat bolt upright as the realisation struck him, shock registering on his face as though he'd been slapped.

'The dragon took us by surprise because it was so unexpected. Even though we know the sarkoe is coming, we won't see it; no matter how ready we are. The serpent was difficult to see, and if the sarkoe is growing in strength and capability, it will be harder to see than the serpent.'

Everyone listened intently as Dane continued.

'It could attack us from anywhere at any time, and we won't be able to adjust our defences. We have to put the Princess in the only place it can't penetrate.'

'And where is that?' asked Medhurst, his voice dripping with contempt.

'Underground,' said Dane.

Heads snapped straight with the realisation of where Dane was thinking.

'You can't be serious!?' said Medhurst.

Dane nodded.

'I couldn't be more serious.'

Lord Frederick and the King looked at each other.

'He's right,' said the King.

'But Sire!' said Medhurst. 'How can he suggest –'

'He's right,' said the King, cutting him off. 'The only access is underground, and there is only one way in or out.'

Everyone but Medhurst was nodding in agreement.

Turning to Salsbury, the King said, 'Have the lower floor of the dungeon converted immediately.'

With a look at Dane, the King said, 'Well thought. It's a sound plan.'

'Thank you, Sire,' said Dane. 'May I ask a small favour – one I think you would agree with in the circumstances?'

The King raised an eyebrow.

'That I be the one to tell her.'

Chapter 19

STRONGER AND WEAKER

Rumours erupted in the city once more ...

'The serpent's dead! Lord Frederick killed it!'

'No, he didn't.'

'Who said that? Everyone says it's dead!'

'We were told Lord Frederick couldn't kill it!'

'Then why have they returned?'

'That was only a few. The regiment hasn't come back.'

'That's because they're looking for the sarkoe, and they're protecting Grelfan and Feryndale.'

'I don't believe you. If Lord Frederick couldn't kill it, it's still out there, and it will only be a matter of time before it kills us all.'

'The dungeon?' said Vanessa, her voice uncertain.

Dane nodded.

'It's the most secure place in the castle. It can't get to you if you're underground.'

'Father has agreed to this?'

'Yes,' said Dane.

Thinking for a moment, Vanessa looked at Marilena.

275

'I think he's right,' said Marilena.

With a deep sigh, sinking back into the pillows behind her, Vanessa nodded.

'Very well.'

'It will be heavily guarded,' said Dane. 'There's only one way in or out; so, you can be sure when it senses you, there will be a lot of knights in the way. We'll kill it before it gets inside the dungeon.'

'How long before it gets here?' asked Vanessa.

'We're not exactly sure,' said Dane. 'But the dungeon will be ready before the end of the day.'

Vanessa and Marilena looked at each other, slivers of anxiety passing between them.

'It will be all right,' said Dane. 'While it won't be lavish accommodation, you'll be safe, and that's more important than anything else.'

The ladies exchanged nervous looks once more.

'We'll be ready,' said Dane, noticing their reaction.

'I know you will,' said Vanessa as Marilena helped her take a few sips of water. 'Tell me about Medhurst.'

'He was really upset when I suggested moving you,' said Dane. 'He wanted you in the tower, and the idea of moving you was so unexpected, he couldn't believe it when it was agreed to.'

'But it does make sense to keep me here,' said Vanessa. 'It's the safest place in the castle.'

'Under normal circumstances,' said Dane. 'But it won't protect you against the sarkoe.'

'But he doesn't control the sarkoe,' said Marilena.

'It doesn't matter,' said Dane. 'This thing can fly - or at least, leap. So, the tower offers no protection. If you're underground, it can't get to you, unless it gets past all the knights guarding the entrance.'

'Very well,' said Vanessa after a few moments.

'And we also have to consider Raegan,' said Dane.

'But –'

'No,' said Dane, raising his hand to object. 'This isn't about me feeling guilty about whether I killed the wolf. He can appear anywhere, at any moment, and we have to be prepared for that.

'When the sarkoe attacks, we'll be vulnerable. No matter what we have to defend you – this creature is going to be unlike anything we've seen before. We will suffer losses until we kill it, and we'll be vulnerable as long as it's alive. While it's doing whatever it can to find you, we have to make sure we don't leave ourselves exposed to another attack.'

The ladies nodded with a nervous glance at each other.

'It's a time such as this when Raegan could appear. He may have been in hiding all this time, waiting for this very opportunity.

'Even if word gets to Raegan about where you are, it will be harder for him to get to you if you're in the dungeon.'

'How many will know she's there?' said Marilena.

'Lord Frederick will take her,' said Dane. 'None in the castle will know. Only the Royal Knights assigned to her, Bowers and a couple of guards, and the King and Council.

'No one guarding you will leave the dungeon. Our meals will be in an antechamber, rather than the dining hall.'

'It's a good plan,' said Vanessa. 'And Commander Hindmarsh is in charge?'

Dane hesitated, looking away for a moment.

'What?' said Vanessa.

'He's dead,' said Dane, staring past her.

Vanessa's eyes widened.

'The serpent killed him,' said Dane, his voice trailing away as he spoke. 'There was nothing we could do. It was striking at random and attacked so quickly.'

Vanessa and Marilena listened in stunned silence.

'We couldn't stop it,' said Dane, losing himself in his words. 'Lord Frederick couldn't kill it, and if not for Will, it would have killed me, too.'

Gasping in the same instant, Vanessa and Marilena's eyes widened in shock.

'But it's dead,' said Dane, seeing the looks on their faces. 'And when the sarkoe attacks, we'll kill it.'

'They were defeated?' asked Mortensen.

'Yes,' said Thurman.

'There were twice as many men,' said Mortensen, his face aghast. 'How is it possible?'

'It was not a co-ordinated attack,' said Thurman. 'Apparently, Lord Frederick saw the Pardosta Knights and destroyed a large number before they had an opportunity to engage.'

Scratching his chin as he pondered this, Mortensen stared straight ahead.

If Lord Raegan were here, that would have been prevented.

'Governor?' said Thurman.

Snapping himself away from his thoughts, Mortensen beckoned him to continue.

'The reports say the serpent attacked. We don't know when – only that it happened at some point in the battle. And as soon as it appeared, everyone fled.'

'The serpent was there?' said Mortensen.

'Yes,' said Thurman.

'It attacked us? So, they *do* control it?'

'We're not sure,' said Thurman. 'Apparently, it attacked Brindabeare Knights, too. We're told they killed it.'

'You're telling me, despite being outnumbered and attacked by the serpent, the Brindabeare Knights prevailed? They killed one of the very creatures we've been unable to kill ourselves?'

Glancing at his fellow councillors, sitting stoically around him, Thurman nodded.

'Did Lord Frederick kill it?' asked Mortensen.

'No, Governor,' said Thurman. 'We're told it was a Royal Knight.'

'Dane Thorburn?' said Mortensen, his mouth gaping in disbelief. 'Again?'

'No, Governor,' said Thurman. 'We're told it was another, by the name of Hevenshire.'

'He would have to be an incredible archer, to have been able to kill that creature.'

'Apparently, he is just so,' said Thurman.

'His arrows had the Princess's blood on them?'

'Yes,' said Thurman. 'I have the report here.'

'I've heard enough,' said Mortensen, raising his hand.

'If I may,' said Thurman, his voice unsteady, anxious at what he was about to say. 'There is one other possibility to consider.'

Staring at the ceiling in despair, Mortensen nodded.

'What is it?'

'We need to consider whether Everidge wanted retribution for the losses Hezabar suffered in earlier events.'

'Are you suggesting he deliberately disobeyed me?'

'We believe it's something we need to consider,' said Thurman, glancing nervously at the other councillors.

His eyes staring menacingly at Thurman, Mortensen's face turned as hard as stone.

'If Everidge disobeyed my orders, he will suffer the same fate as his predecessor.'

Thurman nodded gently in response.

'Send word to both,' said Mortensen.

No one moved for a moment.

'I said, send word to both!' said Mortensen. 'Do you need a formal invitation? I want them here as soon as possible!'

Thurman nodded to a guard, who left the chamber.

Standing, Mortensen stalked around the room.

'Do I have to do everything myself?' he muttered. 'A simple plan; simple orders; an easy victory, and they can't even get that right.'

Thurman and the others waited, none prepared to interrupt as Mortensen continued to pace.

'This can't be happening,' he said. 'The castle was supposed to be a formality. The girl's kidnap was foolproof. One failure after another. No trace of the pulse. It *wasn't* supposed to be this way.'

Instinctively stopping mid-stride, he saw the faces of all the councillors staring at him.

How much did they hear?

'Curse you,' he said to Thurman, looking at him first. 'Curse you all.'

The councillors shifted uneasily in their seats.

'Get out!' Mortensen screamed. '*Curse you all, get out!*'

Chairs scraped as the councillors stood, hurrying themselves from the chamber.

Alone, Mortensen walked towards a window, kicking a chair in frustration. Looking to the city below, he shook his head slowly, lost in thought.

Where are you, My Lord?

Without you, it's only a matter of time.

Turning away from the window, he saw Thurman in the door-way with a message in his hand.

'Yes?'

'We have word,' said Thurman, holding a small parchment.

Mortensen nodded and Thurman entered, crossing the room.

Unsealing the message, he leaned against the window frame as he read, looking from the note to Thurman as he digested the information.

'Well, well,' he said with a smile. 'Isn't that interesting?'

Thurman looked at his Governor, his face filled with hope.

'Very interesting,' said Mortensen. 'Very interesting indeed.'

'Governor?' said Thurman.

'They're putting the girl in the dungeon,' said Mortensen. 'To protect her from the sarkoe.'

Thurman looked at Mortensen uncertainly.

'In the name of the Gods, do I have to explain everything?' said Mortensen, exasperated at his councillor's response. 'By putting her in the dungeon, they think they have her where she's most protected.'

Thurman nodded, still not following.

'And while there may only be one way in for the sarkoe, it also means there is only one way out for her.'

Nodding again, Thurman started to understand.

'Which means, that with the assistance of our allies in Brindabeare –' said Mortensen.

'– we can kill her,' said both at the same time.

The nets were heavy.

It would take both boats to haul in the day's catch.

The smaller boat was already laden with a full net, pulled in moments earlier.

Those on the larger boat had called to their companions, seeking their help.

It wasn't often they needed the other crew's assistance, but when they did, it meant they had enough in the catch to last a few days before venturing out again.

The smaller boat rowed aside the other, side-to-side, the ropes set between them joining the two together.

As the men reached over, dragging the nets towards the boat, they felt a sudden jolt from under the water.

In the next moment, with an extraordinary upward thrust, the entire netting burst clear of the surface, shooting into the air, the force of whatever caused the disturbance tearing the nets completely. The catch of the day rained down, dropping into the boats and the river.

Bewildered for a moment, the men had no time to react before, with another *whoosh!* a huge spray of water leaped out of the water around them, followed by a large, dark shape that sprang into the air from beneath it, hovering for a moment, before falling towards them.

With a shuddering *crash!* it landed on the boats, splintering them to pieces.

Men were thrown everywhere – some found themselves in the river, others crashed onto the decks as they split apart; a few were crushed under the sarkoe as it landed on top of them.

Some in the river found themselves tangled in the debris of the boats and netting, where they were dragged helplessly underwater.

Others suffered as victims of the sarkoe's lustful hunger, torn apart as it lashed its massive head from side to side, its large jaws snapping closed with more force than the heaviest smith's hammer.

Anguished screams were lost in the roiling water as the sarkoe thrashed its way forward, its body swinging from left to right, splitting what remained of the boats to pieces.

As water bubbled around the wreckage, those still in one piece felt a grip behind their necks like an invisible hook, moments before they were thrown backwards, clear of the mayhem and far enough away to be able to swim safely to shore.

As the sarkoe continued thrashing its way through the destruction around it, a greenish-vert light emerged, pulling the torn netting together, turning it into a heavier, stronger material.

Once complete, the netting slid through the water, seemingly of its own accord.

In the next moment it started to close, wrapping itself around the sarkoe.

At first the beast didn't seem affected by what was happening, continuing upstream, dragging netting and pieces of wreckage with it.

As it sought to get clear of it, though, it felt something constricting around it, tighter and tighter, making it harder and harder to move.

Before it could react, the netting started rising slowly towards the surface, the water bubbling once more under the pressure of the creature caught within.

Once it cleared the surface, with a sweeping motion of his hand, Lord Frederick guided his catch towards the shore, well clear of the fishermen struggling to get out of the water.

Gently lowering his prize to the ground, he approached cautiously as the sarkoe continued struggling within the bindings of the netting.

Now a matter of feet away, he beheld the massive creature, some thirty feet long, but quite unlike any sarkoe he had ever seen.

Its legs were different, as though they were able to turn and extend, allowing it to stand upright and run freely on land. Its tail looked as though it could contract if necessary – rather than just being the long, powerful rudder it was in water, it could become much shorter and less of a burden on land. Finally, its huge jaws and snout looked as though they could change their shape and size, so it wouldn't be weighed down out of the water.

Tightening the bindings further, the sarkoe appeared as though it was about to stop struggling, now only moving at its extremities.

With a wave of his hand, a large, steel-like container appeared next to it, an opening at one end.

Lifting the sarkoe off the ground, Lord Frederick guided it towards the container.

If I can get it in here, I'll shrink it and take it to the Great Forest, and we'll kill it once and for all.

Guiding it closer to the container, he felt a vibration in the netting.

Fighting to keep the binding together, tightening it further still, the vibration became greater, before, with a sudden shock and a *BANG!* the netting blasted apart in a bright argent-azure light and a shower of embers and smoke.

As everything cleared, Lord Frederick saw empty pieces of netting scattered on the ground.

In the next moment, a large ball of flame engulfed the container, before, with a giant leap, he saw the sarkoe soaring through the air, landing with a splash in the river, before continuing its journey towards Brindabeare.

'The sarkoe attacked at Grelfan!'

'And now it's coming here!'

'We can't stop it! It's going to destroy us all!'

'We've killed the other three. They'll find a way.'

'But this is more powerful than the others!'

'We have Lord Frederick. He'll find a way.'

'It's too strong! They say he can't kill them!'

'There is no doubt this creature is incredibly powerful,' said Lord Frederick to those assembled.

In addition to the Council, all who were to guard the dungeon were in attendance.

'It's more powerful than the dragon, the kestrel and the serpent. I have been unable to kill or trap it.'

Those in the chamber eyed each other nervously.

'I was able to track it to the Asutvius River, near Grelfan, where it attacked a group of fishermen. While I was initially able to constrain it, it broke free of my bindings, and since that time, I have been unable to find it.'

A nervous chatter broke out in the chamber.

Dane and Will looked at each other.

'Trapping it was always unlikely,' Dane whispered.

'These creatures are more powerful than he is,' said Will, nodding towards Lord Frederick.

Raising his hand, Lord Frederick silenced the noise, before continuing.

'It has not been seen since the attack on the fishermen.'

'What does it look like?' asked Bedcroft.

'Whatever it wants to look like,' said Lord Frederick.

'What do you mean?'

'It has an ability to change its shape, depending on whether it's in water or on land,' said Lord Frederick. 'And once on land, it's said to be able to adapt - running either on four legs or two, as well as being able to leap great distances. In each case it changes its form.'

Nervous looks greeted the news.

'And, like the serpent, it can change its colour and blend with its surroundings,' said Lord Fredrick.

'So, how are we going to be able to see it before it attacks?' asked Harvey.

'It will be difficult,' said Lord Frederick. 'There is no doubt it has sensed the Princess's presence and is making its way here. We don't know how fast it travels, nor do we know how far it can travel in a day. But knowing the distance between Brindabeare and Grelfan, we know it will be a matter of days.'

'None of that matters,' said the King. 'We have to be ready now.'

'Indeed,' said Lord Frederick with a nod to Silvers. 'Our preparations continue. The lower floor of the dungeon has been converted. Only those in this room are aware she is there.'

'And let there be no doubt,' said the King. 'That is to remain so. You are confined to the dungeons until this is over, and there is to be no word to anyone – and I mean *anyone*.'

Murmurs of agreement rippled through the chamber.

'General,' said the King.

Silvers stepped forward.

'We have lookouts at all entrances and on every rampart. We're confident we will be able to raise the alert the moment it arrives. The city is in lock-down until further notice.

'No one will be on the streets unless it's necessary. Farmers are tending crops and livestock, guarded by knights. At the earliest sign of attack, they will move indoors.

'Although we don't expect the sarkoe to attack anywhere but here, we have regiments deployed in the outer and main areas of the city. All gates are closed until further notice.'

The King nodded.

Glancing to Lord Frederick, he said, 'How many weapons have been fused?'

'Enough for those here to kill it,' said Lord Frederick.

'Is there anything else we need to discuss?' asked the King.

Lord Frederick and General Silvers were silent.

'Very well,' said the King. 'Does anyone have any further questions?'

None in the chamber spoke.

'I leave you to your tasks,' said the King. 'I cannot stress to you the importance that we defeat this creature. My daughter's life – the life of your future Queen – the first ruling Queen in the history of this land, is at stake.'

Dane felt his adrenaline rising.

'She is in this position through no fault of her own,' said the King. 'An innocent victim escaping a place she had no right to be. A place she was taken to against her will, having committed no crime.

'As a result of this, nature has decided to send these creatures after her, for reasons only it can comprehend, and to which we can only respond.'

Eyes locking on the King, Dane felt his body tingling.

'We must do whatever is necessary to protect her and ensure her safety. I have no concern for the cost of doing so. We are all aware of the sacrifice we may have to make.

'If I had to lay down my life to protect her, I would do so, without a moment's hesitation.'

Dane felt his heart leap.

As would I!

'My daughter must be protected!' said the King.

'Hear! Hear!' said Lord Frederick.

'Hear! Hear!' said General Silvers.

'I swear to protect the Princess, *in the name of the King!*' yelled Dane.

'*In the name of the King!*' yelled Will.

The chant echoed off the walls as the King, Lord Frederick, Medhurst, Lindstrom and Salsbury left the chamber.

'*In the name of the King!*'

'*In the name of the King!*'

'*In the name of the King!*'

'What happened?' asked Dane.

'We don't know,' said Marilena, worry and concern on her face. 'She collapsed a while ago and hasn't woken up.'

'When?'

'Soon after you were summoned to Council.'

Dane's heart skipped a beat.

That was hours ago.

Looking at the prone body on the bed, his stomach churned.

Vanessa's face was pale, as white and pallid as he'd ever seen her. Sweat gleaned on her forehead, her hair a matted mess.

Sitting next to the bed, taking her hand in his, he leaned over, stroking her forehead gently with his free hand.

Her skin felt hot and clammy.

'She's burning up,' said Dane.

Marilena nodded.

Dipping a cloth in a bowl of water, she sat opposite Dane, wiping Vanessa's face gently.

'Lord Frederick didn't say much,' she said. 'He looked at her briefly and left the room.'

'He said the sarkoe continues to get stronger,' said Dane quietly. 'It's taking more and more of her strength.'

'I know,' said Marilena, a tear trickling down her cheek.

'Mother –'

Dane felt his hand move.

Looking at Vanessa, he felt her arm moving. Releasing his grip, he allowed her to move her hand away, and in the next few moments, he saw her eyes open slowly.

Blinking a couple of times, perhaps unsure where she was, Dane saw her turn her head from side to side, before she looked directly at him, smiling weakly.

Taking her hand once more, he said quietly, 'How are you feeling?'

Vanessa said nothing.

Thinking she hadn't heard him, he squeezed her hand a little tighter and said, 'How are you feel –'

'Hot,' said Vanessa in a dry, croaking voice before he could finish. 'I feel hot.'

Holding out his other hand, he took the cloth from Marilena.

'Here,' he said, reaching over and dabbing her face.

'Thank you,' she said.

Looking at Marilena, he said, 'Find Lord Frederick.'

With a nod, her chin quivering, Marilena stood and left the room.

'Can … I … have … some … water?' said Vanessa.

Moving to sit on the bed beside her, Dane placed his hand behind her. Supporting her back and easing her off the bed to a semi-sitting position, he brought the goblet in his other hand towards her.

Using all her strength, Vanessa leaned forward, taking a couple of sips, before slumping against his arm.

Dane lowered her gently to the bed.

'Thank you,' said Vanessa.

Dane did his best to keep his emotions in check. Seeing her struggle and go limp against him – she was very, *very* weak.

'I'm so … tired,' said Vanessa, her voice soft and broken, as though every word was an effort.

Dane's mind raced.

This can't be happening!

We have to get the sarkoe before it kills her!

He felt tears welling in the backs of his eyes.

'Dane?' said Vanessa, her voice little more than a whisper.

'I'm here,' he said.

'Dane?' she asked again, her voice uncertain, as though she hadn't heard him.

'Yes?'

'Am I going to die?'

'No,' he replied, squeezing her hand and doing his best to keep his voice steady. 'You're not going to die.'

'Dane?' she said once more.

'Yes?'

'I'm scared.'

'It's all right,' he said. 'I'm here.'

'Don't let me die,' she said softly, drifting to sleep once more. 'Please don't let me die.'

Chapter 20
ATTACK FROM ALL SIDES

The city lay in slumber, the streets quiet in the pre-dawn dark.

Knights were stationed on every corner, ready to act at the slightest movement.

Those at gatehouses and on ramparts around the city and the castle gazed anxiously into the blackness surrounding them. Seeing anything at this hour would be hard enough, even without the shape-shifting ability of the unknown creature they knew was approaching.

Security inside and out had increased to a full war-footing.

The King and Queen were safely in their quarters – although not in any immediate danger, additional guards were assigned to them.

Thirty Royal Knights guarded the entry to Vanessa's temporary quarters, waiting patiently for whatever they may be called to do if the creature appeared.

From all reports, she was still weak, but otherwise in good spirits. Entry to her chamber was strictly forbidden, with Marilena the only one allowed in or out over the course of the last day.

The remaining hallways were quiet – even the pre-dawn noise in the kitchens seemed less than normal.

In the dungeon, the knights were changing shifts – a simple nod the only communication needed as new guards replaced old.

The protection around Vanessa's chamber on the lower floor was extremely heavy. Getting there would mean passing all the guards on the upper level, then through a doorway leading down a flight of stairs, past the guards on the lower level, through another door, and finally to the converted room itself where more guards were waiting.

There was only one problem.

All that protection meant nothing against a shape-shifting creature that could blend with its surroundings.

A small flame near the Borsan River Bridge was the only sign of its approach, visible for a moment, then gone. If not for the guard who happened to be looking that way at that exact moment, it would have been missed.

'Where was it?' asked his colleague.

'To the right of the bridge,' he said.

Calling to a couple of others, despite their best efforts, they saw nothing. One saw what appeared to be a ruffle in the grass about halfway between the bridge and the outer city gate, dismissing it as nothing more than the wind.

'Send notice to the castle,' said the Senior Knight of the group. 'They'll be glad we were able to warn them.'

Unfortunately, the message arrived too late.

The change of shift over, all lay quiet in and around the dungeon and outer courtyard.

No one had seen the mysterious shape bounding and leaping through the city.

A loud *CRASH!* was heard at the far end of the courtyard.

In the next moment, a section of wall collapsed.

The sarkoe emerged from the rubble, unscathed; twitching for a moment as it locked its senses on its target, before, with a single leap, it soared through the air from one end of the courtyard to the other, unleashing a ball of flame as it landed.

Screams broke the silence of the night as those in the line of fire were taken, collapsing to the ground.

Struggling to see the shape of the creature against their surroundings, others lunged towards it, swords drawn, hoping to kill it before it crossed the threshold into the dungeon.

'Where is it?' yelled one.

'I can't see it!' yelled another.

'Here!'

'Over here!'

A couple swung their swords in desperation, hoping for a lucky strike.

In the next moment, with a violent tug, the knight nearest the entry was thrown out of the way, seemingly by an invisible force none of them could see. Screaming as the sarkoe bit into him, tossing him away like a piece of rubbish, the stricken knight landed about thirty yards away.

Confusion raged inside the dungeon.

Swords were drawn, but no one could see anything. Apart from the mayhem they heard, there was nothing to give them a hint as to where the creature might be.

Making its way down the hallway, head swinging from side to side, the sarkoe felt the scent getting stronger and stronger, closer and closer than it had ever been before.

With a menacing growl, it ran the length of the hallway, smashing through the door at the end, trampling a couple of knights to the ground in the process.

Guided by the noise, a couple of knights slashed at the empty space in front of them, an instant after the sarkoe crashed through the door, leaping to the floor below.

Drawn by the ever-increasing scent of its prey, it growled again, running the length of the hallway, covering the ground in a matter of bounds, knocking knights out of its way in the process.

The moment it smashed through the door at the end of the hallway, a fireball ripped through Vanessa's chamber, filling the room completely and giving the knights on guard no time to react before they fell; the surrounding furniture little more than a smouldering mess.

Searching blindly for a moment, the essence of its prey filling its senses, the sarkoe leapt on the bed, where it found nothing but a burnt mattress, soiled with trails of blood.

Turning instinctively at the sound of those behind it, it breathed a ball of flame towards the entrance, restraining the knights trying to enter.

Sniffing the empty bed once more, it tilted its head upward, turning to its right.

Picking up an even stronger scent, it turned back towards the entrance, bumping past the furniture in its way.

Sensing an enemy in its way, it turned to its left, in the direction of the new scent. With another burst of flame towards the knights at the entrance, it leapt forward, fragments from the walls falling in its wake as it crashed its way past, retracing its steps and leaping into the courtyard.

One of the few to survive the carnage, Bowers made his way outside, waving a torch in the air.

Up at the tower, Dane and Will saw it instantly.

'It's attacked the dungeon!' said Dane.

'He's waving it again,' said Will. 'They've lost sight of it!'

Stepping back into the room, Dane relayed the information to the others.

A group of ten, including Lord Frederick, were in Vanessa's chambers – her real chambers, still under repair from the attack by the dragon.

'Very well,' said Lord Frederick. 'It went to the dungeon as planned, but they were not able to kill it. I'm certain it will come here next.'

Dane, Will, Harvey and the others nodded.

Stepping to the window, with a wave of his hand, Lord Frederick sent a thin film of gules-red into the air, letting the wind carry it away, towards the dungeon. With another wave of his hand, an image appeared next to him, like Vanessa in every detail.

Like the image in the dungeon, he was sure it would attract the sarkoe.

Stepping back into the room, he said to the group, 'All is ready. When it attacks, we won't have long. It will be hard to see. You will have to react on instinct. When it enters, the veils around the room will drop and keep it here.

'Once they're set, it will not be long before it breaks out. We *must* kill it here. We don't want it sensing the Princess's exact whereabouts.'

Everyone nodded.

Dane felt his body tense, gripping his sword tighter as he and Will nodded to each other; minds focused on what lay ahead.

Hearing the sound of footsteps approaching, everyone looked towards the doorway.

Dane saw Wilfred Chamberlain enter the room, out of breath after making his way from a lower level.

'They couldn't see it,' he panted. 'It attacked the chamber, and after it realised the Princess wasn't there, they lost sight of it.'

'They couldn't see it at all?' said Dane.

'Apart from blurred shapes, they couldn't tell where it was,' said Chamberlain. 'It broke through the entrance and made its way to the lower chamber. Even there, they couldn't see it clearly. It kept breathing fire at them, so they couldn't get near it. Then they lost sight of it.'

'What happened in the courtyard?' said Dane, having seen the rubble on the ground.

'It crashed through the wall,' breathed Chamberlain.

'How do we kill something like that?' said Harvey, aghast.

Before anyone could answer, they heard a growl at the open window.

Barely visible against the image of Vanessa shimmering in front of it, the sarkoe stood in a crouch before them, transfixed by what it saw.

In the next moment it leapt into the chamber, jaws open, as though it intended to swallow the image whole. When its jaws met nothing but air, it swished its head from side to side for a moment, before opening its mouth again.

Dane, Will and a couple of others dived to the floor, moments before a ball of fire swept past them.

Feeling the intensity of the heat of the flame as it passed, Dane's breath caught in his throat for a moment as he realised the enormity of what they were facing.

At the sight of the flames, Lord Frederick produced an argent-grey shield, protecting himself and those nearby. Others, Chamberlain among them, weren't so lucky – taken by the fire and collapsing to the floor.

Leaping to his feet, slashing desperately where he thought the sarkoe to be, Dane found nothing but air.

Lord Frederick waved his hands, lowering the seals around the room and trapping everyone inside.

Swivelling and turning, clearly agitated and annoyed it hadn't found its prey, the sarkoe leapt for the window, only to find itself rebounding back into the room.

Momentarily visible to all, Harvey and Will raced forward, thrusting their swords at it. With inches to spare, the sarkoe shrank itself and both swords swung through emptiness to the floor.

In the next moment it sprang to the ceiling, scanning the room.

Seeing the image of Vanessa in the corner, the scent strong once more, it leapt towards it in one smooth, fluid motion, where, with a *slam!* it met nothing but stone.

Falling to the floor among a shower of cracked stone, stunned for a moment and visible once more, it sprang away, moments before Dane's sword flashed past, missing by inches.

Cursing to himself, Dane swung again, diving away to his right as a fireball loosed itself from the sarkoe's mouth, claiming another of his colleagues in the process.

Turning in the next moment, the sarkoe snapped its jaws tight around the foot of Andred Simplot, wrenching him to the ground as the stricken knight screamed in pain. In the next moment he was flung like a rag against the nearest wall.

Scanning the room, his adrenaline fuelled by a mixture of panic and desperation, Dane saw only he, Will, Harvey and Lord Frederick remained.

No, no, NO!

Leaping towards Vanessa's image again, the sarkoe hit Lord Frederick's veil once more. It fell back, but not as heavily as before, the veil bending slightly.

Dane's heart skipped another beat.

It's weakening!

We have to kill it before it escapes!

Wiping a bead of sweat from his eyes, he lunged towards it again.

Standing on its hind legs, the sarkoe locked onto the image and the scent once more, springing towards it.

Dane saw it pass Will, missing him by inches. In the same moment, Will slashed at it with a knife, a trail of blood spraying into the air.

Expecting to see him to fall to the ground, instead, Dane saw him standing uninjured, and in the next moment, with a dull *thud!* the sarkoe landed on the floor, its dark shape clearly visible for the first time.

Enraged, it unleashed a ball of fire at the space Will had occupied moments before. Sensing what had been about to happen, he dived out of the way, the flames glancing by as he landed on the floor.

Looking at the creature, Dane saw it looked different from any sarkoe he'd seen or heard of; about ten feet long, a short almost horse-like tail, with a considerably shorter snout. He also noticed gloopy spots of blood on the floor.

'It's wounded!' he yelled with a surge of hope.

Will, Harvey and Lord Frederick saw it, too.

Incensed like never before, the sarkoe leaped towards the open window again, throwing itself against Lord Frederick's veil with all its might.

This time the veil bent outward, the sarkoe about to fall from the window, when it contracted again, pushing the creature back into the room.

'It's not going to hold!' Dane yelled, sheathing his sword and throwing a knife at the sarkoe.

Although wounded, the sarkoe jumped effortlessly to the ceiling, easily avoiding Dane's blow.

Leaping past Dane, it landed in the middle of the room, biting down hard on the obstacle in front of him.

With an agonising scream, Harvey fell to his knees, his sword dropping to the floor, moments before the sarkoe walked over him, tearing into his body once more and silencing the screams for good.

Turning to its left, it saw Lord Frederick standing in the open doorway leading to the hallway beyond the chamber.

For a moment, it stood still, utterly transfixed by what it felt.

Looking beyond Lord Frederick, the sarkoe's senses drew it to the source of all it had searched for. Despite everything it had sensed, seen and felt since it had been here, in that moment it felt the true source of it all, and it lay beyond this room, somewhere down the hallway.

With a burst of renewed energy, it sprang towards Lord Frederick.

The fire it unleashed burned a pure, molten gold.

Able to protect himself despite the intensity of the flame, Lord Frederick could do nothing as it seared a hole through the veil.

A moment later, it exploded in a shower of sparks.

Constrained no longer, the sarkoe trampled its way past Lord Frederick, lumbering down the empty hallway.

'No!' said Dane, rushing after it with Will at his heels.

In the next instant, Lord Frederick dematerialised in a flash of light.

Dane and Will raced down the hallway.

Despite its wounds, the sarkoe moved quickly, the guards in the hallway diving clear of the fireballs it sent towards them.

Dane saw it reach the end of the hallway.

'We can't let it get there!' he yelled.

Rounding a corner, they caught sight of the sarkoe ahead, about halfway down the next hallway, guards ducking and falling in its wake.

'No!' Dane screamed.

As Lord Frederick materialised in the hallway, waving Scarafuse in front of him, Dane saw the sarkoe slow to a stop, before raising itself on its hind legs, seemingly transfixed by the wizard's sword.

With no time to think, running for all he was worth, he drew the knife from his other gauntlet and leaped into the air.

At the same time, the sarkoe's head tilted to its left, at last locking its senses on what all hoped it would not.

As it took a step in that direction, Dane crashed into it from behind, the force knocking them over. With a last, desperate effort, he plunged his knife into the sarkoe's throat.

Smacking his face on the floor as he landed, his vision went black for a moment, and he saw stars around him.

Dazed and confused, a dull, throbbing ache in his chin, he turned sideways. He saw flames in front of him, as, like the other creatures, the sarkoe's body became nothing but a smoking pile of ash.

'Are you all right?' asked Lord Frederick, leaning towards him.

Dane nodded, instinctively raising his hand to his chin.

Looking at the blood on his hand, he touched his face again.

'I've split my chin open,' he said.

Lord Frederick and Will helped him to his feet.

'It's dead?'

'It certainly is,' said Will.

'What happened?' asked Dane. 'It was just standing here. I was sure it would sense her and crash through the wall.'

Lord Frederick nodded.

'I distracted it,' he replied.

'How?' asked Will.

'In the same way it was drawn to the dungeon and the chamber. All the images were duplications from Scarafuse, which in turn drew images from the Princess and combined them with the fused blood on the blade.

'Each time, the image and the scent were stronger – all drawn from the one source. The longer it survived, the more likely it would sense her real location.

'Thankfully, I was able to distract it long enough for you to kill it.'

Dane nodded slowly, the ache in his chin becoming more intense.

'Do you think it would have been able to get through?' asked Dane, glancing to the wall beside him.

'I do,' said Lord Frederick. 'If you couple its strength with its heightened sense of the Princess, I'm sure it would have been unstoppable.'

Dane nodded, remembering what it had done to the wall at the end of the courtyard.

'Lord Frederick!' boomed the King's voice.

Dane, Will and Lord Frederick turned down the hallway, and saw the King approaching with Salsbury and two guards.

'It's dead?' said the King.

'Indeed, Sire,' said Lord Frederick.

With a wave of his hand, all the hall guards left.

'Have you seen her?' said the King.

'Not yet,' said Lord Frederick with a beckoning hand towards the wall. 'Shall we?'

The King nodded.

Reaching for the torch next to Dane, Lord Frederick pulled it downwards, opening the doorway to the secret room.

With Lord Frederick leading, they made their way along the passageway to the small room at the end.

A bed had been placed in the centre, where Vanessa lay sleeping.

Rushing to her side, Dane saw the same pale, pallid face, covered in a lather of sweat.

Placing his hand on her forehead, her face felt as hot as the last time he'd seen her.

'But ... she's not ... she's not –'

Leaning over from the opposite side of the bed, Lord Frederick took Vanessa's hand.

Dane stepped back, looking anxiously at the others.

After a few moments Lord Frederick stood, the look on his face telling them everything they needed to know.

'No ...' whimpered Marilena, tears running down her cheeks.

'How?' said the King in disbelief.

'Sire,' said Lord Frederick, 'I'm sorry ... I don't know what happened.'

'It was supposed to cure her!' said Dane, looking at the others desperately. 'It was supposed to cure her!'

In the next instant, everyone in the room felt a vibration from under the floor.

Gentle at first, it began to increase in its intensity.

In the next moment the walls began to shake, the floor trembling more violently, dust falling into the room as the tremors reached the roof.

In the next moment, with a violent shudder, everyone was thrown to one side, then to the other, a thunderous roar growing and growing as the tremors became more and more violent.

'*What's happening?*' Dane yelled, looking around in a panic that mirrored the faces of all in the room.

With a sweep of his hand, Lord Frederick tried in vain to create a protective dome over them all, holding it for a moment before it shattered.

Dane found himself upside down on the floor, lurching helplessly from one side of the room to the other, before slamming into the bed.

In a daze, he found himself looking up and saw an open void, with dark, swirling clouds and angry streaks of lightning criss-crossing the sky as the room shook violently once more.

As he tried to stand, an argent-silver light with tinges of azure, gules and vert shot down from above, slamming into Vanessa with tremendous force, her body going completely limp.

'*NO!*' he screamed.

In the next moment, a glow spread through her body from head to toe, the light gently raising her several feet into the air, where she hovered for a few seconds; her arms and legs dangling beneath her, and her hair fanning out.

Spellbound, Dane watched as the light glowed even brighter, turning her slowly on the spot, before she started to float towards the bed.

As her head touched the pillow, the light, clouds and lightning disappeared, the room stopped shaking and all went quiet.

Struggling to his feet, Dane looked at the stunned faces of everyone around him.

'What in the name of –' said the King.

'*Look!*' said Marilena, pointing to the bed.

Dane and the others looked at Vanessa.

He saw it immediately – her natural colour had replaced the pallid and pale of before; he saw a calmness in her breathing, and she was relaxed – the tension and strain on her face gone.

His body tingling, a moment later he saw her eyes blink a couple of times, before opening and looking nervously around the room.

No one said anything for a moment.

'I'm thirsty,' she said. 'And hungry. Can I get something to eat?'

'Yes!' said Marilena, crying tears of joy. 'Yes! Of course! Anything you want!'

Still gathering himself after all he'd just seen, the King approached his daughter, bending down to give her a kiss on the forehead.

'Are you well?' he asked.

'Yes,' Vanessa replied, sitting herself up in the bed, a warmth and energy flowing through her she hadn't felt in a long time.

'Excellent,' said the King, turning to Lord Frederick. 'Do you have any clue what just happened?'

'My guess would be we just witnessed the Elements of Nature transferring the energy and elements the creatures had drawn back to their rightful owner,' said Lord Frederick.

'She's going to make a full recovery?'

'It will take some time to be certain,' said Lord Frederick, stepping forward and placing a hand first on her arm, then her forehead. 'But the initial signs are promising.'

'Excellent,' said the King, beaming to all in the room.

With a nod to Salsbury and the guards, the four made their way from the room, their footsteps disappearing along the passageway.

'We, too, will prepare for you to be moved back to your rooms,' said Lord Frederick, glancing to Marilena.

With a bow, he turned on his heel, heading towards the entrance, humming as he went.

'Thank you,' Marilena said to Dane and Will, hugging them both in turn.

Looking at the blood on Dane's face, she blinked a moment before saying quietly, 'Have you split your chin again?'

Dane nodded, wiping the blood away once more.

With a final hug for Vanessa, she shuffled out of the room, chasing Lord Frederick along the passageway.

'You're all right?' asked Dane, his mind a mix of wonder, joy and relief.

Vanessa nodded.

'I am. I can't tell you how I know, but I do. In the same way I couldn't tell you what was wrong with me, I know I'm going to be better.'

'I can see it,' said Dane.

Will nodded.

'As can I.'

'You killed it?' asked Vanessa.

Yes,' said Dane. 'And for a moment, we thought we'd killed you.'

'What do you mean?' said Vanessa.

Nodding as Dane told her all that happened after killing the sarkoe, a smile spread on her face when he finished.

'What?' asked Dane.

'Nothing,' said Vanessa. 'I'm just so happy, so relieved. I can't wait to get back to training.'

'Whoa,' said Dane. 'I think we need to be sure there are no lingering effects before you do anything like that. I can just imagine the Queen and Mother squabbling over the many reasons why you shouldn't.'

'Well, perhaps not tomorrow,' said Vanessa. 'Maybe the day after?'

The three friends laughed.

'We'll wait at the entrance for Lord Frederick,' said Dane. 'I'm sure he'll be back shortly.'

'Dane,' said Vanessa as he and Will turned to leave.

Rising from the bed, she approached them both.

'Thank you,' she said, hugging him tightly. 'Thank you for saving me. Both of you.'

'Whatever it takes,' said Dane.

Nodding with a smile, she embraced Will, before walking back to the bed.

Heading up the passageway, Dane noticed the torches flickering more brightly behind him, and in the next moment he heard footsteps from the entrance, heading towards them.

Beckoning Will back to the room, they waited for the others to arrive.

With swords in hand, they reacted the moment Salsbury and the two guards entered.

What happened next was a blur of movement that took place all at once.

Dane swung straight at his opponent, slashing right and left, lunging forward and forcing himself towards the passage. With another swipe, his opponent screamed as a cut opened in his arm, before, with a final thrust, Dane finished him.

In the next moment, Will's foe landed in a heap on the floor.

While this was happening, Salsbury, having snuck around the fighting, approached Vanessa, drawing a knife from his sleeve.

Leaning over the sleeping Princess, he raised the knife above her heart, before slamming it down with all his strength.

At the point of impact Salsbury fell forward, his knife striking nothing but air, before tearing into the mattress, his momentum forcing him to stumble.

Stunned for a moment, he stared in disbelief at the now empty bed in front of him.

'What –'

In the next moment, with a flash of light and a *BANG!* Lord Frederick appeared.

Before Salsbury could react, his arms were manacled.

Dane stepped to one side, behind Salsbury, with Will on the other.

'I'm sorry to disappoint you,' said Lord Frederick.

Salsbury continued to stare in disbelief at the empty bed next to him.

'We knew there was a traitor within,' said Lord Frederick. 'Someone very close to the King, who was sharing our innermost thoughts and secrets with others.

'It took some time to consider who among us would not only hear those conversations, but also have the means to be able to share them. Who better than the King's aide? Someone who was always present, who heard every intimate detail. Someone no one would expect because he never said a word?'

'What –' said Salsbury, looking around the room in disbelief. 'Where? She was *here*.'

'Indeed,' said Lord Frederick.

'But ... how?'

'You know about projected duplications,' said Lord Frederick. 'We've spoken about it several times. Unfortunately for you, until you see one, you really don't know how life-like they are.'

Chapter 21
NEW BEGINNINGS

'And finally,' said Lord Frederick, 'I replaced the Princess with the duplicated image he found when he entered the room.'

'Why?' said the King, eyes wide in disbelief.

Standing before council in shackles, Salsbury said nothing.

'I trusted you with my strictest confidences. In return you have been well looked after, given every privilege, and this is how you repay me?'

Staring back at the King, Salsbury said nothing.

'What have I done that could lead you to do such a thing? To betray me, my family, my daughter – someone you have nurtured her entire life?'

Salsbury remained still, making no move to reply.

'You *will* talk,' said the King. 'In the name of the Gods, even if I have to pry your mouth open myself, you *will* talk.'

Thoughts bubbled around in Dane's mind as he watched on.

Salsbury!

Until Lord Frederick had spoken to him and hatched their plan, he'd been certain it was Medhurst.

That he'd been wrong, so very wrong, made the revelation and impact of Salsbury as the traitor even more shocking.

The news had shocked the entire city.

Looking at Salsbury, beaten yet defiant, Dane saw a look of anger and hate – pursed lips, furrowed brow, tension in cheeks. Now revealed in the light of his true self, they were looks that had always been there.

Back in council once more, seated to the King's right, Vanessa stared coldly at the man before them, her face a mixture of shock, disbelief and simmering rage.

Lord Frederick sat still and impassive, the silent fury in his eyes the only hint of the anger and guilt Dane knew he'd be feeling for not uncovering it sooner.

Medhurst and Lindstrom looked at Salsbury with disgust and burning hatred on their faces, as did Will and Silvers, completing the list of those present.

'How many plots were you involved in?' said the King. 'Did your traitorous acts include arranging my daughter's kidnap? Were you the one who let the Black Knights know when she would be returning from Feryndale? Did you consort with Mortensen to have Fairbrother and Laidlaw killed? The attempt on my life?'

With each question, the temperature in the room grew hotter, the faces of all but Lord Frederick and the accused becoming harder and harder as waves of anger washed over them.

Glancing at Medhurst, breathing heavily, hands digging into his chair, the vein in his neck protruding as he'd never seen before, Dane wondered for a moment if he might pass out.

'Raegan's attack on the castle?' said the King. 'The information Governor Kavendish revealed at the Leader's Convention?'

Salsbury said nothing.

'You will answer me!'

Moving directly behind him, Silvers grabbed hold of Salsbury, squeezing his arm tightly with one hand, pulling his head back with the other.

'You will answer the King, or I will break your neck – right here.'

'Go – right – ahead,' Salsbury gasped as his head tilted towards the ceiling.

Releasing his grip and swivelling Salsbury around to face him, Silvers punched him in the stomach.

Wheezing, Salsbury dropped to the floor.

Grabbing him by the collar, Silvers hauled him to his feet.

Lord Frederick stood, walking towards them, stopping about a foot away. With a nod to Silvers, the General took a step back.

'You hope to enrage the General to the point he kills you,' said Lord Frederick. 'That will not be allowed to happen. At least not until we have extracted what we need from you.

'You can choose to do this co-operatively, or under duress. I suggest the former.'

Salsbury spat on the floor.

Raising his hand, Lord Frederick pointed towards Salsbury.

Salsbury felt his neck tighten, suddenly struggling to breathe.

'I don't know if you have seen Raegan do this, but know that I can do it, too,' said Lord Frederick.

Salsbury felt the invisible grip around his neck getting tighter, constricting the airflow into his lungs.

'I can increase this to the point where you will be barely conscious and hold it there for a considerable time. That would be most unpleasant, and despite whatever strength of will you think you possess, you will not be able to resist it.'

Salsbury's face started to turn red, his breathing faltering more and more as the grip around his neck continued to tighten.

Dane watched as Salsbury started to convulse. He saw Salsbury's face turning blue as the air around him dried up, saw him struggling more and more, before, right at the moment he was sure Salsbury would black out, he fell in a wheezing, gasping heap to the floor.

'I can repeat this as many times as it takes,' said Lord Frederick.

Gulping in breaths of air, Salsbury made no move to reply.

With a nod from Lord Frederick, Silvers reached down and dragged the prisoner off the floor.

Breathing rapidly, Salsbury looked away from the King and Lord Frederick.

Raising his hand again, Lord Frederick repeated the procedure, pointing at Salsbury, constricting his throat and draining the air around him.

Convulsing once more, his body flailing helplessly as it tried to resist the invisible force squeezing the air from him, he collapsed again as Lord Frederick released the hold.

Hauling him to his feet, with a nod from Lord Frederick, this time Silvers held him in a vice-like grip.

'Enough!' Salsbury yelled as his airways were deprived of oxygen once more.

Falling to the floor as Lord Frederick broke the choker-hold and Silvers released him, Salsbury curled himself into a ball, gasping and sucking in air, dry-retching as he struggled to recover.

Dragged to his feet once more, he took a few steadying breaths.

'Why?' asked the King as Salsbury turned to face him.

'Instead of a grovelling servant,' Salsbury gasped between breaths, 'I was to be the High Governor. Instead of pandering to your every need, people would pander to me. Instead of having to stand silent and unheard, people would listen to me, and carry out my instructions.'

'You think Raegan was going to give you this?' asked the King.

Salsbury said nothing.

'I'm afraid you've been misled,' said Lord Frederick. 'While I grant Raegan is very good at painting a picture that looks more attractive than what you see at the moment, he also knows how to manipulate others to serve his own ends. It surprises and somewhat saddens me that you didn't have the intelligence to work this out.'

'He told me I was important to him,' said Salsbury. 'That my thoughts were important to him. That he valued my ideas; how he knew how frustrating it must be, having such valuable insights to offer, while being seen as nothing more than a glorified servant.'

'You sent messages to Candahorn?' asked the King.

Salsbury hesitated.

'Yes,' he said as he saw Lord Frederick raising his hand towards him. 'Governor Mortensen and others.'

'Kavendish?' said the King.

Salsbury nodded.

Dane's mind exploded as he heard this.

Of course!

'Lord Raegan believes he will turn against you,' said Salsbury.

All in the room sat a little straighter as they heard this.

'He's alive?' asked the King.

Silence filled the air as everyone waited, the suspense so sharp it seemingly pulsed through the entire chamber.

Salsbury said nothing.

Lord Frederick raised his hand towards him.

'I don't know,' said Salsbury, reeling back in shock, raising his shackled hands reflexively towards his neck.

Bumping into Silvers, he jumped, looking at the King in fear.

'I swear, I don't know. I haven't seen him in a long time.'

'How long?' said the King.

'Months,' said Salsbury, with a glance at Vanessa. 'Before she was rescued.'

Glancing at one another, the King and Lord Frederick exchanged a nod.

Standing, the King took a step forward.

'Harold Salsbury. Before this council, I find you guilty of the attempted murder of Princess Vanessa, heir to the throne. In light of your confessions of your dealings with Raegan, Candahorn and others, including the sharing of privileged and confidential information, I also find you guilty of treason and hereby sentence you to be hanged at dawn.'

Stepping forward, Silvers and Will walked Salsbury to the rear of the chamber, handing him to guards on the other side of the doorway.

As the chamber door closed, all seemed to let out a collective breath, gathering their thoughts and considering what they had heard.

No one spoke for a moment.

'Sire, forgive me,' said Lord Frederick. 'I should have seen it sooner.'

The King shook his head.

'No,' he replied. 'There are some things even you cannot predict. You are not responsible for this. We all trusted him, which makes us equally liable for the consequences of his actions. We need to think this through and understand how many of our secrets are known by our enemies.'

'Sire, do you think he was telling the truth about Raegan?' asked Medhurst.

'I do,' said the King.

'So, we're no closer to knowing if he's dead?'

'I'm afraid not,' said Lord Frederick.

Dane cringed.

If only ...

'We will inform the city?' asked Lindstrom.

'We will,' said the King. 'At the height of tomorrow's sun.'

Everyone nodded their approval.

'While we are here, we have another matter to resolve,' said the King, nodding to Silvers.

Stepping forward, Silvers addressed the council.

'Sire,' he said. 'As you are aware, Commander Aidan Hindmarsh of the Royal Knights was killed defending the Princess against the serpent.'

The King nodded.

'And we must find a member of the Royal Knights to replace him,' said Silvers.

The King nodded again.

'Before you and the council, it is my recommendation that Royal Knight Dane Thorburn be promoted to the rank of Commander of the Royal Knights.'

Dane's mind and body went numb for a moment.

What? ...

He said what?

Glancing around the chamber, he wondered if he'd heard correctly.

He saw Vanessa looking at him, a broad smile on her face.

I'm to be ...

Looking at Lord Frederick, he saw him raise an approving eyebrow.

'Royal Knight Thorburn has demonstrated his capabilities on many occasions,' said Silvers. 'Firstly, on the field of battle, as witnessed, among other things, by his rescue of the Princess from the City of Lost Souls, and in killing several of the creatures sent to kill her.'

Glancing at Will, Dane saw him tip his head in his direction, a sly grin on his face.

'He has also demonstrated a sound strategic mind,' said Silvers. 'Witnessed most recently in conveying his ideas to move the Princess to the dungeon, which assisted in our planning and killing of the sarkoe, and led to the capture of the traitor.'

Dane couldn't believe what he was hearing.

Commander ...

'I second the motion,' said Vanessa.

'Lord Frederick?' asked the King.

'I agree with the motion.'

Dane's mind raced, his adrenaline pumping.

It's really happening ...

'As do I,' said Medhurst.

Dane couldn't believe his ears.

Medhurst!

'And I,' said Lindstrom.

Rising from his seat, the King stepped away from the table.

'Royal Knight Thorburn, please step forward.'

His adrenaline surging, Dane approached the King.

The King drew his sword as Dane knelt on one knee.

'I, King Winston Meriwether, hereby appoint you to the rank of Commander of the Royal Knights,' he said, tapping Dane on each shoulder as he spoke.

'Rise.'

The formalities of the next morning over, Dane and Vanessa made straight for the stables, escaping the confines of the castle with a ride.

The late-morning sun was warm but comfortable. Together with a clear sky, they were ideal conditions for a ride to the Great Forest and back, just as they had done many so times in the past.

Heading towards the castle once more, they took their time, the others trailing behind them.

'I didn't know if I'd ever get to do this again,' said Vanessa, savouring the sweet, open air.

'You didn't think we'd kill them?' asked Dane in a mocking, semi-shocked tone of voice.

'Not exactly,' said Vanessa. 'I couldn't help wondering what would have happened if killing the creatures wasn't the answer. If nature had some other plan.'

'I don't think we'll ever understand it,' said Dane, shaking his head. 'One creature from each element, gaining strength from you, each absorbing traits from whichever was killed.'

'Although it was a water creature, Lord Frederick was saying the sarkoe reminded him of the Fire-Walkers,' said Vanessa.

Dane's eyes widened.

'Yes,' said Vanessa, noticing his reaction. 'The Fire-Walkers were able to walk through walls and structures and they'd melt from the heat. Although the sarkoe didn't quite do that, the fact it was able to smash its way through suggests it came from a con-nected source.'

'What does that mean?' said Dane.

'We don't know,' said Vanessa. 'Only that there is a source out there somewhere – a true source of everything; somewhere in nature, or the elements, where these creatures come from.'

'That's not very comforting,' said Dane.

'Well, the sun is shining, and the air is fresh,' said Vanessa with a smile. 'For today, that's good enough for me.'

'You really look well,' said Dane. 'Considering what you've been through, and how weak you were.'

Taking another deep, contented breath, Vanessa smiled.

'I feel better than I have in a long while. And now that I think all the way back, I think it all started as early as my journey back from the City of Lost Souls.'

'Raegan,' Dane cursed. 'It's all his doing.'

'And we'll find a way to defeat him,' said Vanessa.

'He should already be dead,' said Dane under his breath.

'Don't,' said Vanessa.

'You don't *know* what I saw,' said Dane. 'How real it looked.'

'It doesn't matter,' said Vanessa. 'Candahorn and the others have to be defeated – with or without Raegan. If we defeat them, he has nothing.'

'I wouldn't be so sure,' said Dane. 'It seems he has allies every-where. Not just the rebels, but in our own city. Those that helped the Black Knights when he tried to take the castle; the Black Knights who tried to kill you – even Salsbury.'

'I know,' said Vanessa, shaking her head at the memory of him at the end of a noose. 'I had no idea.'

'None of us did,' said Dane. 'I was convinced it was Medhurst. I nearly keeled over when he agreed with my promotion.'

'There's more to Medhurst than you know,' said Vanessa.

'Apparently so,' said Dane. 'But it would be nice if he gave me a break every once in a while.'

'Why?' said Vanessa. 'Sometimes, those who challenge us, regardless of the reason, bring out our best.'

'You may be right,' said Dane. 'All the same, it would be nice, just once, if he saw things my way.'

'He did,' said Vanessa. 'Father told me that once he saw your plan to move me to the dungeon was correct, he supported it wholeheartedly.'

'But not in front of me,' said Dane.

'Take it anyway,' said Vanessa. 'You'll be dealing with him more often now. It may be scraps from the table, but sometimes that's enough. I'm told he was the same with your father.'

'Really?' said Dane. 'So, it's Thorburns in general he has a problem with?'

Vanessa smiled.

Arriving at the stables, Dane dismounted, handing Thunder to a stablehand and offering Vanessa his hand.

'No,' she scolded. 'I'm quite capable.'

'You're a Princess today,' said Dane. 'Not a knight.'

With a smile, Vanessa allowed him to help her dismount as a stablehand arrived to take Razor away.

'Executed?' said Mortensen.

'Yes,' Thurman replied. 'At dawn, this morning.'

'He was a valuable ally,' said Mortensen, stroking his chin. 'And his demise is regrettable. But killing the girl was a risk we had to take. Other news?'

'They've promoted Dane Thorburn to Commander of the Royal Knights,' said Thurman.

'Another problem,' said Mortensen. 'I wouldn't be the least bit surprised if we find out he had something to do with saving the girl. *Again.*'

Thurman nodded thoughtfully.

'Not to mention the rumours about ... Lord Raegan,' he said quietly.

'We have no proof of that,' said Mortensen.

'Governor,' said Turman. 'The longer he remains absent?'

'Lord Raegan is alive!' Mortensen boomed, as much to convince himself as anyone else. 'I will hear no more on the subject.'

Standing at the altar, Dane and Will turned together, staring down the aisle as the music commenced, looking past the Maid-of-Honour and locking their eyes on the bride.

Genevieve appeared in a long, flowing gown, her father at her side.

Noticing how stunning she looked; her long blonde hair no longer constrained in a maid's bun; her dress allowing the curves of her body to stand out instead of being hidden away in her dreary maid's outfit, Dane stole a momentary glance at Will, who was gushing with pride as she approached.

The Maid-of-Honour reached the altar, turning to the left with a wink at Dane that went unnoticed.

Genevieve smiled as she arrived at the altar, her father offering her hand to Will, before taking a seat next to his wife.

The music stopped and Oliver Rowell, the new Clerk of Court stepped forward.

'We are gathered on this day, to join this man and woman in the sanctity of marriage,' he said. 'Let all present bear witness to the exchange of vows, and the commitment they offer to each other, now and forever.'

Reaching into a pocket, Dane passed the rings.

Genevieve slid one onto Will's finger.

'Repeat after me,' said Rowell.

Dane looked at Will; everything they'd done together flashing through his mind.

In every one of those situations, Will had remained cool and calm, no matter how intense it had been.

As Dane watched him now, though, he was as nervous as he'd ever seen him.

'I'll mess it up,' he'd said again and again as they'd prepared for the ceremony. 'I'll make a fool of myself in front of everyone.'

'You won't,' Dane had reassured him.

'But what if I do?' he'd countered.

'Do you love her?' Dane had said the last time they'd had this exchange.

'Of course!'

'And she loves you,' said Dane. 'Forget the vows. If you get a word or two wrong, no one will care; and Genevieve will care the least of all. She's marrying you as you are, not on the grounds of whether you can string a few words together.'

'I, Will Hevenshire,' said Will, bringing Dane back to the moment.

Looking into the eyes of his bride, Will felt his heart soar, a calmness descending on him.

'Take you, Genevieve Newbury, for my wife,' said Rowell.

'Take you, Genevieve Newbury, for my wife,' Will repeated.

'To have and to hold, in sickness and health, for as long as I shall live.'

Repeating the vows, Will grinned, giving Genevieve's hand a gentle squeeze as he finished. He felt a burst of energy as he placed the ring on her finger.

With a broad yet gentle smile, her eyes locking with Will's, Genevieve made her vows.

'By witness to all,' said Rowell, 'and by the power granted to me in the name of the King, I pronounce you, man and wife.'

The music commenced as Will kissed his bride to the applause of all present.

Turning to Dane, the two exchanged a handshake and a hug.

'Didn't I say you'd be faultless?' Dane whispered.

'Thanks,' said Will.

Once the guests had passed on their congratulations and made their way to the main hall, the wedding party and parents of the bride and groom were all that remained.

'Shall we?' Walter Hevenshire asked his wife.

Allowing him to take her hand, Isabella Hevenshire smiled at her son and his bride as she made her way away from the altar.

Genevieve's parents followed.

'I guess we should join them,' said Will. 'Ready, Madam Hevenshire?'

'Of course,' said Genevieve, squeezing his hand.

'Very well,' said Dane, stepping forward to take the Maid-of Honour's hand.

Preoccupied with Will, Genevieve and the other guests, he hadn't paid her any attention.

With her back to him, he didn't react until she turned and he found Vanessa looking at him. Dressed in a flowing, crimson gown, and with her plaited and hooped at the sides, he hadn't recognised her until now.

'What in the –'

'Why do you look so surprised?' she said, beaming at him.

'But –'

'You think it beneath me to be the Maid-of-Honour for one of my attendants?'

'No,' said Dane, stumbling for words as he saw the Royal Knights posted around the room for the first time. 'I just didn't expect it.'

'Well, here I am,' said Vanessa, hooking her arm in his. 'Let's not keep the guests waiting.'

After a lavish feast, the music struck up once more, and the bridal party made their way to the centre of the hall for the first dance.

Will and Genevieve moved smoothy and gracefully with the music as the guests looked on.

Dane and Vanessa gave them plenty of space, happy to remain in the background.

Moving around the floor, looking into each other's eyes, neither said a word. Absorbed in the music and the joy of the occasion, each looked at the other as though seeing them for the first time in a different light –

- Vanessa wasn't the Princess, the future ruling Queen of the land; nor was she the friend he'd grown up with, from a young girl to the woman she'd become ...
- Dane wasn't her best friend, the one she'd known all her life, from her mischievous playmate to the man he'd become; nor was he a knight, the Commander of the Royal Knights no less ...

As the music continued, they held each other's eye –

Staring ...

Wondering ...

'Mind if we cut in?'

Snapping out of their trance, blinking anxiously as they regained their bearings, they saw Will and Genevieve standing next to them with slightly bemused looks on their faces.

'Of course,' said Dane, slightly confused.

Vanessa nodded, releasing her grip on Dane's hand, looking at him for a moment, bewildered and unsure about what had just happened.

With a final glance at each other, they joined hands with their new partners and danced once more.

'You look beautiful,' Dane said to Genevieve as they made their way around the floor.

'Thank you,' said Genevieve.

'I'm so happy for you both.'

Genevieve smiled as others joined them on the floor.

Dane lost sight of Vanessa among the crowd twirling around him.

As the festivities continued, among others, he danced with the mothers of the bride and groom, before another, dressed in a gold evening gown stepped forward with a smile.

'May I?' asked Marilena.

'Of course,' said Dane, taking his mother's hand.

Neither said a word as Dane guided her around the floor.

After a minute or so, he saw a tear running down her cheek.

'What's wrong?' he asked.

'Nothing,' said Marilena, smiling as tears streamed down her face. 'It's just – you remind me so much of your father.'

'Except for the scars on my chin,' he said with a gentle smile.

Laughing softly through her tears, Marilena said, 'We had many nights like this, where we'd dance without a care in the world. I miss him terribly.'

'As do I,' said Dane.

'He'd be proud of you,' said Marilena softly.

Looking into his mother's eyes he said, 'If I can achieve half as much in my life as he did, I'll be happy.'

'You already have,' said Marilena, wiping tears from her eyes. 'You already have.'

Epilogue

Passing through the void, the senses attacked his mind, vying for his attention –

– the rich, dirt smell of Earth;
– the soaring, uplifting wind of Air;
– the thirst-quenching coolness of Water;
– but it was the warm, soothing heat of Fire that mattered.

From the very edge of his consciousness, he found it, allowing it to draw him away from the others; slowly at first, then, as the others faded, following the path of warmth, his mind sinking deeper and deeper, surrendering to it.

Pleasant at first, the soothing warmth gave way to a searing heat; hot enough that it took over his entire being – the physical injuries and the thoughts swirling in and out of his mind dissolving to nothing.

Helpless to resist, a scream rang out from the depths of his mind, the agony of the fire so intense he wanted to die.

Somewhere in the midst of the furnace around him, he felt something greater – a searing, scorching ember, that, despite the pain, he could do nothing about.

Unable to resist, he drifted helplessly towards it, like a leaf twirling on a gust of wind.

In the next instant the heat produced a spark that flew along the pathway of his mind, passing through the void and latching onto him.

With a burst of pain, he felt his mind erupt, exploding into pieces ... and in the next moment the intensity of the heat and flame started to fade, and he felt scraps of thought returning.

As the heat drained away, a thought found its way to the wound in his neck, where it sensed a presence, smaller than the tiniest speck of dust.

As the temperature in his mind stabilised, he took comfort in a final thought as he drifted into a deep sleep once more - he would live.

Acknowledgements

First and foremost, as always, I want to thank my family – Caroline, Melissa and Michael, for all their support. I don't know where I would be without you. Words can't describe what it means to have your undying faith and belief in everything I do.

To bring a book to life requires the work and support of a lot of people.

To Kit and the team at MAA who challenge me to explore new ideas that improve the end product – thank you so much.

To William and his team at Inspiring Publishers, thank you for all the edits and rewrites and the amazing work on the covers. I marvel at the job you and your team do.

To Tess and everyone at Invigorate, I thank you for all you've done with marketing and promotion.

And finally, a big thank you to all my readers and everyone who has given me an encouraging word along the way – none of this is possible without you.

To find out more about Matt and his books, visit his website: **www.mattgalanos.com**